Moscow Honey

Moscow Honey

By T.M. Parris

A Clarke and Fairchild Thriller

The Clarke and Fairchild series of novels
is written in British English

Russia

1

Three thousand miles east, the air is different here. God is in heaven and Moscow is far away. Roman's father used to say that to him. But not so far these days. Moscow was getting bigger, reaching further, burying deeper, creeping closer, never stopping until everyone marched to the beat of its drum.

Roman got out of the car and walked to the riverbank. The cold reached out and grabbed him by the face. It sent itchy tendrils up his nose, pressed on his forehead, plunged down the back of his neck, seeped in through the seams of his jacket. So thick you could touch it. This was Siberia cold: stronger, cleaner, drier. It reminded him again how good it felt to be back.

Vadim joined him from the car and stared at the lights on the far bank. He looked like a priest with his long pale face and his mournful eyes. They'd watched each other grow old here. Roman know Irkutsk, every grey street, every scrubby back yard playground, every snow-laden wooden hut. Every spacious boulevard, pavements piled with chipped ice in the winter, shaded from the heat by trees in the summer. Like Paris, so they said. He knew this town and this town knew him. It wasn't personal pride; the fight was necessary, though you paid a price. It didn't happen by itself that the kiosk owner, the night club manager, the traffic officer, the prosecutor, all knew that the Bear was a man of his word, a man to be taken seriously.

He looked down at the black river, flowing here but where it met Lake Baikal it would stop. Baikal was frozen solid for another three months. This yard was unused until the spring.

He looked at Vadim. "Is it true?"

Vadim shrugged, shook his head. He didn't know. It was just a rumour.

"Piotr is there, is he not? Who used to collect from the south? He's in Moscow, now?"

Vadim gazed at him, got his meaning. "Yes," he said simply.

Headlights flashed; the car was here. The engine died. Andrei got out, son of Roman's old friend the locksmith, but all grown up now. He opened the passenger door, reached a burly fist inside and pulled a man out by his shirt. The man shrieked as he landed on the icy ground. Andrei slammed the door and dragged him forward into the beam of the car's headlights. He backed off to take his station, arms folded. The man on the ground scrambled to his feet.

"What are you doing? You just grabbed us off the street!"

He stopped. Roman and Vadim stepped into the beam, onto the stage. The man's eyes widened. He was starting to realise. He glanced back to the car, but his friend on the back seat would be no help.

"You know who I am?" Roman spoke pleasantly. The guy just stared. He started to shiver, from the cold maybe. He was too tall, skinny and folded up, not much more than a boy. A boy with a big mouth. "I heard that you are a man of opinions. Did I hear right?"

He shook his head. "No, not at all."

"Really?" Roman moved in. The man took a step back and looked round to see Andrei hovering just outside the beam of the headlights. The four of them stood spaced in formation, Vadim next to Roman. "Because I heard from my friend, the barman at the Green Palace, that you were there last night. For a long time. Good party, he said. You had a lot to talk about. A lot to say. About my son. About me."

"No, no." Even in this cold, the boy's top lip glowed with sweat. He put his palms up, as if he could calm the Bear down. The Bear was already calm.

"The barman is a good friend of mine," he said. "You're not calling him a liar, are you?"

The boy's breaths were shallow, each producing a puff of mist.

"I was drunk! I was talking nonsense! I don't even remember what!"

"Well, let me remind you." While Roman talked, he took off his jacket and handed it to Vadim. "You said, I'm told, that my son Alexei was in Moscow, pissing away the Morozov obschak on champagne and cars instead of running the business. That I was a fool for putting him in control."

"Oh, no, I didn't say that!" His voice wavered.

"You didn't?"

"No, not that."

"Those were not your exact words?" Roman started to roll up his sleeves. The hairs on his arms prickled with cold.

"It doesn't matter. I just—"

"It doesn't matter?"

He fumbled about. "I just meant that I didn't mean it."

"Well, it matters to me. Alexei is my family, you see. Family is important. You honour your family, you value your family. That's how my father raised me. Do you have family? People who are important to you?"

He was gasping like a fish out of water. "Please don't— please don't—"

"And what else did you say? Something about a woman?" The boy looked around wildly, like a trapped animal. "A particular kind of woman?"

"It was just a joke. I didn't mean it."

"A joke? You think it's funny? What's funny? Me? Or my son?"

"Not a joke, A rumour."

"A rumour? That's interesting. Please, tell me this rumour. I'd like to hear it."

"That he married a whore!" He blurted it out and the words hung in his breath, almost visible.

"A whore?"

His eyes turned skywards as though he were praying. "Yes! A Chechen whore!"

The word sucked the air from Roman's lungs. He sensed Vadim looking across at him.

"Chechen?"

The boy looked straight at him for the first time, curious. "You didn't know?"

Roman punched him hard in the face. He fell onto his back and didn't move. His jaw was a mess, blood and teeth. Roman punched him three more times, fast. The boy's head rolled back. The Bear stood and flexed his hands. It was over already but he kicked him anyway, for the stage show: stomach, ribs, gut. The boy rolled over on his side.

Roman turned away. Vadim handed him his jacket. He put it on and approached the car. Andrei opened the door and he peered in, at the pair of eyes inside.

"You a friend of his?" Another skinny boy. The car smelled of his after-shave and sweat. "Well, I give you some advice. My name is Roman Morozov. People call me the Bear." The eyes didn't blink. "My people are everywhere in this town. You get on a train and go somewhere, I'll know.

You get in a car, a truck, a plane, I'll know. You talk to the police, I'll know. So you don't disappear and you don't squeal. You tell people what happened here. That's your job. That's why you're in this car and not out on the concrete like your friend. Tell everyone you know. Tell them about the Bear. Tell them I'm a serious man. Understand."

It wasn't a question and the boy on the back seat didn't try to answer. Roman nodded to Andrei, who got in the car and they drove off.

Vadim was watching with his priest's eyes. Behind Vadim, the body was slumped in the dark.

Okay, he didn't intend to kill the boy. He didn't kill for enjoyment. Destruction for its own sake? Not if he could see an easier way. But the words repeated, whispered in his ear, shouted in his face: *a Chechen whore*.

He rubbed the blood on his knuckles dry. These days it wasn't respectable to get wet. These days they should be men of authority, in suits behind desks, looking down on this street life, ashamed of it. Well, the Bear was not ashamed. It was never enough just to talk about strength; without blood on the ground there would be no Morozov, no Bear.

"Let's go," he said. Vadim glanced round at the body. Yes, they could haul him over the wall into the freezing river. They'd done it often enough in the past. But this wasn't something to hide. The police would do nothing except talk. Then everyone would talk and those who needed to would learn. So reputation is earned. And reputation was what Roman needed, now more than ever.

They drove off and left the body lying there.

2

Rose climbed the staircase with the confidence of a chick on its first outing out of the nest. Her heels sank into the thick carpet and pushed her weight forward. Her dress rode up, only the thinnest of tights shielding her bare legs from the elements. Her piled-up hair left the back of her neck exposed, and painted nail extensions made everything awkward to handle. Her tiny gold clutch bag was only just big enough for make-up and cash. It was telling, that formal dress rendered a woman next to useless.

This wasn't just any staircase; it was the famous Jordan staircase, leading up into one of the many lavish Winter Palace galleries overlooking the river. She had checked it out on her tourist visit here the previous day. Everything in St Petersburg was a celebration of the era of the Romanovs, the days of the Tsars. Funny how people here preferred to surround themselves with the glories of the past. Moscow seemed much more a city of the present. Most attendees tonight would be Muscovites; this annual VIP event attracted diplomats, business people, journalists, politicians, the great influencers in Russian society.

Inside, tables offered beautifully presented crudités, variations on a theme of caviar. And champagne, of course: real champagne, not the poorly-regarded Soviet variety although plenty of it still remained, apparently, even now. A tuxedoed Peter Craven had located himself strategically next to the rows of glasses constantly being replenished. As Deputy Head of the UK's Mission to Russia, he was officially the second most important Briton in the country, but the most important as far as Rose was concerned, being MI6

Head of Moscow Station and, therefore, her boss. She tottered over to him.

"You look very at home at a shindig like this."

"Well, I've been to a few." Peter's stretch in the country was long enough for him to have experienced its Soviet predecessor. Round-faced and universally liked, Peter was a stalwart Service *good old boy*, perpetually on the brink of retirement. "And you've scrubbed up pretty well yourself, if I'm allowed to say that kind of thing these days."

"Yes, well, it doesn't come naturally. They certainly like to do these things in style."

"They do. You'll have to get used to that, I'm afraid."

"Odd this place is called the Hermitage. It seems the least appropriate name there is."

Rose had left the tour the previous day with a head full of huge volumes of gold and marble, vast canvasses of oil in ornate frames, enormous vases, immaculately polished expanses of patterned wood flooring. Ostentatiously layered wealth, the setting for artwork presenting a view of humanity over the past thousand or more years – birth, love, glory, sickness, terror, death, room upon room, on all sides. The Rembrandt room, dramatic events frozen in time; the father alight with joy, recognising his prodigal son; Jacob with the knife poised over his son's exposed neck, just at the moment the angel arrives to interrupt with God's mercy.

"So, the guests we were expecting have arrived?" While it was part of Rose's official diplomatic role to network at events like this, the clandestine element of her job gave her a more specific reason to be here.

"Yes indeed." Peter had a champagne glass in each hand. "Give me ten minutes then come over. Oh, here's someone you can catch up with in the meantime. I believe you know each other?"

He nudged someone's arm with his elbow. Its owner turned, grey eyes widening with recognition. John Fairchild. The last time Rose saw Fairchild, he was washed out and dejected on a riverbank in Kathmandu. She'd been in a similar state. That was some months ago and things seemed to have improved for him, as they had for her. His face was clean-shaven and slightly tanned, his hair a generous length and tastefully coiffured. Someone else who looked at home in a tux.

He and Craven greeted each other like old buddies. Interesting. Responses to Fairchild within the Service seemed to fall into two camps. A few months ago it was being whispered that Fairchild was selling MI6 secrets to the highest bidder, but to date no one appeared to have acted on those suspicions, and not everyone believed them. Craven clearly belonged in the more favourable camp. As he pulled away with the drinks, Fairchild's handshake with her was less spontaneous. He gave her the briefest sweep of his eyes before fixing on her face with a detached expression.

"Well," said Rose, "I'd be lying to say I'm surprised to see you here. I was wondering when you'd show up in these parts, to be honest."

"I had a few matters to sort out. You know how it is." This was definitely the breezy, suave version of John Fairchild, not the broken, haunted man who awkwardly confided in her on that damp riverside.

"And have you made any progress yet with your mission? Last time we spoke you were looking for a certain Russian monk. One with two missing fingers, if I remember right."

"That's taken a little longer than I thought."

"I see. And I trust you've been occupying your time constructively?" It was always interesting to learn what Fairchild was doing, not that he was naturally prone to sharing. His combination of an impressive global network of contacts, a variety of skills including his famous aptitude for languages, and an ability to know what no one else did, rendered his services in high demand from a colourful range of clients. Most data brokers in the industry were former officers, but Fairchild had acquired his skills in less formal ways.

"I have a number of business interests in Russia, as I'm sure you know."

"Of course." On paper, Fairchild was a businessman with an extensive range of concerns worldwide. She'd asked around at the Embassy as soon as she'd got here and discovered that Fairchild had, amongst other things, a controlling interest in a luxury limousine service operating in several Russian cities. Given the number of luxury limousines she'd seen prowling the streets of Moscow, it looked to be a good line of work. She suggested that might be the case. He responded nonchalantly and changed the subject.

"You've returned to the fold, I see. I hope your role is enabling you to promote British interests abroad. And that you are exporting British values as per your mission statement, even in this inhospitable environment."

Delivered with a knowing smile, it was a reminder that Fairchild was well aware that the description "Trade Delegation" on her name badge didn't quite cover the entirety of her role. Rose was an agent runner. She recruited and managed people who were prepared to pass to the British government the deepest secrets of the Russian state. Fairchild might not know the detail of what she did, but he was familiar enough with the world of secret intelligence to have a pretty good idea.

"Well, the climate does take a lot of getting used to. Frozen solid, moving to icy slush every now and then."

She wasn't talking about the weather. Craven's long-term perspective gave some credence to his view that current "soft war" UK-Russia relations were as close to an all-out war footing as they had been since the days of the actual Cold War, with Russia's seizure of Ukraine's Crimea only the most recent sensitivity. "Still, we try. Always good to have values, mind, even if they're not taken up universally."

"Ah! Of course." Fairchild took this dig at his stateless allegiance-free lifestyle in good humour. "Well, if you'll excuse me. I have some amoral business to attend to." He slid away leaving Rose unsettled, irritated, and none the wiser.

Fairchild's presence in Russia at some point was inevitable. It was Fairchild himself who told her that he'd discovered the identity of a Russian monk with information about the disappearance of Fairchild's parents decades ago. But Rose hadn't been looking forward to seeing him here. It was largely down to Fairchild that she got her job at the Service back at all, and she didn't particularly want him reminding her of that when he needed something. Which tended to be the way Fairchild operated.

The incident in Croatia which led to her dismissal was not her fault. It was just very unfortunate timing, with one of her agents compromised on the eve of a fatal attack on UK soil claimed by the group she should have had eyes on. They needed a scapegoat; she was standing the closest. She'd always felt that way, though it would have been futile to say so at the time. When the mysterious and unspecifically senior Walter Tomlinson arrived shortly afterwards with an offer of an off-the-books job in exchange for re-admission, no way was she going to pass. Fairchild was an unwilling target but in the end she succeeded. As a result, she insisted that her Service record be fully restored. It was – she received the closest MI6 ever gave to an apology – and was promptly posted to one of the most challenging locations in the world. Not a bad outcome, and her fluency in Russian didn't do any harm, although she felt sure it had something to do with Walter's obsession with Fairchild and wanting to keep eyes on him. Until now, though, she'd seen or heard nothing of either Fairchild or Walter, and Craven had never mentioned either. Her work so far seemed unrelated. She'd kind of been hoping it would stay that way. She couldn't afford to have anything, or anyone, mess up the second chance she'd been given.

Her ankles ached. The champagne tasted metallic, the caviar briny. On the other side of the room, a man was laughing too loud. Peter was ready for her.

She wandered over and joined a circle around an expensively-dressed young Russian man, taller, blonder and louder than those around him. The bottom buttons on his waistcoat were undone and his bowtie was loosened. Large-lipped, he waved his glass around as he spoke, letting the champagne slop over the side. He was the only one talking. What may have started as a conversation had become a monologue.

"They buried the statues, you know? To stop the Nazis getting their hands on them. Spread wax all over them and dug holes in the ground. Now look! The biggest collection in the world. The finest, the richest! This is the real Russia, our glorious history! This is what they wanted to take away, those dogs in Finland and their krout masters!"

The embarrassed half-smiles of his audience reflected the crudity of the man's language. "One small loaf of bread they had to eat every day, one loaf, one piece even! The size of my finger. For two years!" He seemed to be talking about the siege of Leningrad, not that anyone here would be unaware of the details. "Do you know what it's like to go hungry? Did you serve in the army? Were you in Chechnya, my friend?" He had turned on one of the men, who humbly shook his head. "No, you see, everyone should do it but people weasel out of it. I was there. I saw men die, women too, children in the street, like they did here. But we survived. We fought back, like we always have. All that Communist nonsense, the collective farming and the purges, that held us back but it's over now. Russia, the real Russia, is even stronger!"

Russia's common enemy seemed to encompass the Nazis, the Chechens and the Soviet-era Communists. The woman by his side stood slightly back from him. He didn't look at her once. She wasn't looking at him, either, instead staring straight in front, her chin high and her face vacant. When he mentioned Chechnya, she glanced at him but let her gaze drift off again. Her silver satin dress plunged at the front, hung low and loose at the back, pinched around her tiny waist and flowed out over her hips. Heavy pearl jewellery glimmered on her neck and wrists. Her young-looking skin, wide dark eyes and small shapely pink mouth gave her an innocent air, although she was immaculately made-up. She seemed detached, standing in the midst of this group of hangers-on, but somehow apart from them. With that combination of desirability and vulnerability, it was easy to see why a man would be drawn to her.

Rose worked her way round to where Peter was standing. As she stepped up to him, her heel gave way and she stumbled against him, spilling champagne onto his sleeve.

"Oh, crap! I'm so sorry!" she said, too loud. The young man looked round, his monologue paused.

"English?" he asked.

"Yes," she replied, then seeing his hesitation switched to Russian. "I work with Peter. I just came over to give him a message." She rubbed her twisted ankle. Peter dabbed his sleeve with his handkerchief, his face pursed. The woman's eye travelled down to Rose's shoes. Her own shoes were strappy silver, every bit as precarious as Rose's. The man was glaring at Rose with flat blue eyes.

"Sorry to interrupt," she said. "I'm Rose Clarke, by the way."

"Alexei Morozov." He offered her his hand without changing his expression. It was large, hot and slimy. Sweat beads had formed around his hairline although the room wasn't overly warm.

"Good to meet you."

"So, how do you like Russia?"

A test question. Rose answered politely and positively, watched throughout. Then a pause, Alexei appraising her with his head on one side.

"You don't like us defending ourselves, though. Claiming land stolen from us." The silence that fell was tinged with embarrassment. Referring directly to an international disagreement was uncomfortably direct for diplomatic circles, provocative in fact. Rose glanced at the woman and caught her eye. It was telling that he hadn't introduced her.

Peter stepped in. "Well, defence, of course, Alexei. But it's sometimes a matter of debate, though, isn't it, what can be considered defence."

The blue eyes narrowed and Alexei seemed to get taller.

"Let me tell you," he said, pointing at Rose, even though Peter had spoken, "let me tell you what defence is. Defence is standing knee deep in water all day waiting for terrorist plotters to come out of hiding behind their women and children. Defence is watching your battalion blown limb from limb by infidel tribal wolfhounds…"

He stopped. Rose saw it too out of the corner of her eye. The woman had flinched, but now seemed completely composed as if she hadn't even been listening. As Alexei turned, she gazed at him calmly. He put his hand under her chin and lifted it, examining her face. She looked back for a few seconds then dropped her eyes. Alexei kept staring.

"There is no need to be ashamed of your birth, Kamila. I took you away from all that. You're a good Christian woman now. Aren't you, my love?"

She looked him in the face. "Of course." A wan smile. "All that is behind me now. You have given me so much, my Alexei." Her voice was quiet, but deeper than Rose expected. Her hand reached out and touched his waist. He seemed to lose his train of thought for a moment. Then he dropped his hand and turned back to Rose.

"Britain is not a Christian country," he said darkly. "You allow all those perversions. Men with men, women with women, disgusting." He took the opportunity to look her up and down. Rose had heard similar sentiments expressed, but not usually so directly.

"Why not live how you want to live, as long as it doesn't do any harm?" She held his gaze.

"Harm!" Alexei snorted and looked around as his huge mouth widened into a grin. Several in the group smiled or laughed with gentle derision. "You think you can tell the whole world what to do. But your country's leaders are weak. They tolerate depravity. It will ruin you."

"Sounds interesting." Fairchild's unaccented Russian cut in. "Maybe I should pay a visit to my country of origin. A bit of depravity might be a nice distraction." He stepped in and held out his hand to Alexei. "John Fairchild."

Typical, thought Rose. To get Alexei's attention I have to sprain my ankle and throw fizz all over my boss. Fairchild just shimmies in. Not that Alexei seemed enamoured of Fairchild's smooth superciliousness. His face took on a sneer when Fairchild mentioned that he knew Alexei's father.

"Roman. Our paths have crossed. We've helped each other from time to time."

"Doing what? Digging potatoes? Making jam? Selling handbags?" Alexei's speech had slowed. "Roman the Bear! Such a man! But what he does is women's work. Morozov is better than that. Some people don't like it when the world changes, Mr Fairchild. We must change with it. You agree, don't you?"

Fairchild's expression remained bland. One of the Morozov retinue approached and muttered something in Alexei's ear, pointing someone out to him. Rose turned to Peter.

"Sorry about your jacket," she said.

"Not to worry. It's not the first time. I'm sure hotel housekeeping will sort it out. I'll be turning in soon."

She watched Peter's eyes scan the room. Alexei moved off with his men, leaving Kamila standing on her own. But not for long: Fairchild approached her. They were standing quite close. Something he said prompted a shy smile, then laughter. Alexei was in a huddle of men, his voice loud and slurred. Kamila looked over at him from time to time, but he didn't look at her. Charming man, thought Rose. Kamila may have started to think so too. Her gaze rested more and more on Fairchild with a particular expression, an intensity. Still standing quite close. Interesting. But things seemed to be going to plan so far. As Peter slipped away, Rose grabbed another champagne to do one last tour of the room before moving onto the next phase of the evening's operation.

3

Inside the men's room Fairchild loosened his tie and leaned over the washbasin. Cold water from a large brass tap filled the basin in seconds. He scooped it up and splashed his face: cooling and shocking at the same time. He picked up a thick cream hand towel that smelled of detergent. Now was not a good time to lose concentration.

It had taken every effort to act normally. Kathmandu was months ago. He could have come to Russia much sooner, sped up the search instead of leaving it to others. It wasn't like him. Before he met Rose, his thirty-year search to find out what happened to his missing parents dictated every decision he'd made. As soon as he discovered where he might find Dimitri, the Russian monk who could give him real answers, the strongest lead he'd ever had, he should have come straight here. Instead he'd made excuses. Bits and pieces of work that took him here and there, and he knew why, although he denied it to himself. It was because he didn't want to see Rose again, wanted her out of his mind.

He wanted to believe his feelings for her were just in the moment, a phase, a leftover from that punishing ordeal they'd both endured. Of course he dwelled on her, but with space, with distance, with time, surely those thoughts would recede? Then Peter nudged him on the arm and he turned round and saw her, stunning in a body-tight dress, and the feelings were back, latching onto him, wrapping themselves around him. It took everything he had not to stare at the curve of her neck and her pale flesh, shoulders, arms: more, so much more than he'd seen before.

He glanced at himself in the mirror. There'd been women in his life of course, liaisons driven by curiosity, gratitude, loneliness, pure attraction. Occasionally he'd felt love but it never lasted. It was simply that other things mattered more. The Morozov wife was an attractive woman; he wasn't against initiating something to serve a purpose. His feelings for Rose served no purpose. They were highly inconvenient. He tried once more to get his mind away from how her legs disappeared up into her clinging little skirt, the shape of her lips as she spoke to him. Did she notice anything? He'd put everything into trying to ensure she didn't.

Had anyone else? From time to time that evening he'd felt that someone was watching, not just in the way that everyone observes everyone at these events: someone *else*. Behind her shoulder somewhere, in the edge of his vision when he turned and saw her, unprepared for the moment, someone was there. But when he looked, he saw no one.

Move on, man. You've got work to do.

He switched off the tap and looked at his watch. Idiot! He'd wasted so much time. Back in there was more small talk, more taps on the shoulder, more introductions, even if he were just passing through to get away. He needed to change his plans, do something drastic. He glanced up at the window, calculating. Behind him, a toilet flushed and a cubicle door opened. Fairchild stepped out of the way and dried his hands slowly. The man, a stranger, washed his hands and left. The room was now empty. Fairchild moved to the window, fumbling with the handle. Come on, concentrate. The inner panes opened towards him and he pushed the palm of his hand onto the external metal latch, wincing from the cold. He loosened the outside panes and pushed them open. Raw air flooded in and he stood with his eyes closed feeling his body cool in the sub-zero blast. His head cleared a little. He rocked back on his heels. His waistcoat felt tight around his waist. He flexed his fingers.

The door of the men's room rattled. Fairchild spun and froze, staring at the handle. Seconds passed. It was the breeze from over the river, nothing more. He took several long breaths and stared out of the window, making out details on the far shore. Then he stepped closer, gripped the sides of the frame, pulled his weight up to get his feet onto the sill, balanced there, squatting, and jumped.

4

From the Winter Palace Rose walked the cobbled pavement alone, dark windows of floodlit imperial frontages like eyes looking down on her. St Petersburg's canals coiled elegantly through the old town behind decorative iron railings, frozen solid or plated with sheets of ice, attracting a heavy clinging mist.

Things had gone according to plan. Alexei had left the reception staggering and shouting, his drunkenness aided by something that Peter slipped into his champagne earlier on, not that his condition seemed particularly surprising to his retinue. The escorts were waiting outside, very tall, very glamorous, very Russian. An afterparty was offered to Alexei in a nearby hotel suite, courtesy of a local businessman who did Peter the odd favour from time to time. So they bundled into the waiting limo and left Kamila to return home on her own. All of which she withstood with the same bland expression. In the meantime, Fairchild had disappeared, so it seemed. Rose discreetly observed events before slipping away herself.

Kamila was not obviously Alexei's type. She seemed to have no particular expectation of fidelity or even respect, even though their marriage was still young. An extremely wealthy criminal businessman and a prostitute, it was clear the marriage wasn't going to be one of equals. Why did Alexei marry her? Maybe his feelings for her were genuine, hard to believe though that was.

Fairchild was a strange one. Walter had formed a view about Fairchild's feelings towards Rose, and shared this with her when they last met in Kathmandu. But Walter was surely mistaken; she'd seen no sign at all that he had feelings for her. On the contrary, Fairchild seemed far more taken up with Kamila. Old family friend Walter might be, but clearly he could get things wrong sometimes. She fought back the uncomfortable idea that this theory of Walter's was the reason she was in Russia right now; that was not a role she wanted at all.

She stopped by a large wooden double door under a wrought iron balcony, and pressed a buzzer while looking into the camera. The door clicked open and she entered. She slipped her shoes off and carried them in her hand up two flights of the wide stone staircase. The steps were warm on the soles of her feet. Chunky pipes clanked hot water into squat radiators on each landing, and carved bronze ceiling lights gave the walls a yellow glow. Rose's ascent was silent and the door of the apartment opened for her without her knocking.

She didn't recognise the young dark-haired man who let her in, but the older bearded guy in the front room sitting behind an array of audio visual equipment was familiar.

"Hello, Larry."

"Hi, Rose. Have a good evening?" said Larry.

"We'll see."

Larry introduced her to his new technical assistant, Charlie. She looked over the bank of equipment.

"Wow. You could make a Hollywood blockbuster with all this."

The room was bare except for the equipment, the tables they were on and two chairs. The curtains were drawn except for a small gap in the middle, where a camera on a tripod was positioned. The only light was a dim desk lamp next to the equipment. They'd been setting up for a while; the small space had filled with the smell of unwashed clothes. Outside, on the other side of the street and the canal, stretched a long building which mirrored this one. Peering through the gap in the curtains, Rose could see that lights were on in most of the rooms.

"The whole thing is the Morozov apartment?" asked Rose.

"Yep, seventeen windows. All these were built for the aristocracy. Most have been sliced and diced into smaller units, like this one. We were lucky to find an empty flat right opposite."

"And she's there?"

"Yep."

"Alone?"

"So far. Ah. Hang on."

Through a small speaker came the distorted sound of a buzzer, like the one Rose had just used. Most of the monitors in front of them were dark.

"No picture?" asked Rose.

"Slight setback," said Larry. "Someone came up to the flat when we were wiring it up."

"Tonight?"

"Yeah. Didn't see who. We had to make a sharp exit. Got most of the bugs in but not the cameras. No visual, except what we can pick up from here." He nodded towards the camera at the window. "I set it up for the bedroom. Seems the most likely place for a floor show, though you never know."

"If there is a floor show," said Rose. They knew Kamila had a lover in St Petersburg, so their plan sought to make it obvious her husband wouldn't be coming back that night. This was Larry's specialism, the full sound and video treatment. It gave him a unique perspective on life that seemed, for some reason, to keep him in very good spirits.

Larry and Charlie, seated in front of the equipment, listened intently. Rose stood at the back straining to hear. Kamila and her visitor were speaking Russian but she couldn't make the words out.

"The sound quality's awful."

"We can clean it up later," said Larry.

The dialogue stopped. Silence. Rose took a step forward and squinted through the gap. She couldn't see any movement in any of the windows opposite. From the speaker came a single, female moan.

"Ah. Looks like it might be audio only," remarked Larry. That was a pity. In Rose's experience the visual part of the package was very influential. There was a long pause. Then came a gasp of breath, very faint.

"Cup of tea?" asked Larry.

"What?"

"Standard equipment. Kettle's just boiled." He nodded towards a plastic kettle and two mugs on a tray. She noticed for the first time that Larry and Charlie both had mugs in front of them. She made herself one. They'd even brought a carton of milk. Charlie got up to peer round the curtain. Suddenly he clicked his finger and nodded to Larry.

"We're on the move," said Larry. Charlie resumed his seat. Through the gap, Rose got a momentary glimpse of swift movement across a window right to left – a bare shoulder and trailing silver satin.

"He's carrying her," she said.

"Do we know who he is?" asked Larry.

Rose shook her head. "It would be useful to find out though. Are they heading for the bedroom?"

"Looks like it."

On a blank screen a dark window lit up with yellow light, illuminating a pair of pale bare breasts. Above that, a dark head lifted and Rose was looking at Kamila's face, flushed but with the same melancholy she'd seen earlier. Rose took an involuntary step back. It seemed freakishly as though Kamila were staring straight at her through the monitor. Her lover was behind her in the shadow of the room. She turned away and was pulled down onto the bed.

"We can't see the bed itself?" asked Rose. She suddenly felt voyeuristic. What a filthy job this was. Animal passions, we all have them, but how vulnerable they make us.

"Nope. The window's too high up. Only above the bed."

"That's a pity."

"The audio's okay, though," said Larry. He adjusted a few dials and the sound got louder, two people's heavy breathing and Kamila moaning in an increasingly regular way. Then there was movement on the screen. Kamila had one hand on the headboard of the bed. The top half of her body was illuminated by the lamp. She looked up, her mouth open and her breasts pert and rounded.

"At times like this I always wonder," said Larry, "why they don't close the curtains."

As they watched, her other hand gripped the headboard and her moans became faster and louder.

"I guess there's no one else at home," said Larry.

"Do we have to have it so loud?" said Rose. Her cheeks were starting to burn. Larry gave her an amused glance before turning the sound level down. The two men stared unashamedly at the monitor while Rose stood behind them. She tried to sip her tea but it was too hot. Some kind of thudding was coming through now, and a man's voice crying out. She felt the hairs on her arms prickle. Kamila rose up slightly, her head back and her neck straining. The man shouted out, briefly, and the noises gave way to heavy panting. Kamila remained motionless for a few seconds, her shoulders back, then she looked down and her face relaxed. A red flush spread down her neck and collar bones, and she was smiling. Rose realised where she had seen that smile before. It was the smile Kamila had when talking to Fairchild.

Kamila reached down with both hands and leaned forward to say something, but it was too quiet for Rose to hear.

"What did she say?" she asked. Larry turned up the sound.

"Spasiba, I think."

"Spasiba?" Thank you? Is that something you'd say to a regular sexual partner? Could it mean this wasn't the boyfriend they knew about? It might be someone else. Someone she'd only just met, even. Kamila was pulled down and disappeared out of sight of the camera. A muffled conversation started up.

"Can you make this out?" asked Rose. Larry picked up a pair of headphones and held them to his ear.

"She's asking him to stay. Says her husband won't be back. He's not so sure."

"Wise man. He'd leave if he had any sense."

"If he had any sense, he wouldn't be there in the first place."

"True."

"Sounds like she might have persuaded him though," said Larry. The conversation had stopped. The screen showed movement again. The back of the lover's head appeared as he half sat up over Kamila.

"He's tall," said Larry. "Long-ish hair. Russian."

"Speaks Russian," said Rose. "Doesn't mean he is."

Larry acquiesced. On screen the lover was looking down at Kamila and reached out to her face. He stroked her cheek gently with his thumb.

"Shit," said Rose. Hot tea burned her fingers and dripped on the floor. She put the mug down and got a tissue out of her bag. Larry looked round, amused again.

"You all right?"

"Sure. Just spilled my tea, that's all." She'd managed to get it on her tights as well. She tried to dab it off and laddered the damn things. It wasn't the sex that bothered her, it was that gesture, that moment of tenderness. Why did she think it was Fairchild in that bed? Why would it bother her if it were him?

Get a grip, Rose, Forget about your tights, just move on.

"An ID on the lover would give us another handle to twist. But there's plenty there without. Alexei Morozov might be nobbing a couple of blond pole-dancers as we speak, but he's not going to tolerate his wife playing away."

Larry nodded sagely. "Way it goes," he observed, turning back to the floor show.

That's for sure, thought Rose, wiping tea off her fingers. In due course, she'd be making that exact same point to Kamila. Female bonding, a powerful tool in the armoury, one she'd used before and would again. The recording was great. All the same, she wished they could be absolutely sure who the lover was. More to the point, who it wasn't.

5

Revolution Square used to be symbolic of the old ideology, but these days Muscovites used it to cross from the Metro to the shops. And shops were the new ideology; Moscow's architecture was grim and boxy compared with the courtliness of St Petersburg, but the department stores started to glow like lanterns when the afternoon sky darkened, and in the displays were sets of shining gold jewellery and luxury perfume, designer coats, stylish leather bags, and on a podium outside, a brand new Mercedes, gift-wrapped with an immense red ribbon. Most people never looked at the display cases and the shelves and the racks and the podium, because they couldn't afford any of it. Sometimes, though, a few would drop in to browse and point and discuss, and every now and then, perhaps, one of them might even buy something.

Fairchild wasn't interested in shopping; he already had what he needed. He crossed the square to the Metropol Hotel and was already lounging in a wide upholstered chair when Zack approached. Zack moved fast for someone of his size. Not that Zack had any excess baggage. Far from it: he was wide but solid, every square inch primed to resist. Fairchild knew that from experience. In jeans, a college sweatshirt and jacket, Zack's colour scheme was more muted than usual but he was clearly still keen to display his Americanness. He'd substituted his usual shades for a designer pair, one small concession to the status-conscious world in which he was currently operating. Fairchild himself was sporting the oligarch's uniform: silk shirt, chinos, expensive leather shoes. With that and his luxury black chauffeur-driven limo, supplied, naturally, through his own firm, he could gain access to pretty much anything he wanted.

"Hey, Fairchild!"

"Hey Zack. Get you something? Budweiser?"

"Christ, you know I hate that stuff. Batlika Number Nine. See you got yours already."

"I didn't know if you were coming." Fairchild was half way through his gin and tonic.

"Yeah, got held up. Had to take a detour. You know how it is."

Fairchild knew how it was. FSB surveillance of diplomatic and military types had become Moscow's number one industry over the past few years, outdoing even its Soviet predecessor, the KGB. Long elaborate routes criss-crossing the city were necessary if you wanted to meet someone without bringing a shadow. He'd had to do the same, but he'd left enough time.

Zack looked him up and down. "You kinda look like you've been here forever."

"In Russia, or just in this bar?"

Fairchild ordered the beer while Zack cased the room as he removed his jacket. Fairchild had chosen seats away from other drinkers but near a speaker playing something orchestral – Tchaikovsky? – loud enough to interfere with any mics, as well as being mildly annoying.

"So, how was St Petersburg?" asked Zack, sitting down. "You know, it kills me when I pay you to go to a party. Especially at your rates. Please tell me it was worth it."

"You pay me for information, Zack. And it was worth it. To a certain extent. The Morozovs were there, Morozov Junior falling about drunk. Didn't react well when I mentioned his father."

"Oh yeah. The Bear! You know him, right?"

"We've been known to drink together from time to time."

"Him being the most notorious gangster in Siberia doesn't put you off, then? Didn't think so. It's amazing he isn't dead by now."

"He's retired. Kind of. Back in Irkutsk while Alexei runs the show from Moscow. They don't see eye to eye, it seems. Anyway, after this reception Alexei ends up staggering off in the company of two glamorous women to a suite at the Empress Hotel. Leaving his wife behind."

"Yeah, well you wouldn't exactly take your wife along to a caper like that, would you? How do you know where they went, anyway?"

"I'm well connected in the limo business, Zack."

"Ah! Course you are. Okay, so you got a chance to check out the apartment while he was otherwise engaged?"

"Nope. I went, but someone was already in there."

"In the apartment? Who?"

"I didn't see. As I was picking the lock at the front, they were making themselves scarce out the back. I caught a glimpse of them in the street, though. A couple of guys, dark clothes, carrying cases."

"Burglars?"

"Nope."

"Spooks, then!"

"A tech team, I'd say. Bugging the place. Or searching it."

"Who do you think it was?" Zack loved all this. Fairchild had known him for more years than he cared to count. With a background in special ops and some never-explained role spanning CIA and military intelligence, Zack partied and womanised to promote his brash Midwest brand, but under all that lurked layers of subtlety. He was also one of Fairchild's best customers.

"Well, I did notice our friend Peter Craven hanging around the champagne earlier on."

"The British! Why are they buzzing around Morozov?"

"Because they've heard the same rumours you have? Concern that such a large criminal empire with international supply lines appears to be attracting attention from the FSB. You're right about that, by the way. Morozov's limo was followed by one of their cars to the hotel. Do people still call them black crows, like the KGB cars?" Fairchild drained his glass. "If the tech crew in the Morozov flat are in the same boat with whoever organised Alexei's little après-ski, you know what that means."

Zack frowned. "The British were running an op! So they may have something. Or someone."

"You should speak to them." He shifted in his seat. "There was someone else at the party. You might remember her from China. Rose Clarke." Did his voice sound casual enough?

"Oh, her. Yeah, sure. When we last met, I was throwing her out of a helicopter. Weird she ends up here."

Zack was probably giving him a meaningful stare, but since he was still wearing his shades, Fairchild couldn't tell.

"She's got her MI6 job back. She's now a bona fide member of the trade delegation, UK Mission to Russia."

"Huh. You didn't tell her you were coming to Russia, did you?"

"She's not interested in me, Zack," Fairchild said, avoiding the question. "She was sent after me in China by Walter. It was a hoop-jumping exercise to get her job back. It worked. Now she's back in the Service she's got other fish to fry. I suspect Alexei Morozov might be one of them."

"Even so. Heck of a coincidence they post her to exactly the place you were intending to go. I mean, I didn't even know myself you were coming here."

"Well, why would you, Zack? I'm not your employee. I just do a bit of work for you every now and then."

"Yeah, yeah. You and your independence. But if it weren't for me, you'd still be in a Chinese prison off the grid somewhere, remember? You owe me."

"Sure, I owe you. But it doesn't make me answerable to you. I go where I please."

"You mean you go where your next *lead* will take you." Disapproving, as ever, of that particular aspect of Fairchild's life.

"Well you don't seem sorry I'm here, Zack. As soon as you tracked me down you offered me work. And I don't remember you sending me a postcard."

"Yeah, well, it's not my favourite place, specially at this time of year." He had a point. Outside, Revolution Square was being spattered by yet more wind-blown snow. "It's those rumours. Folks back home jumping up and down about some possible incursion. On top of the incursions that already happened, that is. We're sensitive about the Black Sea, or at least what's on the other side of it. Those of us with military special ops backgrounds were ordered into the region. Didn't have much say about it."

"Well, crisis or no, I'll be away the next few days, I'm afraid."

"Great. What's the occasion? Vacation? Assignation?"

Fairchild smiled. They both knew he didn't go in for either of those. Zack's face showed the penny dropping.

"Oh! A real life example of you going where you please, is it? In other words, someone's pulled your chain and you're off to 'discover the truth'. Like you've been doing for how many years now? And yet the truth seems kind of elusive, doesn't it?"

Fairchild didn't argue. He'd had plenty of experience batting off this kind of feedback from Zack, who was, to be fair, probably the closest thing he had to a best friend. "I'll let you know when I'm back," he said. "But you should speak to the Brits."

Zack poured himself more beer. "So, are you going to tell me? What this lead is? Where it's dragging you?"

"Tuva."

"Tuva? Where the hell's that?"

"In the south. It's pretty remote."

"And what's in Tuva?"

"A Russian monk called Dimitri."

"And?"

"He was there, Zack." Fairchild couldn't keep the intensity out of his voice. "He was there. In Vienna. The night my parents disappeared."

"He told you that, did he?"

"He told someone I trust. He wasn't just there by accident, Zack. He was waiting. Keeping lookout. He was involved. He knows who was behind it."

"He said that as well, did he?"

"I remember him, Zack! When I came back to the flat that night, when I found it empty, he was in the street outside."

"And you were how old, then? Ten, eleven?"

"I remember everything about him."

"Huh." A non-committal response but he knew Zack believed him. Zack had known for a long time how much that night thirty years ago defined Fairchild's life, how it sang to him like a siren, taunted him to follow the craziest path, to leap into the gorge without caring whether he'd survive, just to find out what happened. Everything Fairchild did was driven by his need to discover the truth. When he'd realised that asking nicely wasn't going to work, he equipped himself with the skills he required to demand answers, and defend himself from those who didn't want him to have them. Those skills also happened to make him a nice living, and he didn't much care who benefitted. But this was more important; finding Dimitri, finding someone who was there, and remembered it, and was willing to talk, gave him the strongest chance he'd had in all these years of discovering the truth.

"Yeah, well, enjoy the journey. I'm sure the New Cold War will hold off till you're back." Zack wasn't pleased, but he'd get over it.

Fairchild got up. "See you, Zack. Like I said, talk to the British. Talk to Rose Clarke."

And with that name echoing round his head, he went out into the freezing darkness for another long journey across Moscow.

6

As soon as Rose pushed open the door of her flat, she realised something was wrong. These few months in Moscow had turned her into a taut wire that hummed to every movement of the air. Peter had said it right at the outset; they were on a war footing. Russia increasingly saw Europe, Britain, NATO, as an enemy intent on thwarting their ambitions to return to USSR-era world superpower status. Moscow was always going to be a challenge. They don't want us here: a thought that seeped into every interaction, every glance from a passer-by, every casual conversation in a shopping queue. We are the enemy, even to ordinary Russians sometimes, and besides, how can you tell who's ordinary and who isn't? It was permanent now, the hotwire between her brain and the hairs on the back of her neck. It exhausted her sometimes. But she was up to the challenge, so she kept telling herself.

Off the train from St Petersburg, she'd got the Metro home. By mid evening she was standing in her front doorway. What stopped her there was the noise of traffic. Her flat was on the third floor above an overpass four lanes wide on either side. Congestion in Moscow was a serious and growing problem, as was air pollution, which was why she would never have opened a window, let alone before leaving the flat unoccupied for two days. And besides, it was December. So why could she hear traffic? She pushed the door wider and the noise intensified. The hallway was empty. The illuminated stairway behind her threw a rectangle of light onto the dark floor.

She stepped in. Outside the bathroom she pushed the door with a finger: no one in there. The kitchen and bedroom were clear. The lounge door was fully closed; this was where the traffic noise was coming from. She paused behind the door and listened. Her mind formed a map of the room – table, rug, sofa. Softly dropping bags, bracing, focusing on the next three moves she had to make – instinct would kick in after that – she counted down in her head. Her hand twisted the handle, the door crashed back. Two steps in, a glance behind the sofa, and she could stop and wait for her heart to race and recover. There were no cupboards, nowhere anyone could hide. Apart from her the flat was empty.

The far window was wide open. The room was as cold as the street outside and smelled of traffic fumes. She stepped over to shut it and the sound deadened. In Russia they at least knew how to build and insulate properly for cold weather, unlike back in damp, draughty Britain. Glancing out into the black sky she saw a ghost of herself, a reflection, small and frightened. She dropped the blind, remembering that it was closed when she left. She drew all the other blinds then flicked on the light.

She perched on the sofa. This was classic FSB, showing its muscle. She'd been warned about what they called 'home incursions' before she'd arrived. Many of the Embassy staff had experienced them, and other expats as well. One person reported that all the toilet paper in the flat had been removed; later it had been found, stuffed behind the fridge. Another staff member realised that one of their kitchen knives had gone missing. Much discussion was had about whether what they did carried any particular meaning. It was all designed to intimidate, that was for sure. Russian nationals employed at the Embassy had it the worst. If it came to it, Rose could simply up and leave, although it would take a lot for that to happen, particularly if that was what the FSB was encouraging.

It did not, Peter was at pains to point out, mean that they knew of Rose's role. They might suspect her of being a spy, but then they suspected most of them of being spies, along with practically all British journos, academics and businesspeople. She had a legitimate job as part of the mission, as they all did. What this meant was that she, like all of them in their close-knit Moscow Station team, had to work that much harder to keep the clandestine elements of their work well and truly hidden. Tricky, as the places MI6 wanted them to go were exactly those places the FSB didn't want anyone to be. Even more tricky now, as she had to assume that her place was bugged, and possibly on film as well. This was the game of mirrors they all played: we spy and eavesdrop on you, you do the same back to us. We corrupt and cajole and bribe your people to spill your secrets, you do exactly the same to ours, or else you trip us up with traps and twists and double-agents. Whoever said the Cold War was over?

Nothing else seemed out of place in the lounge. She checked the bathroom, trying to remember if all the bottles were in exactly the same place as she had left them. It was impossible to be sure. In the kitchen, she opened each cupboard in turn. In the bedroom, she felt inside every drawer, explored the pockets of all of her suits. Back in the lounge, she sat on the sofa again. The room was pretty bare. It was a long way from feeling like home and her personal items didn't fill the room. Her eye kept going back to a small stack of books on a shelf. What was different? She picked them up and went through them. At the bottom was a thin volume she'd never seen before. It was a guidebook in Russian, used and worn: *A Tour of the State Hermitage Museum.*

She'd only just arrived back from St Petersburg. This book contained a very clear message. We know where you've been, the FSB was saying. We're watching you.

She turned the pages of the book without reading it. Her hands were shaking. From the cold? She could tell herself that. She could double, triple check all the doors and windows tonight and sleep with a pepper spray under her pillow. She could be breezy when she told Peter about this, laugh it off. She could make sure she was out of the flat for important phone calls, live a model life while she was here. She could do all that. This was what she wanted, wasn't it? What she'd risked so much to get back? This flat wasn't a home, never had been and never would be now. It was no different from being outside. What she had to do now was put on an act, lie to Peter, lie to whoever was listening, watching, following, convince everyone that she was okay with this, that it wasn't getting to her, that she didn't feel scared and alone.

And that was exactly what she was going to do.

7

Piotr was waiting at the top of ul Lenina. Roman got out of the car and they shook hands, no words needed. They were boys together, their mothers were friends. They drove down to the Central Market.

"Let's take a walk," said Roman.

Vadim pulled in. Roman got out but Piotr hesitated.

"You're afraid of the streets now, Piotr?" asked Roman. "Been in Moscow too long. Come. It's okay. I need to show my face here, show that this is my town. You're afraid, you lose everything."

They wove through the mass of people waiting for buses, tired women carrying their shopping. They went into the market.

"Besides," said Roman as they walked, "I have no enemies here. The enemies are all in Moscow, falling over each other for a taste of Moscow honey. Here is just distant Siberia. This is my retirement, Piotr."

He said it with a smile. Piotr was quiet, on edge. In the narrow aisle shoppers squeezed past his huge form. It smelled like it always did in there, of plastic wrapping, magazines, something sweet.

Oleg was at his stall. He and Roman shook hands. Oleg's fingers were cold outside his worn fingerless gloves. He was here all day, every day, selling candies piled up in colourful heaps. A few roubles a scoop.

"See, those trucks you looked after, Piotr, through the border, this could have been in them." Roman wanted Piotr to understand. When he went south to befriend the border guards and the customs officers, gain their loyalty, it wasn't for nothing. "You think Oleg could make money like this if he bought Russian goods? Sky-high prices because every official takes a cut at every level? He buys them cheap from me, imported, he can make an honest living and I protect him as well. You think the police will care if he's robbed or ripped off? I do."

Oleg energetically insisted they fill their pockets with toffees and fruity chews.

"Small things," Roman said as they walked on. "Small things, but a person's livelihood, a family looked after. That's no small thing, is it?"

Piotr nodded vaguely, his eyes wandering.

Others greeted the Bear as they walked through. It was busy here, always busy. People always needed shopping bags and plastic shoes, DVDs, toys for the children. Lydmilla came out and kissed him. Her jewellery sparkled and pleased the girls and the women. Roman picked up a necklace, a bracelet, and showed them to Piotr.

"Of course it's fake," he said. "Look at these prices! You think people who come here can afford real gold? In Moscow they scoff at such things. They drip with gold, the women there. Our nation is led by snobs, Piotr. Don't you think?"

They came out of the market and stood on the pavement. Roman offered Piotr a cigarette and they stood smoking, watching people and cars crossing the wide junction. A giant advertising hoarding displayed a well-groomed man and an eagle: some brand or other. No one looked at it. Roman felt the sun's winter warmth on his face. His heart filled. This was his home. He made this place; this was what he was.

"So, my friend," he said softly.

Piotr turned to him, his eyes sad. "The world is changing, Roman. This, what you set up here," – he waved towards the market – "it's – small. Modest. In Moscow, you know this, the money, Roman, the money those people have!"

"And Alexei? Morozov is a solid business, Piotr, but he's no oligarch. He thinks he can break into that world simply by spending like them? He will bleed the business dry."

Piotr sucked his cigarette. "He is easily charmed. You were hard on him, Roman."

"I wanted my son to be a man. I raised him as my father raised me."

"It doesn't always work like that."

Roman sighed. "Maybe you're right. If his mother were alive…" Piotr nodded in agreement. "But this woman he has. People are saying she's Chechen. He'd never marry a Muslim dog!"

"She converted to Christianity."

"And they're married?"

"Yes. They're married."

He shook his head. "What is he doing, Piotr? With a woman like that?"

"She's a beautiful girl."

"Fah! Moscow is stuffed with beautiful girls. Girls who will do anything for a few roubles and a night out. I heard that this girl was one of them. Why would he marry her when he can pay so little to have her whenever he likes? What does she want, Piotr? Is she a terrorist? Going to blow you all up?"

"He seems to like her, Roman."

"Well. Maybe he does. Is he faithful?"

Piotr squirmed. "He likes the Moscow life. It's new to him."

"I am a fool. I thought this would change him. The business was too small for both of us. So I gave it all to him and came home. Now the empire is his. But I never thought – I never thought …"

"Roman." Piotr's eyes were fearful now.

"Tell me."

"The lines to the south. The Black Sea lines." He hesitated.

Roman exhaled, felt cold deep inside. "Alexei is pulling out from the south?"

"No, no! He's had approaches. From government men. Making him big offers. They're looking after him, Roman, the men from the Kremlin."

The cold took root, spread. "They want the lines? What for?"

"You know what others would use them for, Roman. What they offered you time after time."

Roman straightened. "I'm not a drug dealer, Piotr. I will not smuggle heroin. I want to make this country great, not get rich destroying it."

"But the money, Roman! So much money! When he's with these businessmen, Alexei has this look in his eye. The government people, they're offering him a way to join all those millionaires, live that life. A way to belong. They know what he wants, Roman."

Roman sighed and looked up at the clouds. "You're sure? You're sure that's what he's doing?"

Piotr shook his head. "No, not sure. I hear things, see the men who visit. One in particular, a solid man, a strong man. Alexei looks up to him."

The image made something inside Roman twist. Piotr, seeing his face, put his hand on the Bear's shoulder.

"You'll find out?" asked Roman. "You'll let me know, what these people want from Morozov?"

Piotr's face was pale. "These men, Roman, they're dangerous."

"We know danger, Piotr. We survived. How many times did our rivals try to get us, during those years, take the business from us? But we fought them off and we won. We got revenge. Remember that."

"The government men are not bandits. They're not robbers with a code, like us. They know everything, see everything. This man, all of them, they're – sure of themselves."

"Well, so are we," Roman said, patting his arm. "Piotr, so are we."

In the car driving home, Vadim caught Roman's eye in the rear view mirror.

"So, it's true?" he asked.

"Yes, Vadim. It's true, all true."

"What do we do now?"

Roman watched the countryside go by, wide and vast. The low sun dazzled on the brow of the hill, casting long shadows through the birch trees. Thin white branches reached up and formed lacy patterns against the blue sky. The snow glittered.

"We go to Moscow," he said.

8

Large, grey and functional, Moscow's British Embassy sat securely behind a cage of steel fencing and a twenty-four hour armed guard. Upstairs, deep inside, it held a long, comfortably equipped conference room with padded walls, suspended in mid-air, so new recruits were told, the only room in the building guaranteed not to be bugged. In this room, in round-backed armchairs that could have been lifted from a hotel, sat Rose and Peter, a laptop open between them on a low table. On it sat the enhanced and edited result of their filthy St Petersburg op: Kamila Morozova displayed to the world over a foggy canal. Rose asked Peter if he wanted to view it. To her relief, he shook his head.

"You know who needs to see it. And we're not looking for a one-off. We need to keep her in place, feeding us what we need. We should have a powerful enough sway over her. If Alexei found out, I don't think we'd be talking about an amicable separation."

"Even though it's okay for him to spend a night with two paid escorts."

"Unfair, isn't it? Still, I'm sure you can make use of it. Female bonding and all that."

"Oh, don't worry, I will."

"And we've no idea who the gentleman might be?"

"We didn't see his face at all." Rose had decided not to mention her suspicion just yet. Fairchild was his own man, and this matter didn't seem to concern him.

"Well, you know what we want from this. The FSB is courting Alexei. What we need to know is why. Morozov has a hand in all kinds of things, but it's the smuggling business that's likely to be of interest to the Kremlin. Morozov trades goods south and west, through Eastern Europe and the Caucasus, down to the Stans as well as east through to China, Korea, Japan. The Kremlin is keen to restore Mother Russia to its rightful place in the world, like the old USSR, challenging the power of the west. We have something of a problem with their proprietorial attitude towards their neighbours, particularly those of the former Soviet Union. And we've seen it in action, not just in the Crimea but in supposedly independent enclaves, troop build-ups along borders, other less direct political pressure. Put those two things together…"

"Does the Russian government really need Alexei? He's a bit of a loose cannon, to put it mildly."

"A liability, but a gift as well. Morozov senior would never have got the firm involved in this way. Bribing minor officials to turn a blind eye is one thing, but acting as a tool of the state something else entirely. That's why Morozov is one of the few crime syndicates left that genuinely stands apart from the Russian state. Alexei taking over is an opportunity to make a lot of things easier. Like moving troops and weapons around without attracting attention, for example."

"Perhaps they just want to muscle in on the revenue. Alexei gets greater status in exchange for a cut."

"It could be as simple as that. We need to know more."

"And we think Kamila will be able to provide this intelligence? She seemed rather passive at the reception." Rose pictured her, a slender decorated waif with a vacant gaze.

"The surveillance spotted her going along to one or two of his business meetings. Surprised?"

"Yes, actually."

"Maybe she doesn't say much, but having ears in the room would help us. She could also plant devices, look things up, report on his movements. Got a plan in place for the first approach?"

Rose filled him in on the detail. He nodded, then sat back.

"I hear you had a home visit."

Rose sighed. "They knew I was in St Petersburg."

"They'll have had a presence at the reception for sure. Files on many of the people there. They have most of us under surveillance. At least they think they do. Get used to having an audience. Don't do anything different. You know how to slip away when necessary. It'll take some getting used to. Your flat will be bugged, of course. Goes without saying."

"Comes with the job, I suppose. The more hostile they get, the more important it is that we keep doing what we do."

"Exactly. They've had a particular space in their hearts for the British since we spoke out about the Salisbury poisonings and so many of their diplomats were expelled worldwide. But that's why we're here, to equip ourselves with the intelligence we need to defend ourselves. And it doesn't matter that there are more of them than us. We just have to be better."

Rose folded her arms. "Are you getting a sense of déjà vu about all this? Is it taking you back to the old days?"

Peter smiled. "It's the same but different. Russia's always done this. A brief period of release following a dominating autocratic regime, and it really looks like things are going to change for good. Then someone gets cold feet and it snaps back again, with even more control than before. And significant casualties, sometimes. The food is better these days, I'll say that."

"Is it?" Rose was not a great fan of the vinegary mush that passed for Russian cuisine.

"Oh, yes. Believe me. And the technology of course. The Kremlin's sponsorship of IT security breaches and social media interference is the world's worst kept secret. That context is all new. So how do you like the place? Settling in?"

For a split-second Rose was tempted to give him an honest answer. But how to put it into words? That growing feeling that she was disconnected, constantly wandering, always watching, spending evenings sitting in empty fluorescently lit burger cafes in front of undrinkable coffee, browsing store shelves then leaving without buying anything, just to put off having to go home? Her flat a doll's house and her an actor playing a role in front of an audience – in the living room, in the kitchen – finally going to bed sleepless because she couldn't stay up all night, then getting out of bed again to pad around checking every door and window, even though she'd already done it three times, and besides, the doors don't keep them out? But this was what she wanted, this job. She'd fought hard, risked her life, to get back into the Service. She had nothing else outside of this job, didn't want anything else.

She nodded slowly. "It's okay. The locals can be a bit – well, they're not the most cheery of people, are they? Everyone has a tragic story. 'Dead, dead, everyone dead!'." She mimicked a Russian babushka, holding her hand out to passers-by in the street.

"Well, there is that element to Russian history, as you'll know from all your background reading. Human life has been valued very cheaply here. Some say it still is."

Rose nodded sagely, wondering if anyone actually got through the diplomatic service pre-posting reading list. She'd managed a few and had even made a start on *War and Peace*. But she was more interested in the present.

"Why are you still here, Peter? They normally move people on by now. Aren't they worried you'll go native?"

Peter smiled again. "I guess I've managed to persuade them that I won't. I like it here. I like the people, sense of tragedy notwithstanding. So does the family. The difference between summer and winter, the vastness of the place, the churches, the countryside. And it matters. There will never be a time when Russia doesn't matter. It's too big. It's got oil, it's got gas. It's got too charged a history. Too many borders, too many neighbours."

"Too many hackers. Too many nuclear warheads." Too many bugs, cameras, FSB snoopers.

"That's the kind of thing I mean." He stood. "If you're worried about the incursions we can transfer you, you know. If this isn't right for you. Some people find it difficult. Understandably."

Great, thought Rose. When did I say I wanted out? This was exactly why she kept her feelings to herself. A man wouldn't have got that.

"Not at all. I'm fine. Enjoying the challenge. As you say, it matters."

She hoped she didn't sound too cold. Peter was old school, but she'd worked for worse.

9

The fluttering of tattered material told Fairchild he'd arrived: a string of prayer flags across the path, their colours almost entirely faded. Beyond that a clearing, outhouses, steps up to large wooden doors, and a man sweeping the steps with short sharp strokes, head bent, intent on the task.

Fairchild called out a greeting. The man stopped and turned. He stared. His jaw hung open.

"I'm looking for a monk called Dimitri."

The man's eyes widened. His mouth clamped shut and he backed away, stumbling on the steps.

"It's all right, Sasha. Carry on." At the top of the steps stood a monk, an older man, the colours of his robes suggesting authority. He didn't move when Fairchild approached and repeated his request.

"We don't have visitors here. This is a closed community. How did you even find us here?"

"Dimitri told a friend of mine. He wanted me to come here. He wanted me to find him."

The man's lips pursed. "That's hard to believe."

"I've been looking for him a long time. Please, I just need to talk to him." How wheedling his voice sounded, like a child's.

"And what do you call a long time?" Said with something like contempt.

"Thirty years."

The man's eyes focused on him. Fairchild stared back. The sweat on his neck and forehead from the long walk was already chilling his skin.

"Wait here." The man came down the steps and walked away.

Fairchild stood in the cold air and watched the sweeper at work, listening to his regular brush strokes. Some time passed. A peal of laughter cut through the quiet. Two young men shot out from behind a building and ran giggling across the clearing between them. Fairchild looked back, and the air stuck in his throat. The figure now standing where the boys had emerged; the shape of his head; his hand, oddly-formed; a slow recognition in his gaze; all this meant that Fairchild had, miraculously, found what he was looking for.

The figure approached.

"You are Dimitri," said Fairchild. It wasn't a question; they both knew. His cheeks were more hollow, his eyes, examining Fairchild, much, much older.

"I thought you would come here eventually. Let's go into the forest."

He walked in a lugubrious, sedate way, as if it were a form of meditation. The woodland path led steeply upward then opened out on a slope opposite a rise of forest, dark green pine lined with fresh snow. Dimitri bent slowly to sit on a log pile. Fairchild joined him. Dimitri, gazing round, nodded to himself, contented recognition on his face: his favourite view.

Fairchild had waited a long time to speak to this man, the greatest part of his life. But now, he couldn't think where to start.

"What happened to your fingers?" he asked eventually. It was something to say at least.

Dimitri looked down at his hand resting on the log, two ugly stumps.

"My sister chopped them off with an axe. If it weren't for that, I'd still be in my village. I'd be herding pigs and rearing horses, living in a cottage with pretty patterned curtains. With a family maybe. But…"

He flexed his remaining fingers, as if it helped to remember. "It was an accident, of course. I was teaching her to swing the handle over her head, and it slipped. I screamed and shouted like a child half my age. The blood spattered in the snow." He looked down at the ground as if he could still see it. "She ran off into the forest. The village men searched for days. When they carried her out, she was stiff and cold. Ice crystals on the tips of her eyelashes." He stared unseeing across the valley. "I stayed for the funeral, then left for Moscow. That was a long time ago."

He looked at Fairchild, waiting. Eventually Fairchild persuaded himself to ask.

"You remember me, don't you?"

Dimitri gave him the kind of smile a grandfather gave a grandson. "Oh yes, I remember you! You were not supposed to be there. You were not supposed to exist. I didn't know what to do, when I saw you. How old were you? Nine, ten?"

"Ten," said Fairchild. It came out as a whisper.

"And you were their child?"

He nodded. Dimitri's brow creased. "And why were you out so late on your own?"

"We were playing cards. The three of us. With forfeits. Questions and riddles. I didn't know one of them. I got angry. I left."

"You ran away! Like I did." In Dimitri's face Fairchild saw indulgence, empathy for his ten-year-old self. "But you came back."

"But they were gone by then. I've been looking for them ever since."

Dimitri's grand-paternal smile faded. "Well, my friend, please don't search for them any more."

Everything around him seemed to magnify, draw closer; the snow balanced on the branches, the faint pine-scented breath of wind, the roughness of the logs under his thighs. Dimitri, talking softly as if to himself.

"It felt like survival, the things I did in Moscow. I was a child. Those men protected me, fed me, kept me from harm. So I did as they asked. But sometimes… they were serious men, hard men. One in particular. A KGB man but a criminal too, a man of the street. Even the toughest of the fighters was afraid of him. He sent us on a special job across the border, through Slovakia to Vienna. It was exciting for me, the West. The cars, so modern-looking! I was young, you understand. There were four of us, in a van and a car. I was the car driver. My job was to stay outside the place and keep the street clear."

He was rubbing his palm with his thumb, as if feeling every callus and wrinkle, calling to mind what those hands had done.

"I waited outside and smoked a cigarette while the other three went in. There were two of them up there, he told us, a man and a woman, to be taken alive. He gave us things to leave hidden in the flat, a radio, documents. We would never ask why; that wasn't our concern. I stood in that street for how long I don't know, gripping my gun every time I thought I heard something. Finally they emerged. The couple were bound up. They didn't struggle or shout, but I could see fear in their eyes. They were messed up, bleeding. They hadn't come easily. The men pushed them into the back of the van and drove off. I was just about to put out my cigarette to follow them when you appeared."

Fairchild was there, in the wide street, walking in the road between symmetrical grey buildings, patches of street light, no sound except his own footsteps. Crossing the road and glancing across, he saw a man standing next to an old car holding a pack of cigarettes. Something strange about his hand. It was just a passing thought.

Dimitri was still speaking. "I could see you clearly in the street light. You looked at me as you walked past, then you pressed the bell. Of course there was no answer, but you had a key. You disappeared inside. I didn't know what to do." The panic was there in his voice. "I didn't know if I should – forgive me – you were a loose end, not part of the plan. But I was on my own. We only had a few minutes to get back to the border. So… I got in the car and drove off. It was some time before I could speak to the others. And by then, I'd decided to say nothing."

He pulled his robe closer and rubbed his arms. Everything he did was slow and thoughtful.

"Our business was with two adults, not a child. No one else saw you. If anyone asked I would say I saw nobody. With him it's a feeling, in here," – pressing his palm to his chest – "him knowing about you would not have been good for you. I have often wondered what became of you."

A clump of snow fell from a tree and pattered onto the ground. Fairchild didn't want to ask, didn't want to hear the answer. But he had to.

"What happened to them?"

Dimitri clasped his hands and drew breath. "There's a place just outside Moscow. We often took people there. It was a secret place, a government place. It's not there now. I went to look for it once, much later. Nothing left. Flat ground. A field."

"Could they have got out? Been released?"

Dimitri shook his head. "Nobody ever came out of that place. I heard rumours about it, stories. People who'd been there to clean up. It was not on any map. You understand what I'm saying."

Fairchild stared at the old man's face, his sad watery eyes, but there was no doubt, no softness, no place for hope. "They died in there, my friend. You can be sure of that."

Tears stung him. This was ridiculous. Of course they were dead. Thirty years and no sign of them anywhere? He expected this. He'd told himself this. He knew this. But still, his lungs heaved for air as he wept like a boy. He couldn't remember when he'd last cried. Dimitri was staring across the valley now. Eventually Fairchild managed to speak.

"This man, the man who sent you. What was his name?"

"His real name I don't know. The men in the street, they called him Grom."

"Grom?" It was the Russian word for thunder.

"A street name. Like the gangsters. They saw him as one of them."

"But he was KGB."

"They would say that he stood apart. That he was his own man. He could be different things to different people. He still is."

Softly said, those last three words, but they grabbed Fairchild by the neck and shook the breath out of him. He'd been watching the film of his past, grainy images from the eighties, faces and sounds seen and heard by a ten-year-old. Those three words froze the screen, yanked him up and slapped him in the face, sent him crashing down right into the present day.

"This man is still alive? Still active?"

Dimitri blinked, uncertain now. "Perhaps I've spoken unwisely. I don't know what your parents did to draw his attention, but I do know that Grom is not a man who forgets."

"Where can I find him?"

"You should be more worried that he will find you. You were lucky, all those years ago. You've evaded his notice. You have a chance to live your life. My advice: find somewhere far away to live. Do the things you want to do, that your parents would want you to do. Treat this chance you have as a gift. Me, many times my life could have ended in the streets of Moscow, but somehow it didn't. I came here and found peace. You could do the same. Think about it."

Dimitri was right. It was Dimitri who had saved him all those years ago. And what had Fairchild done? Turned his entire life into a quest for truth. He'd sacrificed every personal link, every chance of happiness, to search for answers. Every book he read, every journey he took, every friendship he made, one way or another was to further this end. All the things he could have done, and he'd twisted himself up, become this cynical, driven, ruthless machine. Dimitri had given him a life and he'd wasted it.

Dimitri put his hands by his sides and levered himself up. He rested a hand on Fairchild's shoulder.

"I can see you need to be alone. If you want, come back. We can talk again. I'm glad to have met you. It somehow makes things better."

He turned and paced away. Fairchild sat alone, black clouds gathering around him.

10

Gold letters shone on the freshly painted wall above windows that looked out onto a slushy pavement. Formerly Moscow's Gulag museum (now in a remote suburb), the place was just another Gucci now, as the gold letters spelled. Rose went inside and waited, watching the traffic rumble past and people standing at the trolley bus stop by the church opposite.

A car pulled in, long and black with smoked windows. Out of the back door rose a figure in a tight fitting thigh length coat and high heels, with a glimmer of gold. Kamila stared up at the church and lifted her fur-lined hood, even though she was only walking a few steps. The car purred off to sit somewhere and wait, its engine ticking over to warm up the dozing driver who had no purpose in life while awaiting the return of their client.

A man stepped out of the shop door to greet the visitor as she approached. No one else was in the shop. It had been closed for this exclusive 'private viewing', a new habit of the super-rich, emptying a shop of all other customers before deigning to visit themselves. Kamila barely reacted at all to the smartly-dressed salesman's profuse welcome. It must have been something she'd experienced many times. Rose was standing well back as Kamila stepped through the door, eyes already travelling along the racks of clothing in front of her. But she turned sharply at the sound of the door locking behind her. The salesman didn't catch Rose's eye as he slipped past her into a back room. He was trustworthy and had been paid handsomely to provide these few minutes of privacy.

Rose stepped forward. Kamila's startled eyes narrowed in recognition.

"What is this? What do you want?" That low, intense voice again, more powerful than her light frame would suggest.

"Nice to see you, Kamila," said Rose pleasantly, as if they had met by accident. "How did you enjoy the reception? Russian culture is so rich and distinctive, isn't it? I have to say I find it all a little excessive sometimes. The champagne, the caviar, the gold everywhere. But of course I'm a foreigner. Just like you, in some ways. Don't you find? This must all be very different from home."

Kamila's eyes hardened. Rose stepped forward and stroked the sleeve of a fur coat on the rack.

"How did Alexei enjoy the evening? It can be embarrassing, can't it? They like a drink, but then they can't handle it. I've met a few of those, believe me." Kamila's stare became more curious. "And those two women he left with. You know what people say. You can put as much silk and jewellery on a woman as you like but you can still tell a prostitute when you see one. I think it's a bit unfair myself."

Kamila's neck straightened and she pulled her coat more closely round her body, even though the shop was warm.

"Don't you get lonely," asked Rose, "when he doesn't come back at night? In that empty apartment with nothing to do but look out at the canal from that huge bed?" Kamila's eyes started to widen. "Don't you long for company? Someone with time for you, who accepts you as you are? I don't blame you. Family, friends, all far away. Your husband's out satisfying himself with a couple of hookers. It's not right, is it? He can do that, but if you did, it wouldn't be the same at all. These things are always different for a woman."

Rose threw out a regretful look and moved to a table and chairs set in the middle of the store, a hospitality area for VIPs. The laptop was open and ready. She typed the password and the screen opened to reveal a frozen image of the open-mouthed, bare-chested Kamila through the window, just as they'd captured it. Rose pressed Play and the room filled with Kamila's cries of passion at the loudest volume setting, while the body on the screen started moving in time. Kamila stepped forward red-faced and smacked the lid of the laptop down. The sound stopped.

"If he sees that," she said, breathing heavily, "he will kill me." Her lips were trembling.

Rose maintained a pleasant smile. "Well, we'd better make sure he doesn't see it then. That can be done. I do understand it's important to you."

The skin around Kamila's mouth had formed stress lines. "Who are you?" she asked.

"I work for the British Embassy, as I said the other night."

"And what else?"

"Would you like to sit?" Rose sat. Kamila perched. Her skin was white.

"Alexei is a fascinating man," said Rose. "Very different from his father. He seems to be taking the business in quite a new direction. We're very interested in that."

Kamila looked up, then her eyes glazed over. "How would I know?"

"But you go to his business meetings sometimes. That's what I've heard. Maybe you could go to a few more. Or keep an eye on his diary. Or take a look at some of the company files. We can help you. It's the kind of thing we do. We don't want Alexei to suspect anything. It's in our interests to protect you. We want to know a bit more about the operation, that's all. Nothing needs to change. We can help each other here."

Kamila shifted her weight back a little. She looked very sad. It was a difficult position to be in, but she knew who Alexei Morozov was when she got involved. And Rose was genuine. There really was no need for him to find out, if she could coach this woman to be subtle enough.

"They are boring," said Kamila. "The meetings. He takes me because he wants to show me to people. Like his new car. I sit there and smile."

"They'll be more interesting from now on," said Rose. "Now you can listen and observe, and tell me about them afterwards. People will think you're just sitting there but you can fool them."

Did she sound too enthusiastic? She'd always enjoyed being devious and was good at it. Kamila might take a liking to it as well. Was it wrong to feel protective towards this lonely young woman?

Kamila seemed to have calmed down as things sunk in.

"I am not sorry," she said. "A woman has needs, a person has needs. Loneliness is an illness that kills you bit by bit from the inside. If we never feel the heat of another body we will grow cold." She looked up. "Don't you think?"

Rose hesitated. Kamila stared at her, then carried on.

"He was a fine man, my lover, a strong man. You could rely on him. Not falling over himself with vodka." She was half-smiling. "Oh, he is a good lover. He made me feel more human, that we were two human beings, adults, taking pleasure in each other as is natural. It is better to risk everything and be human than safe and locked inside yourself. You agree?"

It wasn't the response Rose had been expecting. Denial, anger, bitterness, those were the kinds of things she was ready to deal with. Personal confidences? Later maybe, when they'd had a chance to build some trust. But here was the difficulty: how to reach out enough that Kamila would reach back, but without giving anything away? Build a bridge without making yourself vulnerable? Kamila, in her soft, emotional way, was challenging her already.

The sad brown eyes were expecting a response.

"We all have our weaknesses, don't we? Our failings," said Rose.

"So being human is a weakness? It's not a strength?"

"That's a big subject. We could discuss it next time we meet. I'd like that. We'll speak again soon, Kamila. That's okay, isn't it? I think we have a lot to talk about." She pulled the laptop towards her. Kamila's eyes followed it into Rose's bag.

"What will you do with that?"

"Nothing. Just keep it somewhere safe. It will always be safe as long as we stay friends."

"So we're friends now?" Kamila still had a half-smile on her face and seemed lost, not at all interested in shopping any more. Maybe she lacked concentration, lived in some dream world. Who could blame her?

"Yes," said Rose. "We're friends now."

11

The car crawled along. Roman didn't like being locked in. Moscow was snarled up now: too many limousines, not enough roads. Vadim edged them forward as the distant traffic lights changed to green then red again. Outside the street was dull, grey pavement and gaudy advertising for western fast food and mobile phones.

Roman rubbed his legs. He'd been in this car too long. The lights changed again. Vadim released the brake, but nothing ahead shifted. Roman couldn't sit any more. He got out and stood on the pavement, stretching his back until it arched. He lit a cigarette. The earthy taste of tobacco filled his mouth. The street had more colour than through the tinted car window. The ground was rough with ice and salt. He paced up and down while Vadim crept along in the BMW. It was a foreign brand, but assembled in Russia. No Bentley for him: none of this snobbish modern preference for imported goods. Of course he couldn't have a Lada now; he still had a reputation.

At the crossroads was a news stand under a small blue awning. He walked up to it, passing Vadim in the car. A good range: newspapers and magazines, chocolate, small gifts for children, umbrellas, kitchen gadgets. The stallholder was young, dressed in bulky clothes. He returned Roman's nod with a grin. Roman picked up a newspaper, looking over the goods and doing a quick calculation of the likely daily take, multiplied upward to weekly, monthly. The street seemed busy enough, passing trade from the Metro. Moscow prices were high, too high. As he handed over the coins he said something about business and the weather. The stallholder smiled and shook his head. Then he saw it. The shape of the nose, the slightly browner skin he had put down to the outdoor work. Uzbek maybe, or Kazakh. That was okay with Roman. But at home they had standards. If you wanted to do business in Russia, take people's money, you spoke Russian. At home it would be made clear. People would get in line. They would know to respect the culture.

He folded the paper and walked on. Round the corner he stood and watched the smoke from his cigarette drift skywards above brown trees and the criss-crossed wires of the trolley bus. Finally the BMW was released from the junction and slid in front of him. He got in and they set off, needing to exchange no words.

They drove out of the city into the suburbs. Following the satnav, Vadim turned off and they pulled up between tower blocks by a children's play area, deserted in the snow.

"This is the one?" Roman looked up at the grey concrete.

Vadim nodded and read out the flat number.

"You tried calling him again?"

"This morning, and again an hour ago."

They walked over and got no answer at the buzzer. A woman with shopping bags passed them and stared, but didn't try to stop them following her in. They went up in the lift, ninth floor. No answer at the door of the flat. Roman leaned on it to think about shoving, but it opened. The lock was broken.

Inside was dark, cramped. It didn't take long to find him. A flat like this was too small for Piotr. He took up most of the floor in the living room. Roman pulled his shoulder to roll him onto his back. Gunshots, but he didn't die quickly. Too much blood. He glanced up. Vadim observed with his priest's eyes. Roman stood and said a silent goodbye. It had been a long time since they last stood like this and mourned a friend. Those days were long ago, so Roman had thought.

He looked round the flat but there was nothing to see. It was clear what they had to do now.

"We go to Alexei," he said.

"Alexei won't see you," said Vadim softly.

Roman folded his arms, looked down at Piotr's body. "Alexei will see me," he said, "whether he likes it or not."

12

Three hours should be long enough to think. Yesterday, it was three hours' walk to the monastery from the town where the bus stopped, and where he'd found a room for the night. And it was three hours back again after Dimitri had torn his world apart. Fairchild lay awake all night and tried to picture another life for himself. Maybe he could do it, now he had the answer and the mystery was solved. He knew now what happened to his parents. He could give this up, as Zack and so many others had told him to do. Instead of being driven, he could think for himself about what he wanted, what he could contribute, even. Be normal. Could he be normal? Stay in one place, build a life? But where? Wherever Rose was, that would be good enough for him. Could he persuade Rose to be a part of it? What would she think? It seemed so impossible. But people did it, didn't they? Most people did it, most of the time. He wasn't so unusual. He was flesh and blood, same as everyone else.

He needed more time to think. He needed to talk to Dimitri again. So the next morning he walked the same route, and thought for another three hours, and his head was full of different things, ideas he'd never considered before, colours entering a monochrome world.

When he got there, Sasha was sweeping the steps again. He was more energetic today, thrusting the broom into the stonework as if digging for something. He didn't seem to hear Fairchild's greeting. Fairchild stopped halfway towards him. Something was different. Yesterday, it had been quiet but there were, he realised, background sounds, the clang of a prayer wheel, distant voices. And the laughing, running young men. But today the silence weighed heavily. Even the prayer flags weren't rustling. The only sound was the scrape of the broom's bristles on the rough stone steps as Sasha gripped the handle and bent low over his task.

Fairchild came close and said his name. Sasha turned and recoiled with a sharp breath.

"I'm looking for Dimitri again."

Sasha shook his head violently. Both his hands gripped the broom and pressed it into the ground. His eyes didn't meet Fairchild's.

"I need to find Dimitri," Fairchild said. Sasha's mouth twisted in a spasm. His breathing was harsh.

Fairchild looked around the courtyard. "Where is everybody?"

Sasha whimpered and spasmed again. Fairchild stepped away. Sasha returned to his sweeping with even more intensity.

Fairchild walked slowly through the complex of wooden buildings. The large doors at the top of the steps were closed as they had been yesterday. Everything else seemed the same, except for the silence. No, not quite the same. The red door of a small building with a pointed roof was closed. It had been open yesterday. He moved towards it. The sweeping noise stopped. He turned round. Sasha was staring at him, but his eyes flicked over to the red door.

"Over there?" Fairchild asked.

Sasha's mouth opened but he said nothing. Fairchild went over to the door. He struggled with the large iron handle. The door was heavy as he pushed. He stepped inside. It was a tiny chapel with a shrine of yellow and gold. His eyes got used to the darkness, and then he saw what was on the ground before the shrine. And as he saw, dread like a deluge of icy water drenched him, pulling some sound out of his mouth. He dropped to his knees and stared, head hammering, chest wrenching, stomach turning at the abomination in front of him. When finally he could move again, he staggered out and leaned against the door frame, looking at the ground, breathing fast.

His head cleared. The silence seemed thicker than before. Sasha was sweeping now but awkwardly, knocking the broom end against the steps over and over again.

The door creaked behind him, moving by itself. The broom came to a halt and Sasha looked up. Fairchild strode over.

"Who did this? Who did this to Dimitri? Who was here?" He grabbed the man's arm. The broom clattered down the steps. Sasha's mouth was twisting again. "Tell me!"

"I can't tell you! I can't tell you!"

Fairchild grabbed him tighter. "Why not?"

"The Rinpoche says, don't say anything! The Rinpoche says, carry on your normal business! Until we come back with the authorities! Just carry on!"

He started crying. Fairchild let go of him. Think straight, man.

"I'm not going to hurt you," he said. "Can you tell me who did this? Who was here?"

Sasha wept, looking down at his feet.

"How did they get here? Did they walk? Were they in a car?"

"Jeep." It was little more than a whisper.

"A jeep? They came in a jeep?"

"Black jeep."

"How many of them?"

The man was mouthing something to himself.

"Two, three, four?"

"Three. Three of them."

"What did they look like?"

Sasha whimpered.

"Okay, okay. Did they ask for Dimitri by name?"

"Dimitri. Where is Dimitri?"

"Did they ask for anyone else? Did they hurt anyone else?"

"Dimitri! Dimitri! Bring Dimitri!" He was shouting to himself now.

"And then they took him in there? How long were they…?"

"No! No! No!" He collapsed onto the step, his hands over both of his ears, sobbing like a child.

Fairchild walked off into the middle of the courtyard. He was exhausted. It was the end of everything. Even the white sky seemed empty. On the steps Sasha was rocking back and forth. Fairchild couldn't help him. He needed to leave. He'd done enough damage here already.

"Don't tell anyone you saw me here," he said.

A loud clattering made him look back as he was going. Sasha had gone over to the chapel and was pulling the red door shut. Then he stumbled back over to the steps, picked up the broom and, head down, started sweeping them all over again.

13

Rose slipped out of her aisle seat. Their row was near the back of the auditorium, so she could creep out while Act One continued. A long soprano aria was in progress, all about how the female character was going to pine away and die now that her loved one was dead. Rose did not have a great deal of patience with opera. She didn't regret having to whisper an apology to her companion, an amiable chap from the Embassy, who had been briefed to expect just that in any case.

Russia involved far too much dressing up. Her long evening gown fell off the shoulders and she was fighting with her shoes again. But for the evening's purposes she felt the need to make an effort. She walked round to the set of ladies' toilets nearest the private boxes. Kamila was already in there, standing in front of the mirror. Rose pushed her palm against each of the doors behind them. All the stalls were empty.

Kamila looked more natural in these surroundings. She was modelling satin and pearls again, a different outfit from St Petersburg, naturally. Rose took the mirror next to her and got her make-up bag out of her clasp. Kamila drew a small object out of her own purse and dropped it into Rose's. Then she took a brush and applied some pink gloss lipstick to her already perfect lips.

"We can't be gone for long," Rose said. "He might get suspicious." The music from the opera rose a level in volume. She picked up an eyeliner pencil.

"I spend a long time in the ladies' room," said Kamila. "He's used to it now. I don't think he cares anyway."

"Has his behaviour towards you changed at all?"

"Don't worry about Alexei. He is a stupid man who drinks too much."

Rose's eyeliner paused mid-air. Kamila's lip brush continued.

"It's all on the drive," she said. "What you asked for. How Morozov helps the government. Tanks, weapons, supplies. There are lists. Bad for Ukraine. Good for Russia. Good for Alexei." She started touching up her mascara.

"Any problems getting it?" Rose asked.

"No, it was easy. I know how to use his computer."

"And you could find it straight away?"

Rose and Kamila had met since their Gucci encounter, to establish terms and discuss practicalities. Kamila greeted every interaction with a serenity that could be taken for a kind of vagueness. Maybe she deliberately detached herself from the present to insulate herself from it. They hadn't made much of a connection, Rose felt. And producing this zip drive in such an effortless way was unexpected.

Kamila's eyes widened as she touched her lashes with the mascara wand. "I searched for it. Like I told you I would. You think I don't know how to use a computer? Why? Because I'm a prostitute or because I'm Chechen?"

Rose gave up on the eyeliner. "No, it's just that Morozov is a large and complex business, and not all of it is entirely legal, so I wouldn't have thought they'd make it all that obvious how to find the more sensitive stuff."

Kamila shrugged. "If the files are the wrong thing, tell me. I can learn." She scrutinised her lashes.

Rose scrabbled about for a stick of lipstick she'd had for about ten years. "Do you know who Alexei is talking to at the FSB?"

"Some older guy," said Kamila, opening a powder compact. "Others too. But he's the important one."

Rose paused the lipstick. "You've met him?"

"One time."

"What's his name?"

Kamila shook her head. "It was in a restaurant, he came in, he and Alexei went back to talk business. The men, you know, have to do such things." She dabbed her nose and chin.

"Would you recognise a photograph of him?"

Kamila looked patronised. "Of course. But a photograph wouldn't show him to you."

"I don't understand. What do you mean?"

Kamila paused. "He is a dangerous man. He never doubts himself and makes others believe him too."

"Really? You could tell all that from a few seconds in a restaurant?"

"You don't need long, if you trust your instincts. Don't you trust yours? And I know my husband. Alexei runs after him like a dog." She stowed the powder compact and inspected the result. "But what do I know? I'm just the pretty wife. Look at the two of us, in here, making ourselves beautiful while discussing all the men."

That calmness again. Was it really coldness, resentment perhaps? Or sheer indifference? Her face gave nothing away. The music was still growing in volume as Act One came to a close.

"You should get back," said Rose. But Kamila had already packed up her make-up. When she opened the door, a blast of passionate soprano burst in. She let it close behind her without turning back.

14

Fairchild wasn't ready for them when they finally approached. He'd known they were there, of course. They stuck out a mile at the small local station. The waiting room was full of thick-legged stoical women wrapped in scarfs pulling substantial packages on trolleys, and men in dusty work gear with tired faces drawing on cheap cigarettes. Everyone wore hats, everyone carried bags of food for the journey, except the two men in leather jackets who tried to stay out of his sightlines but there was nowhere to go. The station building, the single platform and the road outside were their only options.

He hated this bitter cold. He knocked back two strong espressos from the machine, then sat staring at his hands while people dozed on either side. The clock's hands barely moved; they showed Moscow time, morning there, mid-afternoon here. He didn't want to think about Moscow, didn't want to think about anything. When he was on the move it was tolerable, but whenever he stopped the noises invaded his head: shouts, screams, sobbing, *Dimitri, get me Dimitri!* Into his mind came the contorted body, the congealed blood, the unseeing eyes horrifically wide in the dim light of the chapel. Hours of waiting for the bus, and now the same for the train. Poor Dimitri. The old man had remembered Fairchild all this time, had saved him as a boy and could have saved him again as a man. It was because of him that Dimitri was dead. That one rang in his head like the mad clanging of a bell.

On the train it was better. He stared at the passing landscape. Snow started falling, blurring the monotonous birch forests. The soothing rhythm of the train was constant.

At the occasional station stops, other passengers got out and stood, stretching and smoking. He remained seated, willing the motion to begin again. At night he lay down and dozed, thinking that the close proximity of others would protect him. But he'd forgotten about the history of this place, and that it wasn't just history. It was still much, much easier for an ordinary Russian to say nothing, stay out of it. And who could blame them? After all, they were government people, those men; they had that look about them.

He opened his eyes to find them standing over him. In the bunk opposite and above were sleeping bodies. He could have shouted, protested, but it wasn't their problem. No eyes opened as an iron hand pulled him to his feet and prodded him along the narrow compartment and through the door at the end. One was in front, the other behind The man behind pressed into him, making sure Fairchild felt the gun in his pocket and knew they meant business.

The next car along was the restaurant. Usually the dividing doors were locked at night, but not tonight. The man in front pushed the door open. Fairchild could be quick when he needed to be. He shoved him onto the floor and kicked back into the man behind, following up with a punch in the stomach. He slammed the door shut, separating the men. The man behind gripped his shoulders but he lurched and kicked, backing him up against the metal wall. They were in a tiny confined space between carriages, doors to the outside on either side. He couldn't let the man's hands go near his jacket pocket. He grabbed the man's arm and levered down, twisting sharply, prompting an animal yelp. He delved into the jacket pocket. Once his hand was on the gun he realised the danger of using it in this small metal box they were in.

The door opened behind him. An arm circled his neck, wrenching him back. His finger, still in the other man's pocket, found the trigger of the gun. He squeezed. A muffled blast, a shout of pain and the body in front of him crumpled. In the split second of immobility behind him he spun, jabbed up at the face and elbowed the large body. Two thoughts came to him. One, if he stayed on this train he would never make it off alive. Two, the doors were usually locked, but they weren't tonight. With one hand he compressed the large man's neck against the restaurant car door, and with the other he reached back. But the outside door handle needed two hands.

The man lunged. Fairchild rammed with his shoulder, slamming the man's head against the door. He turned and launched himself at the handle, twisting and pushing at the same time. The door swung open and he dropped, hanging onto the handle. His shoulders wrenched. Freezing snow swirled up and around. His legs kicked out: nothing below. Only his arms held him over the moving ground. His grip on the handle was already slipping. The wind rammed the door back, jamming his thighs in the door frame. Strong hands grabbed his upper body and pulled, almost tearing him off the handle. He pushed his feet against the outer frame, propelling the door out against the wind. The door rebounded but he was ready this time. He twisted round and kicked into the carriage, knocking the guy onto his back. Now he was dangling over the moving ground again. He looked down, steadied himself, and let go.

His feet touched the ground. A force slammed him down and rolled him over and over. Something in his face cracked. The train thundered above him. He slowed and slid to a halt. His face was buried in gritty snow. The thundering lessened and receded. He lifted his face, coughing dirt from his mouth. Blood was dripping out of his nose. Snow fell thickly. He started to shiver. He was wearing only shirt sleeves. His skin was already wet. The railway track glimmered in the distance behind the vanishing train. He felt the presence of the forest beside him, a mass of darkness. There was absolute silence.

15

It was just a small gold-trimmed canopy over steps down to a basement. So exclusive it didn't need a name. Black cars hovered, engines droning like bees, drivers ready at a moment's notice while their silk-suited employers sat and drank champagne inside. Roman knew this place. It was just like all the others. So many of them now.

Down the steps and into the bar, the disco dance floor only had female dancers. They paid big sums to get into a place like this. He followed Evgeny through to a private room at the back. Evgeny persuaded the meathead on the door to step aside, and opened it. In a plush room, a blonde and two suits on either side of him, sat Roman's son, legs apart, staring through the window onto the dance floor at a near-topless jiggling bimbo. He turned.

"Who let you in?" he asked. His bouncers finally woke up and stepped forward out of the corners.

"Evgeny did, as a favour. I'm an old customer."

"You used to come to a place like this?" A smile spread across Alexei's face.

"It didn't use to be a place like this."

"Evgeny is a fool. I won't come here again."

"He won't mind. He says you haven't paid for your last three visits."

"He knows I'm good for it."

"He told me how much it is."

"I said I'm good for it."

"Then pay him. Are you going to let me in?"

The smile faded. "What do you want?"

"I want to talk to my son."

"About what?"

"About Piotr."

That made him pause. He nodded his suits away.

"Them too." Roman pointed to the bouncers. "Unless you think you need protecting from your own father."

He waved them off too. Roman sat on the leather armchair next to Alexei's. Through the window hips and buttocks wiggled and swayed. The women sat together and started to look at their mobile phones.

"You're going to introduce me?" asked Roman. "Is one of these ladies your new wife?" They glanced up and laughed, looking at Alexei, not him.

"Kamila is at home," Alexei said. "This isn't her kind of place."

"That's not what I've heard."

He looked annoyed. "Not any more. You want some champagne?" He waved at a bottle on ice on the table. There were no clean glasses and he didn't offer to get one. The room was too warm. It smelled of leather and ladies' perfume.

"This is what Morozov is for now?" Roman couldn't keep the anger out of his voice. "This is what you're spending the money on? Champagne and prostitutes? The obschak isn't for this. It's a fund for security, to help people who need it. Not for your pleasure!"

Alexei glared at him. "Who's telling you I'm spending the obschak? This isn't obschak. This is profit. I'm making a success of your outfit, papa. Realising the potential. No more shopping bags and slippers. I'm making real money." He reached for the champagne bottle and drank from it, wiping a dribble off his face.

"Drugs?" Roman asked. "You're selling heroin now?"

Alexei laughed, a cackle Roman had never heard before. Alexei used to laugh so easily, so freely, when he was a child.

"Is that what you asked Piotr to find out?"

Roman banged his fist on the table. The glass top cracked. The girls looked up.

"Piotr's *dead*, Alexei! You're laughing at that?"

Alexei's face reset. Roman sat back, arms folded. The girls went back to their phones. Alexei picked at the label on the champagne bottle.

"You asked him to spy on me, didn't you? Poke about in the business."

"You blame me, Alexei? I gave you full control but I never hear what you're doing. You don't tell me, you don't ask me, you don't return my calls, you refuse to see me. It's a dangerous business. You know that as well as anyone. I thought – I thought you would want my help."

Alexei looked at him with those pale blue eyes that were once so trusting. "You thought I'd come running to you in a panic? Defer to your wisdom? Ask for your fatherly advice? It's you who got Piotr killed, papa. You compromised him. His blood is on your hands."

"So it was you who ordered it?"

"No! No, of course I didn't! You think I'd do that? He was a family friend! He knew my mother!" He turned away, disgusted.

"Then who did?"

Alexei didn't answer.

"Your new government friends?" He was hiding something. "Those people have no code, Alexei. To them there's no difference between friends and rivals. They put everyone to work to serve themselves."

"You never minded doing business with government men, Father."

"Bribing a border guard? Persuading a customs officer to wave through a consignment? This is different. It's not some stupid unworkable ideology that everyone has to pretend to believe in. We filled the gaps, got the goods where they needed to be when the state was too useless to do it. These days the government has purpose. They want to direct everything, the oligarchs, the other syndicates. Now everyone should dance the Kremlin's dance."

Alexei shrugged. "So? What's good for Russia is good for all of us."

"Oh, my son! Selling off state oil and gas to a handful of businessmen at rock bottom prices? All for Yeltsin's election campaign? Good for Yeltsin, bad for Russia. Now it's even worse. Theft and corruption everywhere. They're bigger criminals than we are, stealing from their own people! Those men you're drinking with tonight, who are they? Those suits?"

Alexei waved his arm. "Businessmen. Authorities. Colleagues."

"Your minders were asleep. Wake them up, Alexei. If you want to stand apart you need to know your people are there. You need to protect yourself."

"We're doing business together. Helping each other. This is how things are now, Father. You don't understand." He lifted the bottle to drink again.

"And Piotr? Did he understand?"

The bottle paused in the air, then he drank and turned his eyes to the dance floor where a tart in hotpants was angling her crotch directly at the window.

"Do you even think about what your mother would say about all this?"

The bottle slammed onto the table. "That's your problem, isn't it? That's why you hate me! Mother was killed in the shooting, but I survived. Your beloved, perfect, Russian wife shot dead in the street, but somehow your puny, weak little son managed to crawl away! Oh, how you wished it was the other way round! You never forgave me, did you? That's why you made me serve in the army. You could have got me out of it like so many others did, people who cared about their sons, but you wanted to punish me. Punish me for being alive. For not being more like you! For not being Mother!"

The two bimbos had looked up from their phones. When Alexei was done, they turned back to their screens.

"I wanted the army to make a man of you. Like it did my father. And me."

Alexei started to laugh, giggling like a girl. "A man of me? A man? Don't you know? The army takes men and turns them into beasts! You have no idea. You think a shoot-out in the streets of Irkutsk is like Grozny? You think that anything that happened during those days was as bad as a month in a training camp? You think that *honour* meant anything there? That there were rules, or codes? You know nothing. You're an old man, Father. That's what you said when you gave the firm to me. It's time I took over, you said. Time for you to retire. You were right. Hey!"

He called the girls over. They draped themselves on either side of him. One nibbled his ear and pressed her tits against him. His hand traced her body down her back. The other one started to stroke his thigh. Through the window the music thumped and more bodies twisted and thrust. Alexei's eyes glazed over as he watched. He reached for the champagne bottle and drained it. He dropped it on the floor and wiped his mouth with the back of his hand. The woman feeling his thigh worked her hand into his crotch.

"For God's sake, Alexei!"

"Go home, Roman," he said, still watching the thrusting women.

Roman stood to go. His son had never called him Roman before, never addressed him as an equal. At the door he turned. Alexei's head was tilted back and his eyes were closed, while the women handled him and the dancers danced on.

16

Something was burning. Crackling, popping noises worked their way under Fairchild's eyelids. He moved; fibres scratched against his chin. A soft stiff lump was massed under the back of his head. He opened his eyes. Wooden walls blurred into thin rugs, pans next to a stove, a figure sitting in a chair. He lifted his head. Something in his stomach swam upwards. His ears roared. He lowered his head again. He was warm: a rough heavy blanket coated him. He pushed it away. He was wearing thick brown work clothes he'd never seen before. The figure in the chair leaned forward and a round red face looked at him. A high-pitched laugh, the laugh of a girl. Then a stream of sounds, some garbled, some words.

"…of course she said her house was best, but I told her…not cold in here. Only when the east wind blows the snow through the hole in the roof. How can she, Olga Petrovna,….the fond idiot she thinks I am. I can put her down when….ten years, it's been. Ten years!"

The words danced and tumbled. Why was he struggling? His Russian was flawless. And why were there dots in front of his eyes? He closed them. What was the last thing that happened before this? Come on, man! Nothing.

Wood scraped on wood as the woman pushed herself off the chair and shuffled towards him. "Have some borscht. My borscht is very good. They all said…best in the village. My husband and my son and my daughter and her son… I kept them healthy. Please! Please!"

The tiny old woman was holding out a bowl of steaming purple liquid. He couldn't seem to lift his head – too dangerous. She bent, wheezing, and put it on the floor next to the narrow little cot he was lying on. He managed inside his head to form a sentence in Russian:

"What is your name?"

"Ha! My name, my name is Olga Grigorievna." She pulled her chair round so that it faced Fairchild and settled as if about to tell a story. "This is my house. I've lived here all my life. I was raised here, and I raised my family here, and they did the same. But now it's only me." That seemed to be the end of the story for now.

He got more words out, but seemed to have forgotten how to form a sentence. "How … come here?"

Olga tilted her head. "You're not Russian? Yet you speak Russian. And you're so pale!" This caused confusion. "Estonian?" Fairchild didn't contradict. "Estonian! And your name is?"

"Ivan," after a slight hesitation.

"Ivan. An Estonian called Ivan! Well, well, well!" She rubbed her hands.

"Can you tell me how I got here?" That was better. The brain seemed to be working better but the mouth was thick.

"Well, Olga Petrovna said that I was going mad. But she always says that. Olga Petrovna says that I shouldn't wander off walking in the snow in case I forget who I am and how to get back. But that's all nonsense. So I still walk in the snow and through the forest where I can think about those times back then, when we were all here together. Sometimes it seems like a dream, it happened so long ago. Only me now."

"You found me?" Memories were starting to stir. Two men on a train, a fight, a gun.

"I almost missed you but I tripped over your boot and fell!"

"Near the train line?"

"Near the train line! You looked very peaceful lying there. But I've lived here all my life. All my life! So I know what that means, when someone is lying peacefully in the snow. I shook you and shouted, but you didn't wake up. Then I broke off a birch stick and prodded you hard. Very hard."

Could he risk trying to sit up again? He got half way; his stomach stayed tame. A sharp pain jabbed him in the ribs. He felt the skin, tender and bruised. Olga pursed her lips.

"Yes. Very hard. And you woke up. But when you tried to stand, you fell again. So I came back to the village. And at first no one believed me, because of Olga Petrovna and what she says about me. But they came to look, and then they saw. And then we went back to the village and brought the cart that Maria Kasparova uses for her apples, and we put you in the cart!"

Fairchild stared at his diminutive hostess. "You lifted me onto a cart?"

"Well, it was myself and Maria and Aleksandra Larionova, and Svetlana Ivanovna and Anastasia Rusakova. And even Olga Petrovna herself came to help to push it up the hill. And then I said that you must come to my house, even though Svetlana's house was nearer and Anastasia's house has more space, and Olga Petrovna said that her house was the warmest, although it is not. Please. The borscht."

Now he was sitting all the way up, leaning back on the wall. Some kind of background humming came and went. There were no straight lines anywhere. Olga heaved herself out of the chair to reach down and pass him the steaming bowl. He took it. It smelled – cabbagey.

"Please." She gazed, nodding, waiting. His gut churned thoughtfully. He picked up the spoon, half-filled it with the dark red fluid and drank.

It was good.

"See! I told you!" She nodded, satisfied, and pulled herself back onto the chair. Fairchild drank some more. A growl from below. That would do, for now. He put the spoon down.

"Ten years," he said. "Earlier. You said ten years."

Olga looked sad. "The last one was Larionov. He was the last. That was the vodka. It was the vodka with most of them. But also the war, the gulag." A regretful smile.

"The last what?"

"The last man, of course! Only us women left now, going on ourselves, for who knows how long!"

"There are no men in this village?" He was starting to doubt his Russian again.

"Not for ten years. Twenty years in this house. Ha! Twenty years! Husband, son, grandson. The war, the gulag, the vodka. The—" She stopped mid-word, closed her eyes and shook her head. "Other things."

Other things. That history again. Black crows, a hammering on the door in the middle of the night, a room at the end of a long corridor. A slow starvation by a window overlooking fallow fields. A scream, a gunshot, a place just outside Moscow. Nothing left, flat ground. Other things.

Her eyes were open again. He pulled the blanket fully aside.

"These clothes I'm wearing…"

"My husband's. I kept a few. I don't know why."

"You really didn't need to…"

"But your clothes were wet. They are drying in front of the stove. And it's good to know that I still remember how to undress a man." She giggled, a girl again.

"When did you find me?"

"Two days ago. But I don't know how long you were there. The trains come through daily. We sometimes find things that have been thrown off the train. Not people, though!"

Fairchild smiled, though it was painful. "I was mugged. On the train. They took everything and threw me off. I went into the forest. After that I don't remember."

"You were going to Moscow?"

"Yes, Moscow." The room lurched. He remembered the chapel. Dimitri, poor Dimitri. The humming came back. His soup slopped over the rim.

"Oh, poor thing!" Olga took the bowl, guided his head to the pillow. "You must rest. You must rest. Moscow can wait, heh? Moscow can wait."

Fairchild breathed slowly and closed his eyes, pushing that memory away.

Yes, Moscow could wait.

17

Rose's feet pounded the road. She sped up, filling her lungs with freezing air. Her chest ached. Checking behind her, she veered into a side street down to the river.

She was running every evening now. It got her out of the flat, away from the invisible watchers, the silent listeners. Her runs were getting longer and longer. The pavements were rough and icy so she found routes quiet enough to run in the road, or where the paths were wider and well gritted. She already knew the streets in her own neighbourhood – standard training – but her knowledge was broadening to other areas as she covered greater and greater distances. Back streets and parks didn't bother her; she wasn't afraid of muggers. What was she afraid of? That was a question she didn't want to answer.

She crossed a bridge by some enormous new cathedral. Here was a former chocolate factory, now regenerated in parts, trendy restaurants concealed within a red brick maze. She powered around the outside keeping to the river. At this time of night it was deserted. She tried to empty her head, focus on her breathing, her pace, maximising the stretch of her legs. The bridges went by as she ran on and on, set in a rhythm, managing, finally, to feel truly alone. She turned back homewards, every sense on overdrive as she neared the flat, every shape, every shadow, every sound registering. But it was only when she entered her apartment building that something jarred.

The light was different. Rose knew it as soon as she pushed open the door. The stairs rose in front of her; to their left the stairwell lurked in shadow. The door closed and a choreography formed in her head. Two steps towards the main staircase, a spin, kicks and jabs into the darkness, leading with hard edges of feet and hands. She met resistance, substantial flesh but unprepared. A male voice groaned as a figure slumped. She took a step back. The body down in front of her was swearing softly – in English. She reached for the light switch.

The man was well-built with slicked back dark hair. He lay crouched, two large hands clutching his groin. The swearing had an American accent.

"Christ's sake! You don't take prisoners, do you?" She struggled to place the voice. The sleek head eventually lifted to reveal accusing brown eyes, melodramatically reproaching. Eyes that Rose recognised.

"Zack!" She crouched down to speak quietly. "I didn't know you were in Moscow."

"Yeah, well, surprise!"

"What are you doing, coming here? This place is being watched."

"Not at the moment it isn't."

Rose glanced at the door. "They've been here. They've been in my flat. You know what that means."

"And that's why I'm waiting for you down here. I know what I'm doing, I'm telling you. I checked the place. There's no one outside. Not tonight. I promise you." Rose stood, not sure whether to believe him. "They can't watch everyone all the time, you know. Not even the FSB."

Maybe she was getting too twitchy. "Well, we can't talk upstairs."

"I know, I know. There's a bar two blocks down on the other side. Irish theme pub. You know it?"

"Sure."

"See you in there in half an hour?"

"What's this about?"

"Come and find out."

The pub was like all other Irish pubs across the world, in that its Irishness had certain limits. It didn't extend to the food menu, for example, and the draught Guinness wasn't the best Rose had tasted. But there were shamrocks and black-and-white photos of Dublin and a bashed up old piano, and a decent number of customers creating a useful hum of conversation.

If Zack had something to say, it was worth finding out what it was. He and Rose hadn't parted on the best of terms last time they met, but he was a man with access to resources and the authority to use them. Last time, on her suggestion, he applied them on a mission to spring Fairchild from a Chinese prison. It had been in both their interests. So she was curious. On the way to the pub she'd given herself a pep talk. No more FSB jitters. She needed to be in control.

He was already in a corner behind a bottle of Russian beer. Rose sat opposite.

"How's the injury?"

"I'll live. Still got the capacity to reproduce. Thanks for that."

"Next time, don't lurk in dark corners near a woman's flat. Can you see anything at all with those things on?"

Zack was now wearing his trademark mirrored shades, making it impossible to read his face. "I can see fine. You want to punch me in the eye as well?"

"Take it as payback for when we last met. Thanks, by the way. For chucking me out of a helicopter in the middle of the jungle. In the middle of the night."

"That was a precaution. As I explained at the time."

"It wasn't a hundred miles to Chengdu, by the way. Only about twenty. And there was a road. But then you knew all of that, didn't you? Do you play games with everyone, or am I special?"

"I didn't like you and I didn't trust you." He necked his beer.

"You don't say. So what's changed?"

"I heard you got your job back. You're back in the fold. That changes things. This isn't a social visit, see? This is work. Sounds like your people and my people are interested in the same target."

"That target being?"

"The charming Alexei Morozov. His dubious business interests. His even more dubious government contacts. I heard you and your pals were actively involved in getting to know the guy."

"And where did you hear that?"

"A mutual friend."

They only had one mutual friend. "I see. I saw him recently, at a reception in St Petersburg. He was working for you? He did disappear quite suddenly during the evening."

"Yeah, well, he does that." She heard irritation in his voice.

"So, has the all-talented Mr Fairchild got inside the Morozov syndicate? He has something of a track record doing business with gangsters, hasn't he? That's what he was doing when he and I first met. He was working for you then, as well."

"That's what he was trying to do. Failing, though, on account of your interference."

"Sorry about that. You both seem to have got over the experience, though. So does he have something?"

"Do you?" Zack's expression was impossible to read.

"Maybe." Rose had no intention of telling him anything of substance. This was interesting news, though, and gave some weight to her theory about Kamila's lover. Would Fairchild sleep with a woman to get information he could sell? She could believe it of him.

"Well, you wanna share? We're supposed to be on the same side, aren't we? Us NATO allies, reluctant to see Russia expanding its influence? Not to mention its borders."

"So you think Morozov is taking on a political role?"

"Don't you? That's what the Kremlin does now. They want all kinds of organisations working to their political agenda, including the less legitimate ones. We should pool our resources on this."

She sipped on her mediocre Guinness. "What you're proposing would involve Fairchild as well, I suppose?"

"That a problem? Can you stand to have him on board? I mean, I know you guys aren't keen on him. Being as he's British, and all."

"Well, you have got to admit, Zack, it's difficult to be sure where his loyalties lie."

Zack shrugged. "I pay him, he does a job."

"That's exactly what I'm talking about. And you're right, he's not flavour of the month with the Service. Particularly our new chief."

"Marcus Salisbury? That's a surprise. Oh, I'm sorry. *Sir* Marcus Salisbury."

"Whatever. Look, I'll run all this past my people. Give me a way to get in touch with you. If I get the green light we can all get together and compare notes."

Zack handed her a business card featuring generic corporate details including a phone number. "One possible hold-up," he said. "You know I said Fairchild had a habit of disappearing?"

"Fairchild's gone off the job?"

"The way he sees it, something more important came up, so he decided to take a few days out. But that was more than a few days ago. More like a week and a half."

"Something more important? Oh, I see." The Russian with the missing fingers, no doubt. Even with his shades, she could tell Zack was observing her.

"So he confides in you now?" he said. "That's cosy."

"He confides in you, doesn't he?"

"We go back years. He knows he can trust me. He knows I'm loyal."

This again. Zack had the idea that Rose wasn't on Fairchild's side. Hence the helicopter incident. And, fair enough, her mission at that time was to deliver Fairchild to MI6 and thereby get her job back.

She leaned forward. "Are you more loyal to him than to your country, Zack?" He didn't answer. "I've nothing against Fairchild. But the job will always come first. He knows that. And I didn't ask him to share. I was pretty surprised, to be honest. You want to be his best buddy, that's fine by me."

She'd only managed half the Guinness, but their business seemed to be concluded. She got up. "See you around, Zack. Don't come to the flat again."

He gave a mini-salute and, as far as she could tell, watched her as she left.

18

Olga Grigorievna was right about her borscht. That and her winter potatoes and her sweet red kompot juice and her stewed apple in jars, made from all the apples she could reach while they were fresh on the trees – fewer every year! Fairchild lay and listened and she apologised for talking – rattling away, Olga Petrovna would say, but she was such a sourface – as she shuffled round the room, her discourse leaping the decades from one family tragedy to another. In his company she spent more time with these memories than she had for years, recalling them more closely, more warmly. A remembered habit or turn of phrase brought a smile and moisture to her cheeks.

When he could walk, he would help her feed the animals then wander around slowly, gathering a few pieces of firewood before returning to rest. But he was getting stronger. The other women of the village stared at him with his oddly-fitting clothes and his fine fingers that showed he didn't belong in the country. Eventually they overcame their shyness and called him over, and if he was gone a long time, Olga would venture out and find him bent over a cold frame or carrying crates of cabbages. Olga Petrovna even got him fixing a wardrobe in the bedroom. The cheek of it! she complained as she shooed him back to sit by the stove. It was she, Olga Grigorievna, that found him. *She* was *his* Olga, not that interfering old shrew.

Sleeping wasn't easy, still. When he woke he'd jump into consciousness, mouth dry, neck strained, sucking air through his teeth, that hideous sight in the chapel coming back over and over again. Olga would tut, and bring more borscht.

He would lie awake and think about those men on the train. Did they think he was dead? He would have been, if a curious old woman hadn't found him by chance half buried in snow. Was anyone looking for him? This was a vast area, mile upon mile of empty frozen land. The whole time he'd been in this village, no one had arrived or left. It felt insulated from the rest of the country, a tiny world in itself where everyone shared the same aim: survive the vicious winter as comfortably as you can.

Time passed differently in the village, too. How long had he been here? One week, two? Perhaps he could stay. He could do some good. He could fix Olga's roof. A small contribution maybe, but not for the woman who'd saved his life in return for nothing. Could it make up for what had happened out there? Out there, where a man died, horribly, because of him. Where people hauled him off while he slept on a train, where someone he'd never met seemed to want him dead. If he stayed here, presumed dead, he could make lives better without making anything worse. He was sick of the life he'd led. He'd been ruthless, cruel, utterly focused. Now he had the answer he'd always craved, it seemed meaningless. He didn't have to be about that any more. He could be someone else, perhaps.

Dimitri's voice came into his mind: *find somewhere far away to live. Treat this chance you have as a gift.* Everyone in the village had seen horrors, but long ago. Life here was about keeping the foxes away from the hens, and finding new places where the mushrooms grow, and keeping warm through the winter, even though firewood melted away in the stove and was so heavy to carry. That could be enough, couldn't it?

But he knew it wasn't. His dreams weren't just memories; they had a present, a future. He thought he was merely digging into the past, unearthing old secrets, but Dimitri's secret triggered something that brought men in the middle of the night. They could come here, with their sullen faces and their guns, and pull him from his wooden cot. Olga and the women here had seen plenty of that in their lives. They'd suffered enough.

One day he went to Olga Petrovna's house to borrow her ladder. When *his* Olga came back from the animals, she found him on top of her house making repairs. Olga had accepted the slow deterioration of her troublesome roof as inevitably as her own decline, and was only hoping that she would reach her end before the roof did. But now it had a new lease of life, and the buckets and bowls so carefully placed everywhere could be tidied away. When it was time to go, his Olga's was not the only house with a well-stocked woodstore or better fitting windows or buckets of onions and cabbages and gherkins peeled and ready for pickling.

The ladies of the village tramped through the forest as far as the railway line, the nearest station stop six miles further on. It seemed that everyone had a box of men's clothing stored away somewhere, and Estonian Ivan had a wide choice of trousers and shirts and sweaters and jackets and woollen hats. Laden down with blinis wrapped in napkins and salted meat and fried potato cakes and apples, he felt a sudden great sadness.

You could stay, Olga said. She'd learned how to read his face. It's not so bad here. You can make yourself useful. The food is good, no? And spring is coming. But he knew he had to go. Moscow beckoned, though with a fist, not a wave.

His posse looking on mournfully, he turned westwards, walking in the middle of the tracks to avoid the snowdrifts. After a while he looked back. The women had gone, back to their snug cottages and their roaring stoves and their bulging winter stores. It wasn't long before all of that would seem like another dream.

19

"Interesting," was what Peter said, when Rose told him of Zack's offer. They were back in the secret room again. "I can't think of any reason why we wouldn't work together, can you?"

"Well, only one," said Rose. "John Fairchild. He's working with Zack on this. That's why he was at the reception. He'd be part of the package if we went with Zack. And he's not flavour of the month with all of our colleagues, is he?"

"He's an interesting character."

"That's one way of putting it."

"You're not keen?" Peter sat back and looked at her.

"He's cynical. He hates MI6. He thinks they covered up the circumstances of his parents' disappearance. You know about that?"

Peter shrugged. "Only the stories. Before my time."

"Well, he's adamant, and determined to find out exactly what happened. In fact, that's where he's gone now. Zack said he'd disappeared. He's gone to track down some Russian who was supposedly there the night it happened. And he hasn't come back. This isn't something you know anything about?"

Peter looked surprised. "Me? Why would I know about that?"

"Well, you and Fairchild seemed pally at the St Petersburg do."

"He's a contact. We've met, occasionally. He can be useful. He's not on my Christmas card list." He paused. Rose could see he knew there was more.

"That job I was doing for Walter Tomlinson, before I came here. You know about that?"

"I knew you were working for Walter, but nothing beyond that."

"Walter sent me after Fairchild, to get a meeting with him. Which I got. After that, Walter asked me to find out where Fairchild was going next. Which I did. Then guess what? I end up being posted to the exact same country."

"Well, it could be that Walter is playing some intricate and long-term strategic game," said Peter. "Or, it could be that we were looking for people with your experience, and you had an excellent Service record as well as already speaking Russian. I don't have any secret motives, Rose, if that's what you mean. You came highly recommended, that's all I know. The reception was the first I've seen or even heard mention of John Fairchild in years."

Peter sounded credible. But he was a spy, and had been for decades. Credible meant nothing. "Well, I guess if there is a Fairchild-related purpose to my being here, someone will tell me at some point. As far as Morozov is concerned, Fairchild may be useful if we think we can trust him. Or indeed, are allowed to trust him. Even if you're happy, I'm not sure what they'd think back home."

"London's a long way away. As long as we keep things discreet there's no need for anyone to know. This guy Zack will be carrying the can anyway. It's the Americans who've contracted with him, not us. Anything goes tits up Fairchild-wise, it'll be Zack's fault. Of course, it would be much better if it didn't go tits-up in the first place."

Rose felt the need to raise the other matter that she'd spent longer thinking about than she wanted to admit. "We need to consider the possibility that we might already be treading on each other's toes. On the night of the reception, did you see Fairchild leave?"

"No. I thought he was still there when I went."

"No one seemed to see him go. But I'm sure he'd gone by the time I left. He just vanished. After spending quite a long time in close conversation with our Kamila Morozova."

"Are you implying something, Rose?"

"The video we have of Kamila, recorded later on that same night. We never see who her lover is."

Peter's eyes widened. "You think it was Fairchild?"

"He was there on a job, Peter. We know that now. He could have had the same idea as us, to get into Alexei's business through his wife. Only in a more direct way."

"Zack didn't give anything away about this?"

"We didn't get into that much detail. But we probably will, if we're working together."

"Well, I wouldn't put it past Fairchild to do a thing like that. No one could describe him as risk-averse. He doesn't have a reputation as a womaniser, though."

Peter's laid-back response bugged her just a little. "But can we be sure what he's really up to? Don't you think it's odd that it was only after St Petersburg that he found out where this Russian is, that he was looking for? When he told me about it in Kathmandu, that was months ago. Zack may think Fairchild is working for him, but maybe it's the other way round, Fairchild taking the opportunity to get something he needs from the Morozovs."

Peter looked nonplussed. "It's worth bearing in mind. But if he brings us something new, maybe it doesn't matter if he took the opportunity to get something for himself as well. He's open about being a free agent, a mercenary of our world if you like."

"I just don't trust him."

"Fair enough. We keep him at arm's length. Heard back from the analysts?"

"It's on its way to you. Everything on Kamila's drive points to what I said before, that the Kremlin is using Morozov's logistics network to get weapons and supplies into eastern Ukraine. They're secretly building up stocks this side of the border and they're arming God knows who within Ukraine itself."

Peter looked doubtful. "If that were happening, you'd have thought our drone and satellite surveillance would have picked up on it. Or social media chatter."

"A lot of the movement's been attributed to military exercises we already knew were going on in the south and west."

"Well, in that case we need to consider the idea that the exercises were deliberately set up to conceal an actual invasion. Any idea when?"

"Soon, according to the data. We're still working on it."

"That doesn't give us much time to verify it. Good work, Rose. Kamila's been useful already."

"Yes."

Peter responded to the flatness in her voice. "You have doubts about her?"

"Perhaps a little too useful this soon, don't you think? I mean, she had no problem finding what we were looking for and putting it all on the drive. Pretty competent for someone who doesn't give an impression of being business or IT savvy."

"You think she's playing us?"

"Maybe. She didn't mind telling me what she really thinks of Alexei. Not favourable."

"Well, rich men marrying prostitutes might make a true love story in Hollywood, but elsewhere motives tend to be a bit more venal. You think she wanted to betray him?"

"She seemed embarrassed about the tape. But she's come round to the idea of helping us pretty quickly."

"The background researchers didn't find anything on her?"

"No. But there wasn't much from before she came to Moscow. It might be worth doing a bit more digging. Her being Chechen is interesting."

"Okay. Research down there is tricky, though. Place is a mess. And we need verification on the double. All teams, all sources. We need to squeeze all our agents and find out if this is genuine or not. And the sooner we can compare notes with our cousins, the better."

"How do we frame this? We've got to pass it on, haven't we?"

For the first time in the months they'd been working together, Peter allowed himself to look slightly perturbed. "If the Russians launch a surprise invasion and we're not ready because we didn't pass on intelligence, that'll be bad. But if we pre-empt an attack on the back of false reports, we and our NATO allies could be painted as aggressors. There's a lot that could go wrong here, Rose. Make sure you stay on top of it."

20

Fairchild rang the buzzer first. No answer, so he went round the back to try the windows. It was one o'clock in the morning, after all.

He'd struggled to sleep since getting back to Moscow. He was staying in a hotel in the outskirts, the kind that didn't ask for ID. Plenty of his contacts would have offered him a bed, but no need to endanger them by bringing the FSB to their door. He'd stay in the wind as long as possible, but how long could anyone hide in Moscow from one of the most active internal security forces in the world? Moscow was saturated with agents; it was only a matter of time before his survival would be discovered. And then? Whatever happened then, it wouldn't be pleasant.

He'd gone out straight away to meet Zack, feeling the need to embark on a half-day tour of Moscow to ensure discretion. It suited his restlessness in any case, his desire not to exist, not to be anywhere. He'd equipped himself for the journey; en route, a red woolly hat became a grey fleece beanie, a leather jacket was obscured by a long dark greatcoat, as he slipped from persona to persona. It was Zack who'd sent him to where he was now.

The Morozov Moscow office was not in a fancy part of town. Just like any local office of any regular import-export business. The place had the smell of Roman about it. Alexei would have wanted something showier, more central. Old Arbat, New Arbat. Painted period charm or glass-fronted commercial modernity. Not a grey square on a featureless street opposite a vacant lot hosting tired, grimy lorries. The real Moscow, Roman would say. Fairchild got the edge of a lever under the window frame and tensed. No give.

Get ahead of the game, was Zack's instruction. When I talk to the Brits, he said, I want something to bring to the table. Going to St Petersburg to get as far as a front door then legging it, only to disappear for two weeks, makes us look kind of unfocused, no? So get over to the House of Morozov and make up for lost time. What about Pops? Renew your acquaintance? Fairchild had put the call out, to discover to his surprise that Roman was already in Moscow. They'd be meeting tomorrow, which left a night and a day to discover what he could and make Zack look focused in front of the Brits. He heaved at the lever again. A piece of window frame splintered off, ramming the back of his hand into the stonework. The graze smarted and oozed blood. The window remained solid. Fairchild swore and missed Olga's stove.

He moved to the next window. Zack had been unimpressed with his news from out east.

"I guess that's the end of the trail for your folks, then," he'd said, displaying his maximum capacity for empathy. In front of him was a can of beer on a plastic tray. They'd met in a fast-food restaurant squeezed between discount stores in a subway off the Metro. Fairchild was sipping substandard tea out of a brown plastic cup.

"Yes," he said, "and for the guy who told me about it."

"What happened to him?"

"He was nailed to the floor in front of a shrine."

"Alive?"

"At the time. Not when I got there."

"By who?"

"Some guys in an SUV. They must have tracked me out there."

"You didn't see anything?"

"I wasn't looking. No one even knew I was going there."

"Someone did. Government people?"

"Must be. The guys who came for me on the train were FSB."

"Why would the Russian government be concerned about this?"

"Because this man Dimitri described is still out there, Zack. This 'Grom' character. He's still active."

"No way! That was thirty years ago. He'll be long gone, or living out a restful retirement somewhere. And what's with the gangster nickname? Mister Thunder! Sounds like a comic book superhero."

"I'm sure he has a real name, but Dimitri didn't give it. He seemed to think he was still around, though."

"And he's got his ear on the ground, has he, this monk who lives in this place that's a three-hour walk from the nearest road?"

"Lived. Not lives. Well, someone didn't like that he'd spoken to me. Or maybe they wanted to know what he told me. And the gentlemen on the train seemed keen to stop me getting back to Moscow. If all of that was about a dead man, why does it matter so much?"

Zack conceded with a nod and finished his beer. "So what are you going to do?"

"Find him. Find Grom."

"Find a man who wants you dead?"

"It beats sitting around waiting for him to find me. And you're going to help."

"I am?"

"Well, you want me to help you, don't you? Ask around. Do some digging."

Zack grumbled, but he'd agreed to it. Probably more than anyone else, Zack knew that the reason Fairchild was in this business was to stay close to the intelligence community.

Fairchild didn't really care about the work he did. But it was only through insider contacts like Zack – and the many others – that Fairchild had a chance of standing up to the conspiracy of silence that was MI6, and getting to the bottom of what really happened. That was always what he'd thought, anyway.

The second window had some give in it. After Fairchild strained for a few seconds, the latch ripped through the frame with a crunch and the window sprung open. Fairchild paused, waiting for the scream of a burglar alarm. Nothing. He lifted himself up onto the sill, his feet getting some purchase on the rough stone wall. One knee up and he paused, half in, half out. Silence. He dropped inside and pulled the window to. A small handheld torch held low gave him a sweep of the room.

It was a messy little back office, metal box files on shelves, a desk piled with papers and an open laptop perched on top. He pressed the space bar and the screen lit up with a password prompt. The keyboard was Russian. That might take some time. Fairchild switched off the torch and gently opened the door a crack. Again he listened. Again silence. He stepped out. A corridor led to the front door he'd buzzed on earlier, with a couple of doors off to the right and stairs up to his left. Faint light from the streetlights outside filtered through the glass panel above the front door.

He went back into the office. Alexei had made his mark here, the careless chaos replacing what before would have been organised neatness. He sat at the desk and tried a couple of obvious passwords on the laptop. No joy. He moved it aside and started going through the papers underneath. General business bureaucracy: invoices, receipts. Nothing obvious to suggest that Morozov was anything other than a standard logistics operator. Fairchild glanced around the room, at the boxes of files. It would take hours to go through all of this.

Something drew his eye back. Tear-off notes, several of them scrawled with large messy writing, were strewn over the desk. Names, phone numbers, dates and times. Some just one word: *Stavropol*, said one. A reminder to do something? His hand hovered over one of them. It said: *Manifest copy to Grom*. He read it again. He'd made no mistake with the Cyrillic. That was what it said.

He sat back and contemplated the ceiling. He'd been accused, by Zack, by Walter, and others, of seeing patterns where there weren't any, connecting random things to try and find the answers he needed. It was the way he'd been brought up. His parents' crazy games, the cryptic tests they set for him, the way they flitted from language to language as if everything in the world were part of a code that needed to be cracked. When he finally realised that this was not normal parenting, he'd put it down to eccentricity, a kind of intellectual high spirits, two great minds enjoying each other's company. It was only later, looking back, that he'd started to wonder if there'd been a purpose to it, some kind of training that should have equipped him to solve the biggest puzzle of them all, that of their own disappearance.

But what purpose could there have been? They were dead. They'd been dead for decades, for most of his life, he now knew. The very idea that their game-playing served a purpose was itself a consequence of their interminable mind-gymnastics. What fools they were! And so was he. They'd turned him into a brooding, obsessed boy who'd grown into a brooding, obsessed man, his life entirely shaped by a hunt for something that didn't exist. And even now here he was, drawing lines in his head, imagining that everything that happened in the world was in some way connected to him and his story. Stupid conceit, the whole thing! He screwed up the note and threw it on the floor.

That was when he noticed the safe, squatting in the corner of the room. A large one, as solid and heavy as they came. Of course there was a safe. Invoices and receipts and manifests were fair enough for legitimate operations, but any syndicate like Morozov also dealt in cash. Cash was the lifeblood, always the easiest and most direct way of extracting value from off-books activity, whatever its nature. And people would know that. Which made it strange – inconceivable – that a ground floor office like this had no security, no alarm system at all.

He got up and went into the corridor. He opened one of the doors. Behind it was a standard office: three desks, computer screens, boxes piled up. Then he opened the door closest to the front entrance. This was slightly grander, the room for receiving visitors. A large wooden desk with nothing much on it sat in front of a leather-backed office chair. Sofas and armchairs formed an arc in front of the window. Pictures on the walls. Carpet on the floor. And on that carpet, in the middle of the room, a body.

Fairchild crouched close to the face which was on its side, one cheek pressed into the floor, a tidy bullet hole in the forehead, its exit wound staining blond hair.

It was Alexei Morozov.

21

There were four of them in the secret room this time: Peter, Rose, Zack, and Nick, a messy-haired bespectacled analyst who'd reviewed the contents of Kamila's zip drive. Zack was updating them.

"He was shot in the head. Single bullet. Whoever did it didn't break in. Alexei must have let them in himself. Which kinda suggests that it wasn't a rival gang."

"Could he have shot himself?" asked Nick.

"Why would he do that? He'd just been gifted a multi-million-dollar enterprise from his pa. He was having a whale of a time. Besides, no gun at the scene, according to – my operative."

Peter's rules: don't even mention Fairchild's name in our discussion. Another way of keeping him deniable. Rose had had to convey this to Zack in advance. "Figures," was his response. Zack hadn't offered any information about Fairchild's disappearance and reappearance in Moscow, but then Rose hadn't asked.

"What else did your operative say?" asked Peter. "Any signs the place had been searched or vandalised?"

"Nope. There was kit lying about. Doesn't sound like a burglary." Zack looked uncomfortable, only just managing to squeeze his mass into a round-backed armchair. At least he'd ditched the shades for the occasion.

"What kind of kit?" asked Rose.

"A laptop. Some burner phones in a drawer. Normal office computer stuff, monitors, printers. Worth something, though."

"The police are presumably working the scene," said Peter.

Nick came in. "According to our police contact, they discovered the body this morning. They'll be working through all of the IT stuff."

"Not the laptop," said Zack. "My operative swiped it. Police won't even know it was there. It's with our technical team right now. We'll share anything interesting, of course."

"That would be greatly appreciated, Zack," said Peter. "The question is, who would do this and why? Clearly it impacts on the whole political exercise that Alexei was involved in."

"Makes no sense for the FSB to get rid of Alexei," said Zack. "He's the one who just handed over the Morozov supply lines. He's their favourite guy." Zack and his colleagues had already been filled in on what was on the zip drive.

"What will happen to the syndicate now?" asked Rose. "There's no obvious successor. It may end up falling apart."

"Roman might come in and babysit," said Zack. "Not what he wanted, as he gave it to his son so's he could retire back home. But he could step in. He's in Moscow right now, so I'm told. My operative is seeing him. They've got some glitzy dacha out by Krylatskoye."

"That might change things," said Peter. "Roman has an old-style *vory* criminal code attitude to co-operating with the government. Once he gets wind of what Alexei's been up to, he could close down the whole arrangement."

"That's good for us," said Rose.

"Except that it's probably too late," said Nick. "If the zip drive information is good, the amount of stuff they've already got in the area is plenty for a major offensive."

"If the government has already got what they wanted out of Morozov, maybe they got rid of Alexei to close it off," said Rose. "I mean, the guy has 'liability' practically tattooed on his forehead. Or maybe he asked for too much, called their bluff, pissed someone off."

Peter looked dubious. "Possibly. I'd expect them to want to stick with it, grow the relationship. There are plenty of other ways the Morozov network could be used to further Russia's interests. Their other supply lines, their profits, their assets. Alexei's no real danger to them, surely."

"He could have squealed. Or threatened to," said Zack.

"Who to?" said Peter. "No Russian law enforcement will take action against the Kremlin in defence of a mafia group. He could have come to us, I suppose, or yourselves. But why?"

"He seemed to be doing very well personally out of the set-up he had with the FSB," said Nick.

"What about Kamila?" asked Rose.

"What about her?" That was Zack.

"Maybe they argued. Alexei was pretty open about his infidelities. Publicly she let it wash over her, but maybe behind closed doors it was a different matter. She really didn't like the guy very much."

"But she still needs him," said Nick. "What is she without him? Young, female, foreign? A former prostitute?"

"I was told Roman's attitude to Chechens is pretty typically Russian," said Zack. "You think he's gonna go out of his way to give her a comfortable widowhood?"

"Spur of the moment?" offered Rose. "Couldn't take the humiliation any more?"

"What would she be doing at his office, though?" This was Nick.

"And does she even know how to handle a gun?" That from Peter.

She wasn't sure why, but this stirred her up. "Why wouldn't she know how to use a gun? She grew up in a war zone. And she went with Alexei to business meetings. And the way she handled that zip drive was pretty impressive. That's why we're looking at her again. Don't we have anything back on her yet?" She directed this at Nick.

"We've got someone in Grozny investigating that right now," he said. "Should hear back soon."

Soothing. Patronising, actually. "Well, if Kamila is so inconsequential," she said to Zack, "it's odd that your operative took so much time getting to know her. Or was that just a bit of research on the side?"

Zack's eyes were as wide as two brown pennies. "'Scuse me?"

"The tape we have of Kamila, in flagrante, in St Petersburg? The one we're using on her? Who do you think her lover is?"

Zack's eyebrows shot skywards. "In that video? That's J— that's our friend?"

"We don't know, Zack," said Peter. "You can't tell who it is from the tape."

"He left the reception early," said Rose. "After flirting with the woman. No one saw him leave. He had plenty of time to hook up with her and get over to the flat."

Zack was shaking his head. "No, that's not what happened. He went over to the apartment straight from the party to check it out. But you guys were already in there. That's how he knows you Brits were onto the Morozovs."

"That's what he told you," said Rose. "He always tells you everything, does he?"

"Oh, come on! You seriously think he'd do that? He's not suicidal enough to sleep with a gangster's newly-wed under the guy's nose. Not even him!"

"You sure? He did some pretty suicidal things when I was with him in China."

"Not when he was working for me. Not when he's on a job. In his own time, maybe. When it's – for something he wants."

"Are you always sure which is which? When he's working for you or when he's working for himself?"

Peter intervened again. "Look, we don't know who it is, and I'm not sure how much that matters now anyway. Let's move forward, shall we?"

Rose hushed up. Losing it with Zack didn't help her credibility any. Peter had taken charge. "The key thing is, what do we do? Do we still have a way into Morozov, or do we need to rethink?"

"I can try and approach Kamila," said Rose. "But the tape won't have the same leverage now Alexei is dead. And she may not be involved in the business any more. That extra background on her will be interesting."

"Good – you follow up on that." Peter turned to Zack. "This meeting with Roman might shed some light. Can you come back to us as soon as that's happened?"

"Sure! Hey, if we're all done here, got a quick question for you."

Everyone stood ready to leave. Rose got her things together slowly, making a play of stopping to write something down. "Ever heard the name *Grom*?" Zack was asking Peter in an undertone. "Possible character within the KGB, back in the day? It's some kind of a nickname. He might have been involved in rendition and interrogation."

Peter was smiling a little. "Oh, I've heard the name. Not for a very long time, though. It's a fake identity, a ghost. There were rumours for years, but it was all just a fairy story, a false lead to get people running around. They played those tricks all the time to put the wind up us all. Who's asking?"

"Oh, one of our new kids. I guess someone was taking him for a ride."

"Yes, sounds like it."

Rose let herself be herded out, as the conversation moved to a who's who of the intelligence world. She lodged that little snippet away, though. Zack's casual air asking the question was just a little bit overdone.

22

The walled compound of luxury dachas was situated prosaically next to a major freeway and opposite a large shopping mall. By the time Rose got there, walking from Krylatskoye Metro station, it was late afternoon and the light was starting to fade. Most of the afternoon had passed on an elaborate tour of Moscow to be certain she was alone.

She approached the compound's manned security gate. Inside she could see an access road winding past a collection of unique purpose-built palaces – the indulgences of the newly rich, sprawling mansions complete with round turrets, Mediterranean balconies, Greco-Roman sculptures and colourfully tiled walls. To the security guards she gave her name and announced her wish to see Roman Morozov.

The guards looked uncertainly at each other, then one of them disappeared inside. He came back out. "No one is expecting you," he said. "What's it about?"

"It's about his son. Alexei. The tragic death of Alexei. I have some information for him. I think he'd want to hear it."

Again the hesitation, then he went inside. A moment later, the gate buzzed and started to open. Rose had to endure a body and bag search before they pointed her up the access road.

"Which one is it?" she asked.

"You will know."

The inner road wound forever past monstrous super-dachas, each one like a Hollywood film set, elaborate and out of context. Many were surrounded by high fences, gated compounds each with a mini Disneyworld rising up inside.

Strange, what people did when they had way too much money.

Beyond a covered entrance area within a row of classical columns, two men stood waiting, watching her as she approached. They made no secret of the fact that they were armed. Rose was not; she'd anticipated the searches. The wood-panelled doors to the house opened as she walked up to them. Inside, a dark-suited man with a long face nodded her towards the back of the house. She walked through, glimpsing up to see a grand spiral staircase and vast chandelier.

A room ran the width of the house at the back. The wall was almost entirely glass. A door led out onto a deep balcony. The ground fell away below. Further back were trees. Behind them must have been the freeway, though it wasn't visible. Against the light of the room, it was almost dark outside. On her left were bookshelves and a sofa. On the right, a table and two chairs. Standing behind one of the chairs was a man in his sixties or seventies, a bulky figure, his open-necked shirt displaying thick grey-brown chest hair, his head shaved and his jawline bristling. His clear blue eyes were watching her carefully.

"You are Roman Morozov?" she asked.

"I am." He waited expectantly.

"My name is Rose Clarke. Please accept my sympathies for your loss. I'd like to speak to you about your son, if I may."

"Do you know who I am?"

She held his gaze. "Yes, I know who you are. People call you the Bear. You have a reputation. You've used that reputation to build an empire."

"And yet you come to see me, just walk in, a woman alone like this?"

"I've heard you're a man of honour. That you have standards of behaviour. I don't mean you any harm or disrespect." Keep your voice low and relaxed, Rose. Never mind your racing pulse, just don't let it show. She was taking a massive risk coming here. But it wasn't the Bear she was afraid of. Not Roman Morozov. It was Peter Craven, if he found out.

He still looked wary. "You knew my son?"

"I met him once. And his wife several times."

That seemed to get him more interested. "Well, join me for a drink. Vadim will take your coat."

The man in the dark suit stepped out of the shadows. She gave him her coat and sat at the table. Opposite, Roman sat and filled both small glasses from the bottle.

"You like vodka?"

"I drink it."

"Why do you drink it, if you don't like it?"

"This is Russia."

Roman laughed, a warm chuckling laugh. He raised his glass. "To your health!"

Their eyes met and they drank. The strong sour taste hit the back of her throat. As they placed their glasses on the table, the burning aftertaste was starting to rise up into her mouth, reminding her of how much she hated the stuff. Never mind: it served a purpose. Roman already seemed more relaxed with her.

"These new Moscow millionaires seem to prefer western champagne. We're losing so many of our old customs. Money changes people, opens up new possibilities, but most of those paths lead nowhere. People forget where they come from."

"You haven't forgotten where you come from?" asked Rose, with the very slightest of glances around the room.

"This place?" said Roman. "This place, this place was bought by my son. I have a dacha near Irkutsk. When I'm at home I go there on weekends. It's a three-room cottage. I grow vegetables. I have an orchard. I go fishing. That is where we are all from. The villages where everyone lived before cities, for thousands of years, surviving the winter and living off the land. Moscow is a mutation, a corruption of Russianness."

He filled the glasses again and they drank, toasting each other silently.

"I'm sorry about Alexei," said Rose, repeating her sympathies of earlier. Roman looked weary.

"It is a terrible thing to lose a child. Do you have children?"

Rose shook her head.

"That is very wise. Having children is a way to fill your life with troubles. How did you know him?"

"I met him at a reception in St Petersburg. I was there for work. My job is promoting trade relations between the UK and Russia."

"You work for the British government?"

"That's right."

Roman laughed, louder this time. "Then you are a spy!"

This was one Rose was well and truly ready for. "Every Russian thinks every British official is a spy. As well as every British journalist and businessperson. I work for the government. That's my job."

Roman's eyes narrowed. "How did you know to find me here?"

"Kamila mentioned a dacha in Krylatskoye. It's not difficult to find these compounds. The people here, they're not making a secret of their wealth, are they? I didn't know if you'd be here or not. Why, you're not hiding, are you?"

"I have no need to hide."

"Exactly."

Roman seemed to accept this. Most of it was actually true. "So, you knew his wife?"

"She was also at the reception. I met her a number of times after that. We went shopping together."

"Shopping?" Roman's eyes were distant, as if picturing this in his mind's eye. "What is she like, this Kamila?"

"What do you mean?"

"I have never met her."

Rose couldn't disguise her surprise.

"Yes, that's right," said Roman. "I have never met my son's wife. Ours was a difficult relationship. It would all have been different if his mother were still with us." He poured each of them a shot. They toasted and drank. "When the Soviet Union collapsed, some of the criminal groups became irresponsible. No more need to hide, they said. We can do what we like now. Who will stop us? So they came out on the streets and started turf wars. In 1991, I was driving with my wife and son in Irkutsk. The city centre. We were ambushed. Several cars, from all directions. They opened fire with machine guns. My wife and I were both shot. Alexei escaped. I survived. My wife did not."

"I'm sorry."

He filled the glasses again. "They thought they could scare me. Frighten the Bear! Then steal my business while I hid away. They realised their mistake. I fought back ten times over. For every life they took, I took ten of theirs, their friends, family, anyone who stood with them. By the end they were all gone. We won. Morozov won. But now I am the only one left."

They toasted. "How old was Alexei?" asked Rose.

"Twelve. A little boy. But nah! He was a little boy even after he grew. He was his mother's son much more than mine. The harder I tried to raise him to be strong, the more he hated me."

Rose nodded. In death, through his father's eyes, Alexei started to make a little more sense.

"Do you have any idea who might have killed him?"

Roman looked up from pouring another shot. It was a bold question. Too bold? Then his face crinkled. For a moment she thought he might cry.

"Betrayal is an evil thing. We all have to trust people, do we not? Who can survive and operate without relying on people around them? We are all vulnerable to traitors, those who will poison the food on their own table." His voice had become hard and bitter.

"You think it was someone within the organisation?"

He looked at her and slowly raised his glass. They toasted again and downed their shots.

"Why did you come here today?" he asked.

"I'm looking for Kamila. I want to see her. She's not returning my calls. I thought you might be able to help. I didn't realise you'd never met."

That was her official response, what she'd say to Peter, if it ever got back to him. She was pursuing an agreed action. Pumping the father-in-law for information about Kamila. It was flimsy, but she'd brazen it out. The real reason? The meeting that morning. You take the prostitute, Rose. The one we don't think is important. The gangster, Fairchild can deal with that. A man we can barely trust, who can't stand MI6, will work for anyone, and hasn't even set foot in the UK for twenty years. But he's a man! So he'll do the man's work. Run along, now.

"Why do you want to see her?" asked Roman.

"She's just lost her husband. I want to check she's okay. Find out if she needs anything."

"You consider yourself a friend of hers."

"A distant one."

He put his head on one side. "So the wife of a big Russian authority and a British government official go shopping together?"

"She was very stylish. She was keen for me to improve my dress sense. She had some specific ideas in mind."

"So! She was more than just a fortune-seeking Muslim slut. Had some ideas. Shopping ideas."

Rose ignored the hatred in his voice. "She'd converted to Christianity. And yes, she was more than that."

Roman smiled sadly. "I fear you may be right. I, too, am looking for Kamila."

"You don't know where she is?"

"Nobody knows where she is."

This was interesting. "She's disappeared? Why, do you think?"

Roman drained the bottle and called Vadim to fetch another one. He sat back. "My son was not a good judge of character. His wife was a whore. That much he knew. But she was also a thief."

"A thief? Who was she stealing from?"

"From Alexei. From all of us. From me."

"She was stealing from the business?"

Roman gave a single nod. "Alexei, he let her into everything, assumed she had no interest. Took her with him when he went on visits, thought she was just sitting there looking pretty on his arm. But she was listening. Planning. I spent most of today going through the accounts. Alexei leaves the detail to other people. Me, I look after things myself. I can see how it was done. Hundreds of thousands of roubles, gone."

"But how do you know it was Kamila? Couldn't it have been someone else, someone more familiar with the operation?"

"I spoke today to everyone who had access. All sad and sorry about what has happened. All surprised and angry that we have been robbed. Unlike my son, I know who to trust, who has honour. They are good people. But Kamila? Kamila, where is she?"

He held up his glass. They toasted, and drained glasses again. Rose was feeling the effects. "Well," she said, putting a steadying hand on the table, "maybe she's not sure of her status now. I mean, her situation without Alexei might be considered quite precarious."

"Precarious? Oh, yes. I would say so. Quite precarious." Roman's voice rumbled with foreboding.

"Do you think she killed him?" Rose hadn't intended to ask that. It was the vodka talking. Roman considered her.

"What do you think? You think she'd do that? You think she could? You know her better. You're her friend."

Before she could answer, the door opened. Vadim said, quietly, "Your visitor is here."

"Ah! Of course! My visitor!" Roman brightened and rose to his feet. "Maybe you know this man! A fellow countryman of yours. He's a good man, this fellow, a friend! You must meet him!"

Rose turned, ready to greet the visitor. Of course, she already knew who it was.

23

Fairchild stood on the threshold. The room was all warm yellow light and wood panelling, thick carpet and bookshelves. Books for show with colour-coordinated spines, unread. A giant vase bedecked with idyllic English hunting scenes perched on a flimsy table. But all of that was background, unimportant, because *she* was there. Unexpectedly, inexplicably, disturbingly, sitting at a table with a shot glass in her hand. She was smiling at him.

"Yes, we do know each other," she was saying to Roman, who was coming over to greet him. Fairchild made the effort to switch into automatic mode.

"Then I don't need to introduce you. My friend!" Roman reached in for a vodka-fumed embrace which lasted some time. By the time they pulled apart, tears had gathered in the old man's eyes.

"I'm sorry," Fairchild said, simply. Roman nodded and turned away. Rose, a little pink in the face, came over to shake hands.

"Fancy seeing you here," she said.

"Indeed, it is a surprise," he said. "How's Peter?"

"Fine," she said. Unaware, was what she meant. What was she doing here? He couldn't envisage ever being in a situation where she would take advice from him. But did she not know what Roman was capable of? Fairchild had known Roman for years and could hide his feelings, but the man still scared the bejesus out of him.

Vadim had brought the new bottle and another glass. Roman was itching to invite him to sit down, but there were only two chairs.

"Rose!" Roman turned to her. "Please, take one of my cars. It will drop you anywhere. My gift to you. Vadim will show you. Please, go with. It's no trouble."

That didn't please Rose at all. But whatever they'd been talking about, as far as Roman was concerned the conversation was over. And most of the time, most people did what Roman wanted. At least they used to. Vadim was shepherding her out. She turned to look at him, perhaps hoping he'd engineer for her to stay. No chance. He wanted her out of there more than anyone. Mainly for his own peace of mind.

The two of them sat. Roman wrapped two hands around the vodka bottle as if finding warmth in it.

"You know, Fairchild, I'm not a huge drinker. Drink has brought this country to its knees, men dying before their time, too weak to stop. But tonight – today, my friend, I lost my son, my only child. Now I am alone in the world. I will drink tonight. You will join me, yes?"

"Of course." Fairchild slid his glass over for Roman to fill it.

"To family!" They drank and the glasses were full again.

"I've had similar news myself," said Fairchild. The gangster's mild blue eyes rested on him. "You remember I told you how my parents disappeared?"

He told Roman what he'd discovered in Tuva, but skipping over the names and the horror of what happened afterwards. Roman was one of his contacts, part of the network he'd built over the years and maintained worldwide. These were people he'd courted and befriended, people he could bring himself to trust. Some were intelligence operatives, many were not. But they could see and hear things, and they wanted to help because they knew that Fairchild could help them in return. He told these people the story of his parents, told them exactly what he wanted to know, asked them to watch and listen, no more, and pass it on if they heard anything. That was all. And for the best part of twenty years this army of observers had nothing for him – until one of them met Dimitri, and realised the significance of the old Russian monk. So in the end Fairchild's patience paid off and he got his answers. That ought to mean his search was at an end and he no longer needed all these helpers. But it didn't feel that way.

Roman nodded sympathetically. "Ha. So you have also found yourself alone in the world. A survivor from the past. We have much in common."

They raised glasses again, and drank.

"Your friend, who was here," said Roman.

"She's not really a friend. Just someone I know." Roman was watching him carefully.

"Someone you work with?"

"Not really. Not exactly."

"Not exactly? But in some inexact way, yes? So she is a spy?"

"Of course she's a spy," said Fairchild. "She's British! We're all spies! You know that, Roman."

"Come now! I'm asking you a question. You know these things, I'm not sure how. Why did she come here?"

"I honestly don't know." That was the truth. "I'm not someone she confides in."

"Ah!" Light dawned in the man's face. "But you'd like to be! Yes, that makes sense."

Since when had he become so easily readable? Not good. He needed to work on that.

Roman poured. They drank.

24

Darkness fell entirely while Rose took the Metro back to the city centre. She'd got Roman's driver to drop her at Krylatskoye. She didn't want a Morozov car dropping her at home for all to see. Besides, traffic being what it was, the Metro was quicker.

She fumed as she sat. Great result: as soon as the man arrives, the woman gets turfed out. Get rid of the chaff, so the guys can get down to the serious business. Her journey wasn't entirely wasted, though; Roman had some interesting things to say about Kamila. It put her in a new light. If Kamila were capable of theft and had the nerve to steal like that from Morozov, she could shoot someone in the head. Would Roman and Fairchild talk about Kamila? Or would they have more important matters to discuss? She wasn't too worried that Peter would find out she'd been there. Instinctively, she knew that Fairchild would keep it to himself.

The train slowed to a halt. The doors opened to let in tired-looking Moscow commuters, hatted, hooded and scarved. Rose looked at her watch. It was mid-evening. After all that vodka she could do with some food. But a night in her goldfish-bowl flat didn't appeal. The background research on Kamila ought to be available by now. She'd have to go into the office to access it; downloading sensitive files onto a laptop at home was a no-no. She pondered the Moscow transit map in front of her, made a decision, and jumped up to get off the train just as the doors were about to close.

25

More vodka, another silent toast and fiery gulp. The bottle was half-empty already. Roman was waxing lyrical on his favourite topic, the Russian tragedy. He sighed.

"Here in Russia we never seem to want to just live in peace. Make some money and look after our own. No, we must create empires and amass huge wealth and wage extravagant wars. Our borders are a threat, our neighbours are a threat, our own people are a threat. The history of Russia! Death and suffering. Then for a while there is hope that we can change. But that hope is extinguished. More death and suffering! Worse than before. In the Russian story, everybody dies."

"And where are we in the story?" asked Fairchild. His tongue seemed thick.

"Fairchild, you know our history! The USSR, such a terrible thing. My father. You know what happened to my father. He was sent to the gulag. You know why?"

Fairchild knew why, but he asked anyway.

"Because he fought for Russia! Because he was captured by the Germans and was a prisoner of war. Him and many others. And when they came back, Stalin decided they were spies for the Germans now! So they went to prison for their service. He became *vor*. A criminal with a code, a black market operator. When he got out, he carried on, passed the business to me. We gave people goods, livelihoods, food sometimes, when the state could not. When the government becomes criminal, criminals become the government."

Roman drank. Fairchild waited for the rest of the history lesson.

"When the Soviet Union came to an end, what an opportunity! Russia could emerge a great nation, with confidence in its people, serving its citizens and putting aside those futile ideologies. But what happened? We descended into gang warfare. Running fights on the streets, when we could have been helping to rebuild our country. Greed, Fairchild, greed. I had to beat them down, but it cost me, it cost me."

Fairchild nodded. He knew about the turf wars and the price Roman paid. "And now?"

"Now, we are being swallowed up. Taken one by one into the big machine, bought like cakes in a shop. My old adversaries. Yes, we were at war sometimes, but we respected each other. We stood on our own feet and lost sometimes, won sometimes. Now everyone is controlled by the invisible strings that all lead back to – you know where they lead."

"The Kremlin."

Roman paused as he was pouring. "I thought we were fierce and proud. But it seems everyone has a price. They may talk in the old way, but they do as they're told, for money. For cars and women and property and currency, hard currency." His eyes tracked around the plush furnishings. "Moscow honey. It attracts everything, the peasants, the dogs, the flies."

He poured. They drank.

"Bears like honey," said Fairchild.

"Not this bear. Not this honey. I would not dance to another's tune. It gets worse all the time, my people tell me. The government seizes businesses just because corrupt officials want the money. No law, no code. Some are leaving, taking their money with them. Me, I will stay and fight."

"You said everyone has a price."

"Not me! I don't care about money or status. I gave it all to my son, for him to do as he pleased. So that I could go home, live in peace."

"And what was Alexei's price?"

Roman shook his head sadly. "Too low, I'm sorry to say. He put the goods on display so eagerly. It is a terrible thing to lose a child. A parent cannot help but invest their hopes and dreams in their children. Then to see them destroyed…"

"You're talking about the FSB? The government people who approached Alexei?"

"Yes, FSB! KGB, FSB, the same, the soldiers of governments who can't trust their own people, the puppeteers!"

"Do you know who it was? Who he was talking to in the FSB?"

"What does it matter? They're all the same."

"Maybe not." Fairchild slid his glass over. Roman poured. "My parents. They were abducted by a crew working for a KGB operative with the nickname Grom. I've been told he may still be active. He had a reputation."

"Grom? He calls himself Grom? What is he, a gangster like me? These people, who do they think they are?"

"He was known on the streets. But he was KGB."

Roman shrugged. "What do your friends say?"

"My friends," said Fairchild, "say that he doesn't exist." He raised his glass. They drank.

"You don't believe your friends?"

"They're not really friends. They're liars. They're government stooges too, just a different government. Trying to cover up the past." He slid his glass towards Roman. "You and I, Roman. We're friends, aren't we?"

Roman smiled as he poured. "Yes, we're friends. We're friends for a long time." He put the bottle down. "But I know of no Grom-KGB-gangster type. The name of the guy Alexei spoke to, the man he trusted, it's in the records. I've seen it. But it's just a name, a Russian name. Maybe real, maybe not."

"And what are you going to do with this name?"

"Nothing. I have no business with the FSB. They come to find me, I tell them to leave Morozov alone. Why? You want the name? I give you the name, if you like."

"Maybe it could help. Maybe this man can lead me to Grom."

"Okay, okay, if it makes you happy. I write it down."

"There's no need."

"My friend, we're both drunk! I write it down, no need to remember! You have paper?"

Fairchild felt in his jacket for a scrap of paper.

26

Rose stared out of the office window at the Embassy, mesmerised by the flow of headlights along the riverside. Behind her, the remains of a McDonald's meal littered her desk. Her laptop sat amongst the detritus, open on the latest intelligence report on Kamila Morozova.

They'd always known that she met Alexei while working in Moscow as an escort. Kamila had been one of many, targeting the most exclusive night clubs, bribing the doormen for an opportunity to come in and display themselves on the dance floor in front of the watching millionaires. They hoped to be installed as someone's mistress, with an apartment and an allowance and free time, and a little money to send home sometimes, in exchange for keeping themselves looking nice and always being available. That had been Kamila's game, and it seemed to have worked out much better for her than that. But what about before? The records from Grozny painted a different picture.

First, Kamila was older than she looked. Rose had put her in her mid-twenties. She was actually forty-two. Why did that change her view of the woman so much? She'd thought that Kamila was a decade younger than her, but in fact she was a few years older. Should it matter? She didn't know, but somehow it did. Alexei was in his early thirties. Would he knowingly have married a woman a good deal older than himself? Was he expecting children? She must have lied to him, and her lie was understandable. But her whole manner, her dismissiveness, her vulnerability – how much of that was real?

The second finding was where exactly the real Kamila was from, a village outside of Grozny. In the war of 2008, the entire area was overrun with Russian troops which successfully besieged Grozny and defeated the Chechen separatists. It had been a bloody war with bitterness and retributions. Kamila's village was occupied by Russian troops. Its population was wiped out. Alexei served in the Russian army, served in Chechnya. Something he was proud of. Now, years later, Kamila was missing and Alexei was dead. Rose shook her head slowly. They should have known about this from the start.

The third revelation was Kamila's career back home in Chechnya. Not everyone who lived in a village was a farmer. Kamila had studied at school and gone on to do a college course. She had a job, in Grozny, although her home address was always back in the village.

Her career? Book-keeping.

She thought back to Kamila in the ladies' room at the opera, calmly applying her make-up while handing over the deepest of Morozov secrets. Earlier, in the clothes store, her round-eyed dismay at the sight of the film. But how quickly she recovered from it. *Better to be human and risk everything than be safe and locked inside yourself.* So philosophical, so blasé. When Rose had done this before, if people didn't regret the act, they at least regretted being caught.

She sat and did what she'd known for several hours she needed to do, but had put off. She opened up the laptop and went to the video.

It took her back to that foggy evening in St Petersburg, standing in the empty flat sipping tea in her uncomfortable shoes. She took it right from the beginning, the door buzzer, the muffled conversation with no picture – the sound quality was still awful. The silence, then the moan in the darkness, the gasp of breath, the light in the bedroom coming on and Kamila, breasts bare to the world, lifting her head. Rose paused the video. She remembered how she'd felt at that moment, her involuntary step backwards as if she were being looked at. Frozen on the screen, Kamila's expression was curiously bland.

Rose resumed playing. This was where Kamila turned and was pulled down onto the bed. Odd, that they never got a glimpse of the man's face. The sound intensified, Kamila's rhythmic moaning. Now she appeared again, facing the window, astride her lover. She was looking down. Rose advanced frame by frame, watching every expression and movement, Kamila looking up, her mouth widening, her head tilting back, her eyes closing. Then all motion came to a halt. Rose rewound, back to when Kamila turned to face the window. She zoomed in on the woman's face and played it again, several times. She focused on the part when Kamila first looked up, her eyes wide open. She played it again and again until she was sure.

Kamila was not just facing the window. Her eyes changed focus, tracking along the building opposite. Kamila was looking out of the window.

Did she know they were there?

27

"It's all my fault, you know." Roman's voice was muffled. His head was resting on the table, his arms outstretched across it. Fairchild was lying on the floor. It was the only way to stop it moving. "I expected too much of him. After his mother died, it all went wrong. She was good with Alexei. She understood him. Maybe I never did."

A pause went on for some unmeasured time. Fairchild felt he should fill it. "You mustn't blame yourself. You did what you thought was best."

The noise from Roman's general direction could have been a snort or a snore. There was a crash: Roman's fist hitting the table. An empty glass fell and rolled on the carpet.

"Women! Women! The women have built Russia, my friend. Us men, we just play games, fight each other, drink too much, die. When she died, she took half of me, too. The better half. I never wanted anyone else. But you, Fairchild!" His voice was less muffled; he'd lifted his head slightly. "Your woman. What does she mean to you?"

This again. "What woman? I don't have a woman."

"No, no! I saw that you like her. You weren't expecting her to be here. You give yourself away, when you're not prepared. Men should be strong, like a fortress, a wall. Of course, love, but don't lose your guard. Could be dangerous."

"That's good advice." Fairchild shifted on the carpet. The ceiling had an interesting overlapping plaster effect. Another long pause. A rushing sound was coming from somewhere.

"Why do you love her? Why?" Roman spoke with a sudden urgency.

There seemed no point denying it. Roman wouldn't have believed him anyway. "What does why mean? Why did you love your wife?"

"Ah! Yes, I loved her…" Silence again. Fairchild lifted his head. Roman was trying to open another bottle. Another one? Vadim had brought the whole case in and left them to it.

"Here!" Roman had unscrewed the lid. Now he leaned dangerously down to pick up the fallen glass. "My wife, she was pretty! Most lovely girl in the village. Very good cook. Very kind mother. We wanted more children but she was ill as a child, lack of food, almost died. Was never healthy. Russia! But she looked after us. Come, come!"

Fairchild climbed with difficulty to his knees and leaned on the table to take the offered glass. They toasted silently and drank. He could barely taste it now.

"So, your woman!" Roman insisted. "What was her name? Rosa, yes?"

"Rose," said Fairchild, while the room started to spin again.

"Why you like Rose?"

"Why do I like her?" Fairchild clambered back down to the floor. All the words, images, that rushed into his head. What could he say?

"She's…" A force, an energy, the centre of everything but she doesn't even know. When she looks at me with those eyes, judging me, shaming me, I see my miserable, shambling self and my meaningless farce of a life. Centred, grounded, true, loyal, she's everything I'm not, I could never please her.

"She's…" The gangster was waiting. What was in his mind that moment in Kathmandu, when the pieces fell into place, when he realised what she was to him?

"…magnificent," he said.

A silence. "Magnificent?"

"Magnificent."

Roman chuckled. He laughed. He threw back his head and roared. His chair rocked under him. Fairchild lay and listened. Then he started laughing as well.

It was pretty fucking funny, after all.

28

Rose was out running again. She needed to think. The office was silent and oppressive, the flat unsettling. It was well beyond midnight, but so what? Chest heaving, arms pumping, she ran flat out for as long as she could along the eight-lane highway, only stopping for a red light at a crossroads where she bent, hands on knees, wheezing to get her breath back. It wasn't ideal running alongside all the taxis and limos and beat-up vans and trucks, but the pavements were clear of ice and it saved thinking about where she was going.

Who was Kamila? What game was she playing? One thing was certain; she was putting on some kind of an act. Before Rose left the office she'd called Peter and alerted him to the report findings and her own observations reviewing the video. He would notch up the 'health warning' they had already passed to London about the contents of the zip drive. They were still in the process of trying to verify the intel. The Americans were doing the same. No reason had yet come to light to suggest that the information was bad, but they needed to understand why Kamila had been so keen to pass it to them.

A simple act of sabotage? She'd seen an opportunity in Rose's approach to work against her husband? Damage his relations with his new government friends and cut off his new income? That would be Kamila the scorned wife, abandoned night after night while Alexei went out to be entertained with his oligarch friends. Maybe: but in that scenario, she would have been unaware of the trap they were laying for her in St Petersburg. And why did she marry Alexei in the first place? The money, Peter would say, but would money really persuade you to marry someone you hated so intensely? Would it be enough to persuade a Chechen war survivor to marry a Russian ex-conscript? It happened. People were extraordinarily good sometimes at separating out politics from individuals.

Rose recalled Kamila's calculated stare out of the window in St Petersburg. If Rose was right, if Kamila had really been that far ahead of them, then she already knew what was going on, why Alexei left so early and in such a state, and what was likely to happen later. Two possibilities there: one, Moscow Station had a mole. The idea that their tight-knit little team harboured a traitor, or even a reluctant victim of coercion, seemed inconceivable. But then it probably always did. And it happened. Two, Kamila was conspiring with someone very clever, with substantial knowledge of how a covert sting operation might work, and who had managed to turn the whole thing around on its head for their own benefit. A terrifying prospect. And what was the benefit? Who would benefit? They needed to know a lot more to untangle this mess.

Was Kamila's lover in on it? Fairchild certainly had the knowledge and skills, the instinctive ability to anticipate. He'd need to be a pretty good actor, too. It was much easier for a woman to fake a good time than a man. Maybe they were both faking. But it looked more to Rose like neither of them were. They'd have no sure-fire way of knowing exactly where the cameras were. And what was it all for? She had the uneasy feeling that they were all walking into a trap, but had no idea yet what it was.

She drew up at another red light. She crouched to stretch. Her heart was pumping steadily, fingers tingling, blood flowing to all limbs. Heat radiating from her body competed with the cold air on her skin. The sweat on her neck was already starting to cool.

She needed to find Kamila.

29

Roman was laughing again. It was unacceptable, uncouth, unbearable! The carpet was fuzzy against Fairchild's mouth. The room throbbed when he lifted his head. And still the Russian was sitting there, sniggering, mocking, humiliating.

He'd been tricked. This was all a trap and he'd been too stupid to see it, as usual. The gangster had poisoned him! Disabled him to strip him of his secrets. What secrets? He couldn't even remember. But he was laughing about it now, the bastard! Enough of this! He had to get out.

Fairchild focused on his hands, pushing down on them to lift up his body. Never mind the throbbing, this is important. Get away from here, before it's too late! He was on hands and knees. Sick rose in his throat. He was going to spew. He breathed fast through his mouth. Okay. He wasn't going to spew. He climbed to his feet and the room lurched. He tottered. His shoulder hit the wall.

"Hee hee hee hee!" That bastard Russian just wouldn't shut the fuck up. It had to end. He would end it. Now! He needed a weapon. He lurched forward and grabbed the giant vase by the neck. It was heavier than he thought.

The laughter stopped. "Fairchild! What are you doing?" Now he had the bastard's attention. He swung the vase wide through the air. It carried him in a circle, like a shot-put. He staggered and rested the vase on the floor. "Fairchild! Stop that nonsense! Come, sit!" But Roman wasn't at the table any more. He was standing, backed up against the wall.

Coward! Fairchild swung again. Idiot, fool! Get yourself out of here! He hurled it into the door pane. The glass smashed with a noise like a hundred breaking bottles. The panel turned opaque with tiny crack marks. Shards pattered on the carpet and scattered across the balcony decking. The vase swung in his hand, still in one piece.

"Fairchild! Who are you fighting, my friend? You're with friends here!" Fairchild tensed, ready to punch and kick, but Roman's voice was calm. He breathed in cold air, coming in through the broken pane. Why had he been so angry? The vase was an unbearable weight.

Running footsteps. A dark suit and a thin pale face, coming towards him.

"Vadim, stop." The older man's swift order halted the assault. Vadim, breathing heavily, stood staring at him. "It's okay, Vadim, everything is under control. It's no problem."

Fairchild forgot to keep holding the vase. It dropped on the floor and broke, two halves of a cracked egg.

"Not now, Vadim. Leave it. Leave it!" Vadim was making for the vase, or maybe for him. But on Roman's curt order he straightened and left the room, reeking of disapproval.

"Come, my friend!" The Russian was approaching. "Come." The inside of the vase was a dirty white. Dusty. It was something to focus on. "Never mind that thing. Some old antique. I hated it. Sit down."

A hand was on his back steering him towards the table. "You know, you cannot always be alone in life. You must know who to trust, my friend. Everyone must trust. None of us can survive without others." The man turned to face him. His breathing was slow and heavy. "I am your friend, John Fairchild," he said. "I trust you. You can trust me. Come now."

Roman's arms were around him. He was buried in the Russian's solid, sweaty embrace. Tears came to his eyes. It was all okay, after all. It was all okay.

30

As Rose had expected, a police car was parked opposite the front door of the Morozov Moscow office, its unlucky occupants well wrapped against the cold. There was no obvious way of getting in at the front anyway. Also as expected, no one was posted round the back. She tried each of the windows; one of them gave as soon as she pulled on it. The catch was broken. This was presumably how Fairchild had got in. She climbed up, paused on the sill, heard nothing and dropped quietly to the floor inside.

She had no precise plan. She was after anything that might lead her to Kamila, progress having come to an abrupt halt with the Bear himself. Addresses, correspondence, names, whatever might get her a step closer to the woman. Peter didn't know she was here. Having gone off-reservation once that evening, it didn't seem a big deal to do it again. She was wired, as far from sleep as it was possible to be. The more she thought about it, the more urgent it seemed to get to the bottom of this. And it could only be done at night. Already, after getting the right gear together and double-backing on the way here, it was four in the morning. So it was now, or wait another fourteen hours at least, just to ask permission. And what if he said no? At times it was better just to get it done and explain yourself later.

A furtive swing of the torch told her there was nothing much in this room. A desk with empty drawers, a chair, empty shelves. The torchlight fell on a hefty safe in the corner. The door was open and it was empty. In the corridor she went upstairs first. Same story there, empty offices. No computers, monitors, phones, just furniture. Back downstairs was another empty office, then a room at the front. The door was ajar. Rose poked her head inside. Out of the window, she could see the cop car across the street. She played the torch briefly along the floor. An ominous dark stain betrayed where Alexei had fallen. But that didn't matter now. This was a meeting room, not an office: no files in here.

Those poor souls outside. Cold, tired and bored, yet everything inside of any value or interest had already been cleaned out. It was just an empty shell.

Rose left the way she came.

31

Fairchild woke. He was shivering. Where was his jacket? The carpet smelled of vomit. He rubbed his cheek and looked at his hand. There was blood on it.

He lifted his head. A blackness descended with an edge of pain. The blackness cleared; the pain didn't. His mouth was sticky. It was getting light outside. Light and cold. He looked round. A body was lying on the floor, on the other side of the room. Someone he recognised. A big guy. The Russian. Roman, his Russian friend. He was slumped awkwardly, unnaturally, an arm outstretched, facing away.

His friend! The only one he trusted. Everyone else lied, or used him, or wanted him dead. And now Roman was gone too. The blood on his hand: what did it mean? What had he done? Concentrate, man! But no memories came. No, wait! He remembered a long embrace. *You can trust me.* Nothing since.

You can trust me. But Fairchild trusted nobody. That was why he was alone. No friends, no woman, no love. So alone, so cold. He curled up, wrapped his face in his arms and sobbed.

32

Getting through the wire fence into the compound wasn't difficult. Rose had spotted it looking out from the Morozov balcony the previous evening. She'd seen the whole route laid out in front of her: a corner where the land rose up against the external wall, masked from the road by trees; a shallow area of ditch; a gap between two internal fences. Still once fence to cross, into the Morozov complex itself, but that wasn't hard with the right equipment and an idea of what was coming.

The climb onto the balcony was more tricky. She had to throw a rope awkwardly above her head to loop it through one of the struts. She tried it again and again. She was starting to wonder if she needed a new plan when finally she managed it. Once up the rope, she grabbed onto the strut and worked her way monkey-style out to the railings one hand at a time. They'd done this kind of thing during training but that was a long time ago and Rose felt it.

She transferred her weight to her arms, gripping the railings, and lifted herself up, straining, until she could see onto the balcony. Nobody there, but it was strewn with broken glass. No sound or movement outside. It was eight in the morning, light but not yet sunrise. She climbed over the railings and crept up to the balcony door, her feet crunching on broken glass. The door pane had a massive hole in it. Something large had smashed the glass. She peered inside. A body was lying on the floor. She tried the balcony door. It was locked. Gently she snapped off the biggest shards round the hole, and climbed through. Sharp edges tugged her clothes and nicked the skin on her back and stomach. Pieces of broken glass littered the carpet inside. She eased through slowly, but straightened too soon and knocked her foot on a shard. She stumbled and her foot banged into the door pane. She froze. She could hear nothing. But there was another body, lying on the other side of the room. The first one she'd recognised from outside: John Fairchild. And the other, judging from its solid form, was Roman Morozov.

She reached her hand out to Fairchild's neck to check for a pulse, but a sound made her stop. It was a snore. The man was snoring. Rose withdrew her hand and looked around. Vodka bottles, some on the table, some on the floor. An aroma in the air, fumes of alcohol, sweat, possibly vomit. She checked up on Roman; his chest was moving steadily up and down. A large vase was in pieces in the middle of the floor. Both chairs lay on their side. The room was freezing cold. Fairchild snored again. A very Russian evening, clearly.

Rose remembered from her visit earlier that this room had no desk, files, devices. She padded softly towards the door. Fairchild's jacket was on the floor, fallen off the back of a chair. Rose picked it up and went through the pockets. Wallet, phone, another phone. Nothing unusual. But her hand felt something in an inside pocket: a piece of paper. She drew it out. It had been torn from a notepad and was very creased, as if it had been scrunched up and straightened out again. The writing on it was in Russian. On one side were the words: *Manifest to Grom*. On the other, in a different hand, was a Russian name: *Mikhail Lebedev Khovansky*.

Grom. The name Zack had been asking Peter about, in his oh-so-casual way. Peter said there was no such person, but whoever wrote this seemed to think there was, unless she was mistaking the meaning. The other name she'd never heard before. She put the paper in her own pocket.

Something moved. She looked up. Standing in the doorway was Vadim, Roman's dour-faced minder. She hadn't heard him approach.

"What are you doing here?" His voice was grainy. She backed into the centre of the room. She really didn't want a confrontation now.

"Just came back to pick something up. I'll be leaving now."

She edged towards the balcony door. Vadim watched, hostile. As she started to turn away he stepped up and grabbed her arm.

"How did you get in?" He had a thin build but his grip was solid. Rose twisted her arm up and aimed a kick at his stomach. His grasp slipped but the kick barely registered. His fist came out and almost got her face but she ducked. She lashed out again at his body and hit something soft. He grunted, but recovered. In a split second he had her arm again, but up behind her back this time. He jerked it, sending a spasm of pain through her shoulder.

"You're not going anywhere." He dragged her backwards towards the door. He stepped back and looked down to avoid tripping on the prostrate body of his boss. Rose seized her chance. She lunged backwards and aimed an elbow at his face. He let go and in that second she grabbed an empty bottle from the table and swung. Vadim ducked but she caught him on the top of the head, a glancing blow. He staggered. She raised the bottle and brought it down sharply on the edge of the table. It smashed, giving her jagged edges. She advanced, swiping aggressively. Vadim jumped back, just avoiding the glass slicing his stomach. He held his hands up. She launched the entire bottle right at him and made for the balcony. She had a couple of seconds on him, no more.

Her clothes ripped on the glass as she scrambled through the hole. She reached the balcony railing but Vadim was already half way through the hole, slower because he was bigger. She climbed over and lowered herself down. A final glance told her that neither of the bodies in the room had moved. Hand over hand she traversed the strut to get to the rope which she'd left there from earlier. Vadim was directly above her now. She dropped to the ground and ran, adrenaline powering her over the first fence, down into the ditch, then up the other side.

The crack of a gunshot stopped her. She rolled back into the ditch. Vadim had got his hands on a gun, or it was one of the other security guards. If she tried to scale the fence where she came in, they would have a clear shot. She was lying flat in the bottom of the ditch. She rose to her hands and knees to crawl along. A barrage of bullets pinged on the metal enclosure above her. She dropped again. Vadim wasn't alone in the house; she had to get off this compound before they came in to get her. No time to wriggle along. She braced, then got to her feet and ran flat out along the bottom of the ditch. Shots rebounded above her. Five seconds and she was out of range from the Morozov balcony, behind another fence.

Lungs heaving, she threw herself onto the wire fence and climbed up. It was a long way down on the other side now, and she was in full view of the road and the traffic. No time to waste: she prepared to roll onto her side as soon as she dropped, but her ankle jarred and she gasped from the pain. A second or two lying, clenching her teeth, then she got to her feet, brushed the snow off and started to jog, expecting any moment the sound of screeching tyres as they came to find her.

The road bent round and the compound fencing gave way to blocks of flats. A crowd of commuters waited for a bus. Rose slowed to join them, getting a black fleece hat out of her bag and shoving it on her head. She faced away from the road, shielded by the other passengers, expecting to hear car doors slam, shouted warnings, bracing herself to run again. Her ankle throbbed. She started to feel stinging pains on her front, back and legs from the glass cuts. She didn't meet anyone's eye; she must look a sight but no one would say anything. This was Russia.

Eventually a bus pulled up and they all filed on. Rose's heart was still thumping as the bus pulled away. Her phone vibrated in her bag. She pulled it out.

After all that, Kamila was calling her.

33

She got there as soon as she could. The address Kamila gave her was on the outskirts of the city within an industrial zone. An open yard sat in the middle of a ragbag of small warehouses, some with doors yawning open, others shuttered. Pallets were piled up by the gate. No one was about, no obvious security cameras. Rose approached the largest building, which had an ordinary door next to a goods entrance. The door was ajar. Someone was inside, back turned, wearing a headscarf. Rose pushed the door open and waited at the threshold. The person was standing, thumbing through a pile of dockets. As the door swung open, the room brightened and the figure turned.

It was Kamila, but a different kind of Kamila. In ordinary working clothes and no make-up, she looked closer to her real age. There was no coy innocence about her. She seemed sharp, business-like, pre-occupied, maybe a little tired. Seeing Rose, she nodded a greeting, the papers still in her hand.

"I'm surprised you're still in Moscow," said Rose. "You know Roman Morozov is looking for you? He thinks you stole money from the business." No change of expression. "And possibly, that you killed his son." Her chin lifted but she said nothing. She opened a filing cabinet and stashed the dockets inside.

Rose looked around. The tiny office had just enough space for two chairs, one rammed between the loaded desk and the wall, the other piled up with boxes.

"What is this place?"

"It's my place. Bought with Morozov money." She spoke with pride. "Roman doesn't know about it."

"And Alexei didn't either?"

"Alexei didn't know anything. You are alone, like I asked?"

"Yes. And no one followed me here."

"Well. Let's walk."

She locked the door behind them but the gate was wide open as they walked out together. They paced slowly with no destination, just for the sake of moving.

"Your village in Chechnya," said Rose. "It was destroyed during the war. Did Alexei know that?"

"Nobody knows that. No one wants to know. Once you've been a prostitute, there is nothing more worth knowing. Everything before is irrelevant."

"Alexei served in Chechnya." She let the question ask itself. Kamila continued in the same tone.

"It was his battalion. These people are called Russian Heroes here. They had no need to overrun our village. Grozny was already taken. The officers let them as a reward. They stood by, smoking, seeing nothing. Their soldiers went from house to house, rounding up the men and taking them off to shoot them. Then they helped themselves to what was left."

"You were there?"

"Yes, I was there. Why not?"

"You worked in Grozny. For a company. As a book-keeper."

Kamila looked at her. "You know that?"

"We do our research." Eventually, she could have added, after I persuaded them. But she didn't.

"I went back to my family home often. To see my mother and father, my sister and brothers. They were all killed. All of them. I got away. I ran into the woods. I was lucky."

"And Alexei was there?"

Her voice tightened. "When I saw him in Moscow, I knew it was him. I remembered his big stupid mouth and his hands all over everything that wasn't his. Pushing his way through the doorway. He didn't remember me."

Rose neck prickled. This was much more personal than she'd thought.

"So it was a long term plan, to come to Moscow and find him?"

Kamila smiled thinly. "No, no plan. I came to Moscow to survive, like so many lost people do. I saw Alexei in a night club. I recognised him. He didn't recognise me. I had an idea. It all fell into place. It was easy. I stole from him. Roman is right. Alexei couldn't manage things. He was going to lose all the money anyway. I helped, like a secretary, so he thought. But I kept a track of where the money went."

"Did you kill him?"

Kamila glanced over again, but looked away unfazed. "Alexei was shot in the head. I read that on the news. A good death, tidy and quick. In the village, my mother was raped three times. My sister five. My brothers had to watch. When one of them broke in to intervene, a Russian Hero shot his hand off. He bled to death. It took hours."

"You said you ran away." Rose spoke gently.

"I did. But not straight away. I was one of the goods the Russian Heroes handled. My mother, my sister and I. Much later, when those glorious soldiers were sleeping it off, I broke out and ran off. The others were too badly injured. I had to abandon them."

"Was Alexei…?"

"He was one of them. He had all of us. He didn't remember me. He was drunk, they all were! He never remembered me at all."

"You married a man who raped you?"

"I have thought many times about how I would kill Alexei Morozov. I wanted to punish him. Humiliate him. Bleed him dry. If I decided to kill him, I wouldn't do it with a simple bullet in the head. You believe me?"

Rose thought she probably did. "And the FSB? You knew of their involvement in the business, didn't you?"

"That fool Alexei would strip naked in Red Square in return for flattery. Once they're in, you can never get them out. Once they know your secrets they will take whatever they want. They win everything in the end."

"The information on the zip drive. Where did it come from, exactly?"

Kamila went quiet. She was weighing things up.

Rose pushed. "You knew, didn't you? You knew all along. You knew in St Petersburg that we were watching the flat." Kamila had a mischievous smile on her face. "You knew that Alexei was being set up. Who told you?"

Kamila fell silent again. They were walking in a big circle through the industrial zone, past storage depots, empty lots, piles of tyres. Try not to sound needy, Rose. But this is important. Whoever this person is, they made a fool out of me and my colleagues, my country actually. I want to know who and I need to know why.

She prompted once more. "How did it happen, Kamila? You can tell me now, can't you?"

Finally Kamila spoke. "The man who came to Alexei. The man Alexei admired so much. He came to find me, when Alexei wasn't around."

"Khovansky? Mikhail Khovansky?" It was the name on the notepaper in Fairchild's jacket. But Kamila shook her head.

"That's not what people called him."

"Grom? Was it Grom?"

"That's what Alexei called him. A silly name, like his father the Bear. This man, he told me he's been working in the FSB for years. An important guy. But he's from the old time. The KGB. He doesn't like all this, what Russia is becoming. All the wealth being squandered by boys like Alexei, just interested in clothes and cars and women. Russia could be a powerful nation like the USA, but it's too decadent and corrupt. It's rotten, this man says. No ambitions now except for money and power for the few. And they don't like him any more. He's too old. They want younger people who will do anything without questioning. He's important now, but it will not last. He will soon be gone. That's what he said to me."

Rose was working it through in her head. "He deliberately played into our trap to weaken the Kremlin?"

"Yes. And to show you what he knows. What he can do. To show *you*."

Her emphasis was clear. "Me? What do you mean?"

"He wants to meet you. He wants to help you more. To talk to you directly. Me, I'm no longer involved in Morozov. I have to run now, hide away. He says he will help me do that. He knows I stole. He will keep that a secret from his colleagues, keep this place hidden from Roman. If I contact you. If you meet him."

This was big news, a rare thing. A senior FSB officer wanting to pass on secrets. If it wasn't a hoax. "Why us? Why the British?"

"Because you came to the reception, you wanted information about Alexei. This man Grom realised what was happening. He's clever like that."

"He was in St Petersburg?"

"Yes, he was there, watching. Watching and listening. He understood everything. He gave me my instructions."

"Which you followed because he promised to keep quiet about how you were stealing."

"Yes. And now he wants to talk to you. You tell her, he said. Tell her to come and meet me. Only her, no one else. He is very careful who he trusts."

Rose's mind was in overdrive. "When and where?"

"Not Moscow. Not Russia. Abroad."

"Abroad?"

"To be safe. Away from his so-called colleagues."

"Where abroad?"

"Tbilisi."

"Tbilisi? Georgia?"

"Yes. Georgia. He is going there for work. He can meet you there safely. You should go immediately. He will send instructions when you arrive."

It was a long way to go. But this man knew how the FSB operated. If he thought they had to get out of the country to have a private conversation, it said a lot about Russia.

"I'll need to speak to my boss."

"You should hurry. He may not be there long. They could call him back. Any day they might get rid of him. Some day they will, but he doesn't know when. So hurry. Then tell me. I will pass on to him."

"I can't contact him directly?"

"In Tbilisi, yes. Not until then. He is a careful man."

They reached the dead end of an access road and turned to walk back again, at the same steady pace. Kamila was wearing flat-soled leather boots and a padded winter coat. Without the glamour she had in St Petersburg and Moscow, she looked more at home here.

"Why are you still here, Kamila? Why not go back to Chechnya?"

"What's in Chechnya? All my family is dead. It's run by Russians. And it's so backward. I can't do there what I can do here. I like business. I'm good at it. I just need a little help to get started. But who would help me? That's why I help myself. Besides, after what I've done, what was done to me, I would not be accepted now in Chechnya. I am tainted. You know how it is."

Rose had to ask what was on her mind. "The man you were with in St Petersburg. Your lover. Was it John Fairchild?"

Kamila glanced across. "The man at the reception? The businessman with the car company? I remember him. He is an attractive man, very charming. But he was not my lover."

She seemed amused. Rose felt herself flush. After a pause Kamila continued.

"When I first came to Moscow I knew nobody. The other girls, we all stuck together, but that's not the same. Then I met someone. Just a guy working in a bar. Serving rich people. Calling their cabs, being discreet, wiping their mouths when they couldn't hold their drink. Not so different from what I was doing. He had nothing, just like me. He came to Moscow to survive. He didn't care about my past, and I didn't care about his. He's Russian, I'm Chechen, but we are just two people. We fell in love." She was smiling. "What I did with Alexei, getting married, taking his money, that's for both of us. We will set up together. We will build a life together."

"He doesn't live in St Petersburg?"

"He has family there. He goes there often. If I went there without Alexei, we used the flat. This time we were going to meet somewhere else, but Grom told me to go to the flat. My lover, he didn't want to, but if we hadn't done what Grom wanted, we would have lost everything."

They were back at the warehouse. They stopped by the gate and Kamila looked her up and down. "You are too thin. Losing weight. All bones. It's not healthy. You should eat more."

Did it show that much? She probably didn't look her best; she'd been up all night after all.

"You will go to meet him, this man?" It was the old Kamila again, vulnerable, small. "If you do, maybe we can be together, my lover and I. Live as we want to. Make something good from all of this. If not…"

She didn't have to finish. With both Roman Morozov and the FSB after her, it was clear what would happen if Grom gave her away.

"I'll try," said Rose.

34

"So he's cautious. But he's reaching out to us, Peter. We need to consider it at the very least." Rose heard her boss sigh. "Come on, Peter. How many people must have thought Penkovsky was a hoax, when he came along? But he wasn't, and with him we prevented the Cuban missile crisis becoming Armageddon. Sure, it might be a set-up, but they all might. We go in and investigate, check it out. It's our job, isn't it?"

She took a sip of coffee from the paper cup she was holding, but it was already cold. She'd come back to her flat after leaving Kamila, hopefully to pack and set off for Tbilisi. To speak to Peter she came out to a tiny park a block away, next to a busy road creating useful background noise and not-so-useful fumes. A mobile van sold hot drinks and snacks. A handful of people had come out for a quick smoke. Not a place you'd spend a lot of time, but it had enough space to talk without being overheard. She hadn't forgotten the watchers. Any of these people could be FSB.

"But going all that way without any kind of verification whatsoever?" Peter was saying. "You don't even have a name for the guy."

Rose hadn't actually mentioned Grom. Naming someone Peter thought didn't exist wouldn't have helped her argument. "There's a name associated with Morozov, though. A possible connection. It might be the same person but I can't be sure. Mikhail Khovansky."

"Okay." Peter was making a note. "We'll see what comes back. Where did this come from?"

"John Fairchild." She said it lightly.

"Oh, I didn't know you two were talking directly."

"It was a chance encounter. I can explain more later, but if we're going to do this we need to hurry, Peter. The last flight to Tbilisi leaves in two hours."

"There are more flights tomorrow, Rose."

"If he's still there. He could be called back at any time, Kamila said. Look, I'm ready to go. If it's a wasted journey, so what? I'll just come back again."

"There are worse things than wasted journeys. Look, stay by the phone. I'll see if we can check on this name. And calm down!"

Rose pocketed her phone and paced to the nearest bin to throw away the cold coffee. Another night in Moscow spinning her wheels? Please, no. She should be tired after her sleepless night but it hadn't kicked in yet. She left the park and walked along the street. She went into a tiny grocery store and bought a couple of lurid candy bars just to be seen to have a purpose for the journey. Back at the park she joined the small queue at the mobile kiosk and had a careful look around.

Bingo. The man sitting on the bench was still there. All the other faces were new. And it was faces she was looking at, not hats or hoods or coats. The guy on the bench had no hat, or hood, or coat. No cigarette, no hot drink, no phone. White hair, a dark suit and tie. He was just sitting, hands on his knees, as if contemplating the meaning of life. Pretty cocky, not to even try to blend in. That or just unprofessional.

She bought cigarettes and was fumbling around lighting one when her phone rang. It was Peter again. His voice sounded different.

"Where did you say you got that name from?"

"John Fairchild."

"And where did he get it from?"

"I assume through his investigations into Morozov. Beyond that I don't know."

A pause. "And what are the chances that this is the guy who wants to talk to us?"

"I don't know for sure. He's connected in some way. That's all I know." An even longer pause. "This is someone we'd be interested in?"

"Yes. It is." She'd never heard him sound so emphatic. "He's a very senior figure, Rose. He's been there for years, since before the regime change. His name has come up numerous times."

"That ties in completely with what Kamila said about Grom. Sounds like it may well be the same guy." Silence from the other end. "Come on, Peter. Do you really want to miss out on this? If it's a ruse we'll find out. But if it's not, it could be a game-changer for us."

More silence. Then, eventually: "Okay, get your flight. Make contact with the Tbilisi Head as soon as you get there. They'll be expecting you. I'll talk to them about getting a team together for you. And take care!"

It was all Rose could do not to punch the air. They'd struck gold, by the sound of it. This Khovansky must be quite someone. But she kept her euphoria well hidden. She had a flight to catch.

She set off for home. The man on the bench was still there. Not only that, but he seemed to have given up all attempts at subtlety and was staring straight at her. Their eyes met for a fraction of a second. His blasé behaviour was unsettling.

But she had no time to worry about that. She had to get moving.

35

Fairchild didn't have to wait. He knew exactly which room Walter was staying in, but chose to sit in an armchair in the plush lobby and wait for the man to make an appearance, as he no doubt would about now, since he'd booked a table for dinner in half an hour's time. Iconic city hotels were something of a specialism of Fairchild's. Particularly for keeping tabs on people of interest. Watching the watchers. Impressive what you could learn with a friend or two on the front desk.

He stared up at a heavy chandelier feeling sick. Sick? No, sick didn't cover it. Ill, diseased, poisoned. Pain whenever his eyes moved, guts twisted, senses floating, disconnected, disoriented, like his brain was detached and moving around inside his skull. The session with Roman started twenty-four hours ago, but he felt just as bad as he had this morning. Bloody vodka. Bloody Russians. And here was Walter now, looking typically old-school British, although his jawline was shadowed and his waistcoat creased. He slowed when he saw Fairchild. Not so much surprised as wary. Possibly even a little afraid.

"I don't suppose this is a coincidence, is it, John?"

"Good to see you too, Walter. Fancy a pre-prandial?" Fairchild nodded towards the bar, though the mere idea of alcohol made his stomach catapult. Walter sighed.

"Would I regret it if I asked how you knew I was here?" he asked as they settled at a table. Fairchild had already checked out the bar for possible eavesdroppers, and the waiter had been paid generously to alert him to any suspicious newcomers.

"You always stay here when you come to Moscow."

"Yes, but it's rather more about knowing that I'd be coming to Moscow. I only arrived three hours ago."

"Scotch?" Fairchild suggested. The waiter was hovering.

"Anything but Johnnie Walker." Walter addressed the waiter directly. He spoke Russian, of course; back in his era it was obligatory. Fairchild ordered a tonic water.

"I'm surprised you're not more pleased to see me, Walter. You were very keen to speak to me a few months ago. So much so that you sent Rose Clarke to track me down."

"Things have moved on. That was part of a probe into a possible leak. I had to be seen to be investigating you. Orders from the top."

"Ah, so it was all Marcus Salisbury's doing."

"That tends to be the way it works, John, if you're part of an organisation. He is the boss after all. Anyway, the focus of the investigation has moved elsewhere, since there was never any evidence you were involved."

"Such a relief."

"And you made your views about the Service clear at the time, as I'm sure you recall. I regret that you wouldn't consider my offer of an approach to Salisbury. I'm sure he can be persuaded to abandon any preconceptions he might have if you expressed an interest in working more constructively with us."

"Working constructively with you of course would involve abandoning any attempt to find out what happened to my parents."

"Well, you've made your views on the matter quite clear. I take it you want to talk about some other matter?"

"I do. You remember the conversation we had on my sixteenth birthday?"

Walter's face set itself to a resigned blandness. "Yes, I remember. You didn't like what I had to say."

"I found that man. I found him, Walter! You said you'd looked. The Service. You put everything into it. That's what you said."

"And we did. But there wasn't much to go on, was there? A physical description, no more."

"A good physical description. And a likely nationality. I went to a speciality tobacconist and found the make of cigarette he was smoking. A Russian brand. Only for sale in Russia. New information, Walter! What did you do with it?"

"The make of cigarette on a pack you got a partial glimpse of, in passing, in a dark street. Not exactly fool-proof, is it? And I don't need to remind you that you were ten years old at the time. MI6 is a big organisation, with stretched resources. If you're going to open up an old line of enquiry like that, you need a strong enough reason, a justification in the here and now. Besides, what did his being Russian tell us exactly? It wouldn't in itself clear their names, would it? And there's the equipment that was found inside the flat."

"That was planted."

"He said that, did he, this fellow?"

"Yes, he did. You're saying now that you think my parents were double agents?"

"No, John. I've told you, I've never thought that! They were working for me at the time, remember? But what was found was found. And we never heard from them again. Some people were never convinced after that, though I tried."

That whining voice again. He'd heard these excuses most of his life. "So the problem went away. How convenient. Well, I met him, Walter. I've spoken to him. Stick that in your Scotch and drink it."

Already he'd reverted to a sulky teenager, as he so often did with Walter. The drinks arrived. Unfortunately, the barman explained, they had no Scotch except for Johnnie Walker but he hoped Sir would be okay with Black Label, a fine premium? Failing to mention it was also the most expensive in the range. Fairchild's tonic was miniscule.

"Are you expecting me to say well done?" asked Walter after the waiter had gone. "You've made this your life, John. You've let it twist you up. All the things you might have done if you could just let it go."

"I can see how that would have suited you."

"Well, let's hear it, then. What did this man have to say for himself? That's what you want to tell me, isn't it?"

"But you already know what he said, Walter! Every time I find anything out and bring it to you, it turns out you knew already."

"Don't be ridiculous. How could I possibly know what some Russian said to you about something that happened thirty years ago?"

Fairchild drained his tonic. "He said that my parents were abducted on the orders of a senior KGB agent who used the street name Grom. Are you going to tell me you've never heard of that person?"

Walter sighed. "Grom doesn't exist. He's a scare story, a ghost identity the KGB used to frighten their own recruits in case any of them felt like turning."

"That's exactly what Peter Craven said. And yet, within days of the Moscow Head of Station hearing mention of that name, you show up. That's a coincidence, is it? Or are you here for some other purpose entirely?"

No response.

"It's a lot of trouble to go to for someone who doesn't exist. When I asked Zack to throw the name around, I wondered how long it would take for you to make an appearance. And here you are."

"Well, that's all very clever of you, John. I can tell you're pleased with yourself." Walter sipped his Johnnie Walker as though it were lemon juice.

"So," said Fairchild, "are you going to treat me like a grown-up? Or are you going to make me look elsewhere for someone who will? You know I'll find out. Some of you people will help. Of course, that means spreading the word. Whispering the name Grom in the ears of spooks far and wide. And I get the impression you don't want this particular body dug up."

"Can I remind you," said Walter, "that persuading or coercing intelligence officers to give out secrets makes you a significant security threat and could be considered treasonous?"

"You can. I also know how embarrassing it would be if it were to become public knowledge that a breach like that had happened. Not to mention if the information itself also got out. I know you don't want a big fuss, Walter. You've spent the past three decades trying to drop this in the deepest well you can find. But I'm not going away. I will find out. If not from you, then from someone else."

He waited. Walter sighed and began.

"Earlier in their MI6 careers, your parents were involved in an internal investigation. After a series of operational blow-outs, a senior officer came under suspicion of working for the Soviets. Edward and Elizabeth were sufficiently distant from his activities to be trusted with it. They were on the verge of amassing enough information to proceed, but before he could be detained he was killed in a car accident in the Scottish Highlands. At least, that was how things appeared. The leaks seemed to stop."

Walter swilled the ice cubes around in his drink, apparently having lost the will to drink it.

"Years later, the Fairchilds were working for me. I was a rising star at that time, you know, fast promotion and all that. Anyway, this case niggled at them. They kept going back to it. You know how they liked to theorise. I told them to forget about it and move on, but they developed this idea of a new presence in the KGB, someone whose information seemed to lead right back along all those same trails. They starting talking about his death being a decoy and that he'd crossed into the USSR. They were based in Vienna at the time, to screen and recruit defectors crossing the Hungarian border. Then they disappeared."

"So of course you diligently investigated the idea that they may have been right?"

"John, you need to develop a sense of realism. Without the two of them I couldn't make a case. They were the ones who'd pulled it all together, but most people dismissed the idea as fantasy. A few thought there might be something in it, but there weren't enough of us, I'm afraid. So I did try, although I'm sure you won't believe me."

He sounded like he wanted his dinner. Fairchild was unsympathetic.

"This person calling himself Grom might be a former British intelligence officer?"

"That's what your parents thought. But the problem with that idea is that other defectors – Philby, Burgess and so on – never earned enough trust from the Soviets to play an influential role in the intelligence world in the East. They were sidelined, frozen out. Left to live out dreary unimportant lives in tatty communist apartment blocks, and serves them right. Which made the Fairchilds consider something else."

Fairchild was already there. "He wasn't British at all. He was Russian all along, with some cover that was deep enough to fool all the checkers."

"I went through every element of his back story, John. I couldn't find anything amiss. It all checked out. I have to say, this idea that he was Russian didn't exactly make the Fairchilds' theory more popular within the Service. But if they were right, it would explain how he established himself in the KGB."

Fairchild remembered Dimitri's words: *Grom is not a man who forgets.*

"He had my parents killed because it was their investigation that blew his cover. He never forgave them for it, even though he got away."

"Maybe. Or perhaps he saw them as a threat. He thought they might still track him down somehow."

"But he framed them as well. He wanted to destroy their reputation as well as take their lives."

"Well, some on our side argued the Fairchilds were in on it. That they were working with him the whole time, and took a suitable opportunity to go over as well. Not me, John! I always backed them up. But we were in the dark, really."

Fairchild's mouth was dry. The tonic had had no effect. "They would have taken me with them," he managed. "They wouldn't have left me behind."

"Unless they thought you'd have a better life in the west. You were at boarding school most of the time anyway. Maybe they were told they couldn't bring you. Maybe you just happened to leave the flat at a very unfortunate time."

Fairchild thought back to that evening, the card game they were playing, his parents' stupid forfeits, tricks and puzzles they were always foisting on him. Don't go, his mother had said to him as he stormed off. Please don't go, John.

"What's his name?" he asked.

"Nobody knows his name. Theories floating about, that's all we ever had."

"His name in MI6! His name in the Service. What was he called?"

"That won't mean anything to anyone, John. The man died, so everyone thinks. It's just a file in the archives now."

"Then it won't matter me knowing, will it? Come on, Walter."

Walter sighed. "His name was Sutherland. Gregory Sutherland. For what it's worth. But careful what you do with all this, John. There may be good reasons for not digging these things up."

Careful, careful. Walter had been careful all right. He could have told Fairchild this at any point during his life instead of watching him risk everything time and again to find out for himself. And now here he was, his lean, worn face, his sharp eyes tinged with concern, telling Fairchild to be careful. What a fraud.

He couldn't stand to be in the old man's company any more. He got up and left.

36

Fairchild walked out, too impatient to stop and chat at the front desk, too furious to check for shadows. With no destination he headed into the Metro. Knowing in advance that Walter was a two-faced schemer didn't make it hurt any less. Years of his life he'd spent on this. Jinpa, his Tibetan friend, risked everything to pass him Dimitri's identity, and after all that, why had Walter been so secretive all these years? To avoid the Service being embarrassed by its own incompetence. It really was that tawdry.

He paced along the platform, not even caring where the train was going. Walter was framing this as a thing of the past. But Walter didn't know that Dimitri had been murdered. Or that Fairchild had almost been shot on a train. This was not history. It was live, happening now. The man was still active, this Russian who'd fooled MI6 and infiltrated its highest ranks. Even now capable of carrying out acts of revenge and settling old scores, just as he had with Fairchild's mother and father. Walter hadn't even asked what Dimitri had said about their fate. He probably already knew that as well.

The train pulled in and he got on. He stood and stared at his own reflection in the glass as it picked up speed. Grom, who killed his parents, was somehow involved in the Morozov business. Maybe it was the same person as Roman's FSB contact, maybe not. Leaving the Morozov office the evening he'd discovered Alexei's body, Fairchild had, on a whim, picked up the notepaper he'd thrown on the floor earlier and taken it with him, along with the laptop. He was sure that this piece of paper was still in his pocket when he'd gone to see Roman. Which meant that it was the same piece of paper Roman had used to scribble his contact name on. Which was why he was so enraged that he couldn't now find this piece of paper. Normally, if someone gave him a name he'd commit it to memory. But last night he was drunk. They were both unspeakably drunk, and he couldn't remember the name for the life of him, even though he'd seen it written down. Idiot, Fairchild! A wasted evening. Using self-pity as an excuse to lose focus. He'd never get anywhere acting like that.

He got off at the next interchange. On the way up the steps, his phone vibrated. It was a text from Zack: *Call me when you can.* Fairchild made for the exit. He emerged at Okhotny Ryad Metro, and once he'd walked far enough not to be overheard he was in Red Square. A funfair was still going, chattering groups gathering around the rides and stalls, strings of lights glowing against the night sky, bright colours penetrating lightly falling snow.

He made the call, following the agreed procedures for a secure line.

"Hey, Zack!"

"Can you talk?"

Tinny music played from a carousel. The massive wall of the Kremlin stretched out across the length of the square. Children squealed. It was as good a place as any.

"Sure."

"Want to know what's new?"

"Of course."

"This is big. Seriously. You know the files we got from your lover Kamila?"

"My *what?*"

"Your lover. You went to bed with her in St Petersburg. That's what Rose Clarke seems to think anyway. They were filming the whole damn thing."

She thought *that*? Jesus. He fought to moderate his response. "Well, I don't know what they filmed, but it certainly wasn't me. Like I said, I left once I'd seen the technicians floating about."

"Have it your way. She seemed pretty sure, though."

"Zack, would you do that if you thought someone was watching? I'm not that nuts."

"Yeah, that's what I said. That Clarke woman, though, she seems to think you are."

"Really?" His delicate insides were reconfiguring. Was it good or bad? That she thought he was nuts, or that she gave a damn about who he slept with?

"Anyway, that's not what I'm calling about. Those files on the zip drive Kamila provided. It's all bogus. I mean, completely wrong. Intended to deceive."

"You're joking."

"Nope."

"This is about the supply lines, right? Using them to prep for military ops?"

"Yes. And they are. But not in Ukraine. We sent our teams out on the ground to look for all this gear and all these troops. Nothing. Checked it out by satellite as well. Looked at social media, any chatter in posts by Russian troops. These training exercises they were doing in the south were part of the deception. Confused us for a while. But Ukraine's not the target."

"So what is the target?"

"Georgia."

"Georgia?"

"Morozov has plenty of contacts there as well, right through the region. Russia's had its eye on Georgia since forever. They never exactly left after they invaded in 2008, setting up those enclaves and all. We've made it clear what we'd think if they tried anything. So's the EU, so's NATO. But they want it."

"And how do we know this?"

"Because they've just launched a land invasion."

"What? When?"

"Tonight. Now. Their tanks are rolling through Georgia as we speak."

He was desperately trying to process it all through his thudding head. "Zack, who the hell knew about this?"

"Nobody. I mean, nobody. This is a complete surprise, believe me. Georgia's tiny, Fairchild. They'll be at Tbilisi by morning."

"Christ."

"You can say that again. My people are asking why we had no heads up, the Brits are in the same boat. We deliberately had the wool pulled over our eyes. This was calculated misdirection. And you want to know what else?"

"What?"

"I just spoke to Peter. Rose Clarke is in Tbilisi."

A moment of blackness. The fairground music seemed to fade. "What for?"

"She was told about a potential FSB source who wanted to meet her there. All so urgent that she went straight away. She left this afternoon."

Icy tendrils reached out, coiling around his skin. "And who told her that?"

"Guess who? The lovely Kamila. She's been leading us all a merry ride. But it's the Kremlin pulling her strings of course. Just as well you didn't do the deed with her."

"Who did Rose think she was going to meet?"

"Peter says some senior guy who's been inside the government for years. He was pretty excited about it, which is why he let her go, even though it sounded dicey."

"It was a trap, for God's sake! A set-up!"

"Must be. Someone with the inside track on the invasion thought they'd make mischief with it. But here's the weird thing. It was Kamila who passed on the message from this guy. But the name she had, his actual name, Rose told Peter she got it from you."

The tendrils gripped, squeezed, turning everything numb. "Zack, do you have the name?"

He paused. "You mean it wasn't from you?"

"I – it's a long story." Bloody vodka. Bloody Russia. Bloody stupid Fairchild. "Did Peter give you the name?"

"Yeah, it's a – here we go – Mikhail Khovansky. That's what Peter got so worked up about. Khovansky's a real insider, massively influential. He'd be a hell of a target to recruit. Wonder where she got it from, then."

That was the name. That was the blasted name, he knew it as soon as he heard it. How the hell did Rose have it? She'd long gone by that time. Unless she came back later, when they were… A vomit-stained carpet came to mind, almost making him retch.

Zack was still talking but Fairchild wasn't listening. However Rose got it, she'd been set up nicely, helped by his own self-indulgent ineptitude. And now she was in danger.

Georgia

37

The door opened.

"Boris! Boris!"

Boris heard his name echo around the washroom. He didn't move a muscle. He knew they would find him there. He just needed some time to rest his throbbing, bleeding feet. He stayed perched on the toilet seat, covered in grime, knees bent, bare feet up on the pan.

The sergeant shoved the first cubicle door open. It crashed against the side. Metal smashed into metal. The noise surrounded and compressed Boris' head, smothered his skull, pricked the backs of his flickering eyes, a stab of pain with the peak of every echo. Then the next door, and the next, the echoes building, points of pain sharper and sharper. He covered his ears though he knew it wouldn't make any difference. The sergeant got to his cubicle. The lock rattled.

"So there you are, you snivelling coward!" He moved right up to the door and spoke through it. "You think you can get out of marching by cowering in here? I'll send you out without even slippers this time! I'll have you marching up and down all night, when everyone else is lying in bed!"

Boris' army slippers fell apart long ago; they weren't meant for marching. He'd been barefoot for hours. His feet had been covered in pus and sores for months. He held his arms up and braced. The lock ripped away. The door slammed against the side of the cubicle right in front of him. A tidal wave of noise, suffocating. His throat made a sound like an animal. The sergeant grabbed him and dragged him out. He threw Boris across the floor and kicked him in the ribs. Boris fought to breathe.

"Stand up!" He kicked again, on the knee. "I said get up, soldier!"

Boris hauled himself to his feet, trying not to catch the sergeant's eye. His neck and face started to flush.

"Blushing again? What kind of a girl are you?"

His cheeks burned. A movement in the corner of his eye. The sergeant punched him on the nose. He heard it crunch, felt warm blood on his mouth. The sergeant punched again, on the jaw this time. His lip split. The room swayed. Boris staggered. He should be used to this. After months of training, there was no inch of his body which hadn't been bruised. How did he not know it would be like this? So many people warned him, so many! But it was for Russia, for glory, father and mother, for pride, for Tatiana! That was what he expected.

The sergeant punched him in the stomach. The blow made him retch and he doubled up. A shove knocked him to the ground. His teeth clashed against the tile floor.

"Press-ups! Now!" A boot landed on his ribs. "Press-ups, you lazy little girl!" Boris turned face-down and started to lift himself up. "Count!"

"One!" he shouted. The sergeant kicked him in the mouth. His arms collapsed.

"Again!"

"Two!" He raised himself up. The sergeant kicked again. Blood was dripping onto the floor.

"Come on, little blond Boris! Time you grew some muscle! Faster!"

"Three!" He raised himself expecting the kick but there was a voice at the door.

"Stop that! We've got to go, now!" Another of the older conscripts.

The sergeant paused. "Why?"

"We're all being called. They're loading up the trucks now."

"What for?"

"We're going to war."

38

Rose was already in her hotel room when she heard the news. After landing at Tbilisi, she had a message on her phone from Kamila telling her that Khovansky was in Lali, but only for another day. It was already evening, as she'd had to take a long indirect flight. Lali was a town outside Tbilisi, just over an hour away in a taxi. So she went straight there. She checked in by phone with Tbilisi Station on the way, updated them and got a hotel recommendation. They would work on a plan to support her during the meet, and they'd speak again in the morning. She wouldn't try and make contact with Khovansky this evening, but if she were already in Lali, things could move more quickly tomorrow.

A few minutes after she arrived, Peter called.

"Switch on your TV. Look at the news."

"What's happening?" Rose reached for the remote control.

"The Russians are coming. Land invasion. From the South Ossetia enclave. They're going straight for Tbilisi."

"A land invasion? Here? That can't be right."

"It is, I'm afraid."

Rose realised he was right when she found Russia Today and saw image of tanks rolling along roads. She read the headlines.

"They're talking about Georgian encroachment," she said.

"They're always talking about that. It's just an excuse. That's how they justified seizing South Ossetia in 2008, last time all this flared up."

"How serious is it?"

"Very. They've amassed huge resources and are unleashing it all. The Georgians will mobilise all they've got, but it's not enough."

Rose glanced out of the window. It was just an ordinary street down there, just an ordinary town.

"How long have I got here?" She was still thinking about Grom.

"Get out as soon as you can. It doesn't matter how or where to, just leave. There are still flights from Tbilisi but that could stop any time."

"I'm not in Tbilisi. I'm in Lali. It's an hour away."

"Lali? Why?"

"I got a message from Kamila. She said Khovansky was here, but only for another day. It was a taxi journey from the airport, Peter. I checked in with Tbilisi Station. We were going to finalise everything first thing tomorrow."

"I'm looking at a map right now. Lali is between South Ossetia and Tbilisi. You're in the path of the invasion. You're right in the middle of it, Rose. Every piece of information Kamila gave us is false. This guy isn't going to be there. It's a set-up. Time to wake up."

Rose's mouth was dry. "But why? For what purpose?"

"Let's hope some day we'll find out. Just get out, Rose. Any way you can. I'll see what I can do from here."

Rose grabbed what she could easily carry and went downstairs. The lobby was busy with worried faces and people wheeling suitcases. Outside, a long line of people waited at the taxi rank. One flustered concierge was trying to fill taxis as they arrived one by one. Another was on the phone. They were cramming as many people as they could into each car, but Rose counted twenty people in front of her, and minutes went by between each taxi arriving.

In front of her in the line was a tall westerner with brown hair and gold-rimmed glasses. They caught each other's eye.

"Are you a journalist too?" he asked in a European accent, Dutch maybe.

"No, I work for the British Embassy."

"Wow. So the diplomats didn't know about this either."

"I wouldn't be here if we knew."

"Same with us. I've been freelancing here for years, they kept this completely secret. I'm going to cover the story from Tbilisi. Too dangerous here, with the barracks and the citadel."

"Citadel?"

"That's what they call the old town, the river island." He pointed off into the distance. "The fort at the top is an army barracks. Troops, supplies, ammunition. The Russians will try to take it. And they'll want the river crossing as well. It's too close for comfort here!"

Another taxi arrived and was loaded up beyond its limit with people. It drove off, leaving the queue looking as long as it was before. The concierge did a kind of "calm down" semaphore for everyone's benefit, but he looked stressed and muttered to his colleague.

"I'm hoping I don't need this taxi," said the journalist. "My interpreter offered me a lift with some people they're going with. If there's space you can come too."

"Thanks." Rose's mind had already started on the alternatives to the taxi. There was still the odd parked car in the street. Most of them were too modern to hot-wire but one or two might be old enough.

Her phone rang. It was Kamila. She hesitated, then picked up.

"Kamila."

"You are in Lali?"

"You know what's going on down here, right?"

"You tell me where you are, please."

"Why?"

"Grom wants to know."

"I bet he does."

"No, you don't understand. He didn't know this would happen."

"He didn't know? How could he possibly not know about this?"

"I mean, he thought it was in a few days. That was the plan. But it happened early. Tonight, he didn't think tonight."

"Why on earth should I believe a word you say, Kamila?"

"Grom has a car. Grom is in Lali. He can come and find you. Pick you up. Take you somewhere safe. Just tell me where you are, please."

While she was talking, three taxis pulled up at once and were mobbed by the front of the line. With five or six people in each one, it was looking good for her for the very next taxi.

"Kamila, I just can't trust you any more."

"Please! You have to. You know what will happen to me!" Her voice was cracking.

"I'll make my own arrangements."

Kamila was pleading for her life, but Rose had to think about her own life. The taxis were just pulling off, leaving the journalist and her at the front of the line.

"No! Don't do that! He is on his way. You are in Lali? He can be there soon. Just wait. Wait and tell me where you are. Please, Rose!"

Rose hung up.

An overloaded car pulled up in front of them. A man jumped out, greeted the journalist, and pointed into the back where there were already three people. It was clear there wasn't space for Rose as well.

"Don't worry, I'll be in the next taxi," said Rose.

"Well, if you end up back in Tbilisi, look me up. We can compare notes." He gave her his card. Jannes, his name was.

"Thanks, Jannes. Good luck!"

"You too!"

The laden car drove off. Perhaps a dozen people were now waiting for a taxi. The concierge and his colleague talked between themselves. The concierge turned to Rose.

"Five minutes!" he said. "Five minutes. Wait here, please."

Both the front desk staff disappeared inside. The minutes dragged out. The street was becoming more and more busy with people walking, family groups carrying bags and cases, all heading in the same direction. The group behind Rose in the queue sounded like German tourists. The stunned looks on their faces summed up the general atmosphere. They'd trotted the globe assuming their country would always help them if they got into such a fix, but what could anyone do in these kinds of timescales? With her background, Rose at least had more options than they did.

The five minutes had turned more into fifteen, and no sign of the staff. Rose didn't blame them for leaving; they had their own affairs to deal with. She abandoned the taxi queue and walked off, taking the same direction as all the others but going into side streets, hoping to get away from prying eyes.

She passed an elderly couple in the process of pulling the shutters down on a small convenience store. It reminded Rose that she was hungry and had no idea when she might next have something to eat. The couple spoke no English, but Rose tried Russian and they understood. She showed them some cash and persuaded them to let her grab a few items: nuts, dried fruit, semi-stale bread. It would have to do for now.

"Where are you going?" she asked them. Home, they said. They shrugged. We have no family, no car, no way to leave.

In the days that came, she wondered from time to time what became of those people – the shopkeepers, the Germans.

Outside she continued a winding route, peering into the dashboards of cars to see if they might be stealable. Something made her stop, concentrate. Then, a sound which would over the coming weeks define her life and stay with her for years to come: a high whistle, impossible to place in the sky; a silence; a flash; a thud; a crash, splintering tile, smashing glass; shouts carried on the wind.

They were here.

39

Crammed into the back of a truck, Boris could feel the soldiers' hot breath and smell their unwashed bodies. They were squeezed together, legs, arms, bulky uniforms, all the gear. The gear they didn't know how to use, the guns they hadn't been taught how to fire. No one had much to say. They stared down at their feet. The road was bumpy. They were part of a convoy, constantly stopping and starting.

They pulled in and were ordered off. It was dark. They walked along the road. No one knew for how long or where they were going. Every step Boris took was painful, his feet crammed into hard boots. He wanted to whimper. He could still feel dried blood on his face. He couldn't breathe through his nose. Tanks thundered past them on the road, towering above, spraying grit. A lightning flash in the distance, a crackling like a firework. Then again and again, getting louder and brighter as they marched, deep thuds with every flash making his heart race.

They converged on a bridge, a whole mass of them. Men shouted orders but he could hear nothing except the crashing and booming above. A convoy of tanks was ahead, crossing the river towards the town. He had no idea what town this was. When the sky lit up for a second he saw a hill, a wall at the top, rectangular buildings along the river's edge. They piled onto the bridge. He couldn't see the water swirling below but imagined how cold and icy it was. They walked towards the thundering and the flashes, with the tanks grinding and the bridge vibrating. More soldiers packed in behind them. They had to go onward, onward.

A new sound, a juddering rattle, low-level flashes on the hill. Cries from around, then yelps and screams of pain. Oh

Christ, they were firing! Someone in front turned and fell, his face a bloody mess. People crouched down, tried to help him but what could they do? Shouts from behind: we can't help him, we have to keep moving. More cries, more falling bodies in front.

They slowed down. Then, a kind of pop, and a massive bang which lit up everyone's faces. Shouts: a tank has been hit! The vast thing was skewed and blackened. Smoke leached out. Soldiers were squeezing themselves out of it and running, running towards them. But they couldn't make any headway because the bridge was so crammed. The tanks had stopped and were disgorging people like vomiting beasts. But the soldiers were being pushed forward, more and more troops coming onto the bridge.

Boris was jostled towards the side. Or maybe he was pushing to get there, he wasn't sure which. The swirl of people had a momentum of its own. Then word went round: Retreat! Retreat? How? We can't, the space is full of people. But there was a wild desperation in men's eyes and they started pushing and shoving back the way they came. A man shouldered Boris into the railing of the bridge. Another squeezed past, stepping on the toes of his boots. He felt sick with pain. He leaned out over the water.

He couldn't see what was below. Behind, on one side the terrible sounds of destruction, the blackened tank, the smell of burning. On the other, the grabbing, shoving men, desperate to push their way through and back. Back to the barracks and the beatings and the humiliation. Back to Blushing Boris.

Many ran away in the early days. He didn't want to bring shame to his family. In his letters home he painted the picture they would have wanted to see. He lost himself in those letters, living a daydream of foolish hope, imagining it was real. But to meet his end during a conflict? They would be sad, his family, but proud also. He'd be remembered as a hero. He grabbed the railing. He said their names out loud: mother, father, sisters. Tatiana. He swung one leg over, expecting someone to shout: "Boris, what are you doing?" To reach out to try and stop him. Or to lambast him with their sarcasm and point him back to the line. But no one cared. They were all too taken up with their own survival.

He swung the other leg. He didn't look down. He simply let go, and fell.

The water slammed into him like a hard object. Oh, so freezing cold! It knocked all the breath out of him. He was flailing, flailing. He kicked up against objects, maybe other people, bodies, but he couldn't see. His eyes were squeezed shut. His chest was tight. He couldn't get back up to the surface. He was fighting but going nowhere. Bit by bit, everything started to go numb.

40

Rose needed to know what was going on. The main street was crowded now with people walking. A man in army uniform went past in the opposite direction, giving instructions to anyone who approached, pointing back behind him. Rose tried to stop someone and ask what was going on, but they waved her away. Sirens approached: a fire engine flashed by, its sound distorting in passing. The hill beyond the river lit up over and over again, each flash accompanied by an ominous thudding. Some of the hits were much closer, coming from the opposite side. A long whistle split the air right above, then a boom shook the ground and a plume of dust rose against the night sky. That was no more than one or two blocks away. A young girl stopped to turn and look up at it. Her mother grabbed her by the arm and spoke to her, pulling her along. On the mother's other side was a wide-eyed boy, older than the girl. Rose caught the mother's eye.

"Can you tell me what's happening?" she asked in English. The woman hesitated and looked to the boy.

"Citadel," he said, pointing to the hillock. "Everyone is going to the citadel."

Rose looked again at the mother, who shrugged. "Do you speak Russian?" she asked, in Russian.

"Russian? Yes, yes!" The woman's face was suddenly animated.

"Why is everyone going there?" It seemed to Rose that they were heading straight for where the attack was worst.

"It's safer. The river goes right round. But we must get across the bridge before the Russians."

"People aren't trying to leave the town?"

"We can't leave now, the Russians have blocked the roads."

Already? "How do you know that?"

"They told us." She pointed to the soldier giving instructions. She was hurrying the children along, one in each hand. Rose kept pace with them.

"You don't live here?" the woman asked.

"No, I was staying at the hotel. I've only just arrived."

"The Russians are trying to take the bridge on the northern side, but our soldiers are stopping them. My husband is up there now. They can't cross the river, but they've crossed at the next road bridge and they're coming into the town from the south. Our soldiers can't defend the whole town. We cross the south bridge into the citadel and maybe there…"

She tailed off. The children didn't react to their Russian.

"Where are you from?" asked the woman.

"I'm British." They introduced themselves, rather incongruously; the woman was Marta, children Ilya and Katya.

"What are you going to do in the citadel?" asked Rose.

"Go to the fort. My husband is there." That was all. Rose looked around. The crowd was getting thicker all the time. "The bridge is just up there." Marta pointed beyond them to a mass of heads.

"So many people!"

"There was not enough time to leave. Not everyone has a car. Many have nowhere to go. Many didn't believe the rumours at first. Or they have family here who are fighting. Like us." Marta pulled the children closer towards her. Crowds were filling the pavement and road now. They had to slow down. "Besides," she said. "You're here, aren't you?"

"I didn't hear the rumours," said Rose. She could have added, even though it's my job to hear rumours.

By the bridge the road was jammed. More people were joining, pushing from behind. Sirens were going off in the streets around them. An explosion a block away prompted gasps and moans of fear all around. In front, cars were trying to get out across the bridge: residents of the citadel in a last-ditch attempt to clear the town, not realising it was already too late, or determined to try it anyway. Horns were beeping like mad. Some drivers stuck their heads out of windows, waving people out of the way, but there was nowhere for them to go. Arguments erupted as the cars tried to edge forward, nudging people out of the way. What would have been easy an hour ago now seemed almost impossible. The artillery fire was much louder now, almost above. At every flash and boom people stared up then tried to hurry even more.

At the other end of the bridge it became clear what the hold-up was. Most of the width of the road had been blocked by metal barriers. Georgian soldiers were lined up on either side, standing and waiting, heavily armed. Others were corralling civilians in through a small opening in the middle, beckoning and at times pushing people along. The bridge was still full of people.

As they waited, something changed. The soldiers' attention was drawn by something on the south shore. Some started to move into position. Others came running down from the streets behind. Rose was almost at the opening. A murmur travelled through the crowd behind them. People started pushing forward more urgently. Rose turned again, and realised why. Across the shore, further upriver, dark shapes crawled along in the street light. A line of tanks was making its way along the riverside towards the bridge. They had no more than a few minutes.

Someone grabbed her arm. She turned, controlling an instinct to lash out. It was a soldier trying to hurry her through the gap. The pressure from behind was growing. The soldier pushed her forward, barely looking at her. Rose could see Marta and the two children just in front of her. Doing anything else was impossible. She squeezed through the gate after them.

Once through, the crowd thinned as the road branched in different directions, east and west around the island then up into the old town itself.

"The fort is this way," said Marta. Rose went along; she had no other plan. But they never got to the fort. Two streets further up they ran into a waiting queue. Everyone had the same idea, everyone was trying to get to the same place. Marta had some hurried conversations with some of them, many of whom also had family up there. Getting into the fort was impossible. Marta had checked her phone repeatedly too. Either there was no signal or her husband was too caught up in the fighting to respond. Rose was getting no signal either.

No one seemed to know where to go. People were wandering off in all directions. Katya started crying. They walked upwards into the old town and stopped to sit on some steps wedged between two tall buildings. Now they weren't packed into a crowd any more, Rose realised how cold it was. It was around midnight. The family huddled together. As if on cue, it started to snow very lightly. Marta checked her phone and put it away again. Rose stood apart and rubbed her arms.

"The shelling has stopped," she said. Marta shrugged. The enormity of their situation seemed to be sinking in. "I'm going to have a look around." Rose got some of her food out of the bag, and a spare scarf and hat. She handed them to Marta.

"Thanks for your help today."

Marta nodded. Both the children had their eyes closed. Rose turned and left. Marta was probably expecting not to see her again.

Rose embarked on an exploration of what they were calling the citadel. At the top somewhere was the fort, a permanent barracks, so Marta said. This was bearing the brunt of the artillery attack which seemed to have ceased for now. She worked her way through the narrow streets, winding down to riverside level where the ground flattened out and more modern blocks lined the river. In normal times it would be a pretty little place. Everywhere she went she saw people kipping down in doorways and alleyways. A couple of times she heard glass smashing: looters, or the desperate. It was getting quieter and quieter; groups of people hurried past each other without looking. The snow kept falling. She climbed up and found a viewpoint towards the south bridge where they'd entered. There were no cars or people on it now. A line of tanks blocked the far end. The Russians hadn't tried to cross the bridge, but no one was going in or out that way.

A similar view over the north bridge revealed a convoy of tanks across the bridge, the one at the very front a burned-out wreck, neatly blocking the road. The victim of a grenade, or an incendiary device launched from some high position overlooking the river. From the fort, the Georgian militia would have excellent vantage points over both these bridges, and the island's raised position put them above the invaders right round. Clearly they had a stock of weapons. With anti-aircraft fire they could also hold off airborne attacks. They weren't calling it the citadel for no reason. It was defensible. But the Russians didn't look like they were going anywhere.

Her phone still wasn't getting any signal. She looked up at the windows of the flats above her. Some of these would be empty, their occupants having taken their chances elsewhere. She worked along the streets, trying the entrance doors. One of them gave when she pushed. She looked closer and saw that it had been forced. She glanced around and slid inside. Each floor had two flats. Both the ground floor flats had lights on, she'd noticed from outside. On the next floor up, one door was locked and the other wide open. Rose stepped up to it, heard voices coming from inside, and retreated. On the top floor, both doors were locked. She chose one at random, dug her lock-picking implements out from her toiletries bag and set to work. It took a while but eventually the latch clicked and the door swung open. Rose paused, straining to pick up any sound. Nothing. The interior chain was hanging undrawn: an indication, no more, that the place was empty. She crept in. Moving carefully in the dark, she could see lace table mats, neatly placed embroidered cushions, a clean wooden floor from which all objects had been put away or tidily placed, a large box in the corner full of plastic toys. But in the kitchen, dirty plates lay stacked in the sink, the table hadn't been wiped, pans sat on the cooker with food still in them. She checked the bedrooms: a double bed in one room was neatly made, in the other room a child's bed had rumpled blue sheets. In both rooms clothes lay on the floor: clean, folded garments from a drawer or wardrobe, not clothes someone had been wearing. She stood and imagined the last scene that happened here: a phone call or a news report, a hastily-finished meal, essential packing, waking the child from slumber. These people had heard the rumours.

She heard footsteps in the stairway. She ran back to the door of the flat, closed and locked it, and drew the chain across. A couple of young men, dark-haired, in track suits and trainers, appeared through the eye hole. The owners of the voices from the flat downstairs. One of them carried a bag. A couple of chancers after easy pickings. Heart-warming, that there always seemed to be people happy to take advantage in a crisis. They took a door each. The lad on Rose's door tried shoving it sideways with his shoulder. After a couple of goes he stepped back and landed the sole of his boot directly on the deadbolt lock. A slight crunch suggested it could give way. He booted it several more times. Rose crept to the kitchen and grabbed the sharpest knife she could find. She returned to the front door and stood, knife in hand, in the dark, watching the door judder with each solid kick.

A splintering sound and a shout. The lad turned. His friend had just got through the neighbouring door. They disappeared into the other flat. Rose waited, watching the open door opposite. Presently they emerged with more bags stuffed full, and made off. Rose waited for all sound to fade, then came out and entered the flat opposite herself, its doorway swinging open. There was plenty still to take: clothes, food, drink, ornaments, DVDs. She touched nothing and returned to the first flat. A cursory search of kitchen drawers revealed a set of keys which she verified were front door keys. She went out and locked up carefully behind her. The other door remained hanging open, a much more attractive target for any more passing looters.

She didn't know if they'd still be there, but they were, huddled tightly together, snow gathering in the folds of their coats. She touched Marta's arm to wake her.

"How would you like a bed for the night?" Rose asked.

41

He thought that would be the end, that he would just fade away in the freezing water. But something, some instinct, made him reach out and struggle. He swam, then his legs felt land and he staggered up a bank and collapsed inside a filthy great pipe. The bridge was a distant line of lights suspended in the dark. It looked harmless, a piece of jewellery decorating the horizon, but his heart thumped when he thought about being on it. No noises now: all he could hear was the chattering of his own teeth.

If he closed his eyes and relaxed, then eventually everything would stop. Boris would drift away. Boris would be no more. He pictured the scene back in the village when they heard the news: his mother, florid in her grief, his sisters quiet and stoical. His father comforting, saying that he died in action, while on manoeuvre, fighting for Russia. A hero! Knocked down by treacherous Georgian guns while leading the brave assault, although the body was never found. And Tatiana, would tears fill her large brown eyes? Would she come to his funeral dressed in black lace with a pale face and a trembling lip? He relaxed and stilled his shivering, willing himself away. But as he drifted off, some wretched force within him jerked him awake and shouted in his head, I'm so cold, I'm so cold! But he forced it down and tried again and again.

He jerked awake. It was longer that time. The riverbank was white with a dusting of snow. The sky was velvet blue, no longer black. His hands didn't exist. He could see his legs trembling. When he moved, flakes of ice fell from his uniform, tinkling like tiny coins.

He shifted forward and fell out of the pipe. His body no longer worked. He lay on the snow and rubbed his ankles and legs. He sat, then stood, shifting weight from foot to foot. He couldn't feel his feet or ankles. He walked, stumbling like a clown in oversized boots. The movement eased the stiffness through his body. He saw the bridge now, its railings visible in the dawn light. He wanted to creep away into a corner somewhere, some warm corner where his body would allow sleep to take over. A sleep from which he wouldn't wake.

Steps led up away from the riverside, between high brick walls, into a street. He weaved from side to side like a drunk. Shop doorways, tiny alleyways, bodies were huddled away. Dead? He didn't know. He kept walking. He found a doorway with enough space in front to curl up. But when he sat to lean back, the door opened. He went inside. Two closed doors, stairs up. More stairs up, then two doors, one closed, one open. He went in through the open door, and it was like entering heaven.

Soft, clean carpet. A chair. A sofa. A clock ticking on the wall. Cups and saucers in the kitchen. A bed made up with soft sheets.

He stood there in that place, and started to sob.

42

From Moscow to Nalchik, Fairchild drove. Or rather, he commandeered a car and driver from his Moscow fleet, and they took turns driving to continue through the night. A high-spec limo was more luxury than the journey required, but in some ways it formed its own passport. A sleek black car meant, to the average passer-by, someone with money, someone I don't want to argue with.

It was a thousand miles. At some point during the journey, Zack phoned with news from Peter. Rose was in Lali, the last time anyone had heard from her. This resulted in some rethinking of Fairchild's plan. Tbilisi he knew; the word summoned up squat Orthodox Christian churches, outdoor cafes sheltering under trailing vines, tumbledown back streets, a casual late-night vibe. Lali drew a blank; he'd be learning as he went.

On arrival in Nalchik he sent his driver with a generous pocketful of cash back to Moscow, and equipped himself with supplies. Anyone crossing from Russia to Georgia would face scrutiny right now. Even with a false ID Fairchild didn't rate his chances. But you could get through the mountains if you knew how. Taking a bus from the city to the end of the line, Fairchild walked south, up above a frozen stream to a farm complex, where the woman who came out to greet him nodded and sent him over to the barn. There he waited.

Passing through hostile territory was something he'd done before. He was young when he realised that to get anywhere he needed to skill up. Walter, in informal loco parentis, shipped him off to summer camps and university, but didn't check if Fairchild was actually there or not. Once

Fairchild graduated he stopped communicating with Walter entirely.

Fairchild learned how to shoot aged seventeen, spending a summer at a Vietnam veteran's isolated homestead in Colorado. He learned how to operate covertly in enemy terrain from a former SAS officer who trained him up in exchange for making himself useful in various ways. And for money. Fairchild had always had money thanks to his parents' trust fund. During his teenage and early adult years he soaked up knowledge, information and physical skills like a sponge, reading widely, accumulating languages and nurturing contacts, including names from the intelligence world that he'd stolen from Walter. How to get his hands on a false identity. How to follow without being seen. How to fight with weapons, and without. How to kill someone if need be. Fairchild had all this at his fingertips, and over time he'd used it all.

If all this came off, and he wasn't too late, and he managed to find Rose and she was still alive, would she welcome his presence? Probably not: he couldn't imagine Rose asking for help from him, unless she absolutely had to. But this wasn't just about Rose. Some deception had been worked here, and Grom was at the centre of it. Fairchild didn't yet have a clear idea of why, but Grom had brought Fairchild into this somehow, made him part of some game. Fairchild wasn't going to let himself be played by the man. Particularly when other people were involved. Particularly when one of them was Rose.

The knock came after dark. Fairchild was ready. The bearded young man shook him by the hand.

"Levan would come himself, but he's on the front line like everybody else."

"Where is the front line?" They were speaking Georgian.

"Changing by the hour. I can get you over the border, but after that…"

"After that is my business. Just point me in the direction of Lali and go home to your grandmother."

"Lali? You're not going to Tbilisi?"

"Not any more. You know anything about Lali?"

"It's surrounded. We're holding them back. But no one can get in or out. The Russians have spread beyond it now, but they're not giving up on it. They want the bridge and the barracks."

Fairchild heard the stress in the man's voice. "It doesn't sound good."

"Us alone against Russia? Fairchild, without some help on the ground, what does everyone think will happen? Georgia is a small country! We're not Russia!"

There was pleading in his voice. People mistook Fairchild for all kinds of things. A fixer, a diplomat, an ambassador even. But he didn't get caught up in affairs of state. He moved between states, following his own path. Selling his services, yes, but to pursue his own ends. He could offer little comfort to this young man. But he tried.

"You'll get help. The international community won't let this happen. Georgia's of strategic importance with its routes to the Black Sea."

"They let it happen in Ukraine."

"Crimea is full of Russians. They had sympathisers on the inside. It's different here."

"Even so. Us against Russia? Alone?" He wasn't bitter, just desperate. He clasped Fairchild's arm. "Levan told me you know people. People everywhere. People of influence. Can you help us? Will you try? You will, won't you?"

His eyes were wide, pools of hope and fear. "I'll try," said Fairchild. It was mere goodwill, feeding the hope, nothing more. "But I can't promise. Just get me into Georgia. Then look after your own."

He nodded up towards the mountains: they had a long walk ahead of them. His guide shrugged, turned, and led the way.

43

Boris sat on the sofa. Outside were distant mountains white with snow. But he was looking down at the socks on his feet. The carpet was soft and the socks so thick he could barely feel his sores. His trousers were made of cotton and the bottoms were rolled up because they were too long. He was wearing a shirt and a thick woollen sweater. He was comfortable and warm with a full stomach.

Yesterday when he found this place he locked the door and piled furniture up to stop anybody coming in. He slept for hours in a warm bed. He washed and scrubbed every inch of his body. He sat at a table and had breakfast. Pastries and jam and coffee. This place could be his home, his and Tatiana's. She would want him to clear away the breakfast things, wash and dry the plates and cups, pick up any crumbs off the carpet. She would want him to put all the crockery back where it belonged and wipe down the table with a cloth and replace the vase with the plastic flowers in the centre of the table.

So he got up from the sofa to do all those things. But then the bombing started.

A screaming howl above, like a frenzied devil. A tearing blast that wiped away all his thoughts. He threw himself to the ground. The sound travelled through him, pulled skin from his body, reached into his brain and kneaded it. The windows shattered. Pieces of glass rained down on him and all over the carpet. Outside a siren went off and he heard wailing, shouts for help. He covered his ears. He couldn't move. He lay there trying not to listen to the chaos outside. Another squeal and crash, further away. He mustn't cry, he mustn't cry. The carpet was covered in shards of glass and twisted metal pieces. He reached out and picked one up. It was hot. Shrapnel. The back of his hand was bleeding.

Oh, Tatiana, where are you? Why aren't you here with me, holding me, telling me it will be okay? I would stroke your shiny dark hair and kiss your soft white skin, feel the warmth of your body. But it wasn't warm. It was cold now, the air from outside coming through the windows. He heard crackling, angry rattling like on the bridge. He crawled over the broken glass and the hot shrapnel. At the door he stood. The cups on the breakfast table were broken. The sounds would never stop. He had to make them stop. In the kitchen was a vodka bottle. He returned with it and pulled the sofa right back away from the window. He sat again. Looking at the mountains through broken glass, he opened the bottle and took a swig. Its fiery taste filled his mouth and throat.

When he was a little boy, his mother said, he would run and hide at anything: a sudden knock at the door, the bark of the neighbour's dog. He was still a little boy even now. He thought the army would give him courage. But here he was, still running, still hiding.

He drank. The vodka made his head buzz. He swilled the bottle in his hand. He shouldn't drink it so quickly. Tatiana wouldn't like it. She would put her hand on his arm and look at him with her large brown eyes and implore him to drink less, so that they could both live long lives together. She would say that she didn't want to be alone again, that she wanted them both to grow old together, that she loved him, and her eyes would well up with tears.

Boris would do things to please her and make her happy. He would clear all this mess up. He would wash the floors with the mop that was in the cupboard in the hall. He would think about what to make them for dinner. Perhaps some meat out of a tin, made into a stew or soup. Perhaps some borscht from the cabbage that was in the larder with the other vegetables. That's what he would think about, all day. And he imagined Tatiana returning in the evening, when she would smile and kiss him on the cheek and say how lucky she was to be with someone who took such care over things. He was going to do all that. But he needed another swig from the vodka bottle first. He just needed one more swig and then he would start.

He lifted the bottle to his lips.

44

Fairchild wasn't concentrating properly, when he wandered into the village. He was stretching himself too far. It was three nights since the Russian incursion began. From occasional text exchanges, he knew the Lali siege was continuing, with constant bombardment and entrenched positions on both sides. The Russians wanted the river crossing; the Georgians weren't giving up. No word from Rose. So Fairchild was rushing, walking for hours when he should be sleeping, risking exposed short cuts when he should be staying unseen. He had no plan for when he got there. Just get there, was all that was in his mind, driving him onwards.

He'd used up his supplies and needed to bargain for some more, or steal some. So when he came over the brow of a hill and saw a rough track leading to run-down farm buildings; when he surveyed the whole village from the hill and saw nothing unusual; when he wandered out into the road after an hour of watching, too impatient to wait until after dark, that was when it went wrong.

The man in the distance was leaning against a wall smoking a cigarette. His uniform was Russian army. Fairchild turned and ran, but he'd been seen. Before the soldier started to shout Fairchild was half way back up the grassy hillock to the trees beyond. But it was too late. More soldiers surged up in front and behind, cutting him off. They screamed and pointed guns at him. They led him back to the village and forced him face down in the middle of the road.

"Who are you?" asked a man who carried himself with authority. A captain, maybe. "What's your business here?"

The men emptied out his pockets then tipped his backpack out on the roadside and went through the contents.

"Where's your ID?" barked the captain.

"I don't have any." Fairchild answered quietly in Russian, turning his face to the side to free his mouth from the grit of the road. The captain bent over him.

"What's your nationality?"

Nationality, why was it always about that? Why did it matter so much where you were born, where your parents were born, things that nobody could help? And yet it determined whether someone would kill you or let you live.

The captain kicked him in the thigh. "I asked you a question!"

"I'm Estonian. My name is Ivan."

"What are you doing here?"

"Looking for a friend."

"A friend?" Laughter all round. There were half a dozen of them. "Don't you know there's a war going on?"

Fairchild tried to look up and make eye contact, but the captain was standing upright now, arms folded.

"I don't care about the war. I'm not Russian or Georgian and neither is my friend. We're just caught up in it. We just want to get out of the place."

"And where is your friend?"

"Lali."

"Lali?" More laughter. "You're just going to walk into Lali, are you? In front of the tanks and past all the snipers? 'Excuse me, I'm looking for my friend'?" He kicked him twice in the side. "You are a spy! Who are you working for, eh?"

Fairchild tensed for the next kick. But one of the soldiers cried out. He held up a plastic wallet: Fairchild's stash of US dollars.

"American? You're American! You're spying for the USA!" The captain spat. The globule landed on Fairchild's cheek and dribbled down his neck.

"I'm not spying for anyone." He kept his voice low. He glanced at the formation around him. Even from lying down, he'd have a chance against one or two. But not this many. And they were armed. The captain was looking down at him with a new curiosity.

"How did you get here?"

"From the north. Over the mountains. I crossed the border."

"The border's closed. You can't cross there."

"Well, I did," said Fairchild. "I can show you where, on a map. If you let me go. You can have the dollars, too."

The captain raised his eyes skywards, as if thinking about it. He drew a gun and pointed it at Fairchild's head. "Or I could kill you! And take the dollars too!" He grinned. His hand tensed on the trigger.

"Wait!" said Fairchild. "Okay, you were right. I am a spy. I'm spying for the Americans. They don't like what you're doing. They have plans. I'll tell you about their plans. I'll tell you everything they know. But not to you. To a military intelligence officer. A big guy. Not you."

A smile spread. The gun stayed pointing at him. "You think I'm stupid?"

"And what will they think when they find out you could have got all this intelligence but shot me dead before I could speak? They'll think you're the stupid one."

The smile disappeared. Fairchild had a few seconds, no more, to persuade him.

"You've got nothing to lose. All you have to do is keep me here. Lock me up and summon your superiors. If they think I'm a fraud they can shoot me anyway. But I'm telling the truth. The information I have could win Russia the war. You could be a hero."

The men were standing, listening. All eyes were on the captain. Time passed.

"You," he said finally, "are a lying dog."

He squeezed the trigger.

45

They were still in the flat days later. A cellar would have been safer, but with the influx of people into the citadel, cellars were crammed solid. Once, they took sleeping gear and talked themselves into one. Inside was gloomy and airless, people staring at them from rows of mats that filled every inch of the floor. There was no space for the children to pitch down together with Marta. Katya started screaming and wouldn't stop until they were out of there. So they took their chances in the flat.

The barrage was constant. One morning a mortar hit the block opposite and smashed all their windows in a deafening, splintering crash. Anyone standing near them would have been blasted with shrapnel. After that they spent all their time in the kitchen, as far from the windows as possible. They slept there too, Marta, Ilya and Katya curled up together on mattresses. Rose made a nest out of sofa cushions, but she often went out at night. It was the best time for scavenging.

No windows, no gas, no electricity: it was cold even after the snow had melted. Rose slunk through the streets in the dark and came back with planks and boards, nails and fixings to hammer the boards across the window frames and cover with blankets and curtains. Marta's husband came by several times; pale and quiet, his manner didn't bode well for the state of events up at the fort. They would all sit together, the family unit, in a shared embrace, saying very little, until he had to go again. Rose would make herself scarce as best she could. One time he brought a stove and a gas canister. The stove became the central point, the only source of heat for themselves, for cooking, and for heating water to wash.

When the taps stopped working, a medical centre became a base for distributing boiled river water. Ilya and Marta would take turns, laden with buckets and plastic bottles. By day the snipers ruled the streets; they could shoot you in the eye, the rumours said, from a mile away. Don't stand still, hug walls and buildings. If you have to cross an exposed area, run. If you can see the river, they can see you.

The area around the medical centre became an informal market for swaps. Marta was by default in charge of all food arrangements and had raided the cupboards and taken luxury biscuits, tinned artichoke hearts and stuffed vine leaves, coming back with larger quantities of dried beans and flour and powdered milk. No electricity, no refrigeration, no freezers. In the cold, some food had kept for a while, but then the snow melted and the weather grew warmer, in an unwelcome twist of climatic timing. But this was where Rose could help.

She went out like a hunter-gatherer after nightfall, and came back with supplies from wherever she could, going further and further afield. The flat opposite had been barricaded shut right from that very first night, but she found other places: shops, bars, restaurants, hotels, other empty homes. Fresh food to start with, canned and dried as the days went by. Her advantage: she could climb further, crack a secure lock, help herself to the best before anyone else showed up. Meat and fish, vegetables, sweet things sometimes, chocolate for the children. Whatever they didn't want, Marta could swap for something else. Rose would come back in the dark laden with tins and jars, and lie down silently while the family still slumbered. It was only fair; she needed them to find out what was going on, and this was her contribution. They ate well, compared with some out there relying on the dwindling army handouts. This was hell, for sure, but her little unit wasn't starving at least.

Katya hated it when Marta went out, so Ilya stepped in. He became the scout, bringing news from the barracks and from friends he'd found. Some of them were acting as informal watchers, finding observation points along the riverside where they could see Russian positions, and reporting back to the fort. The boy was developing a quiet confidence; Marta watched him come and go with an expression of both pride and terror. Marta and Ilya going out at the same time was a no-no; Katya screamed herself hoarse the first time they tried it. Rose had an English-Russian language triangle going with Marta and Ilya, but Katya only spoke Georgian and still went to hide behind one of the others when Rose tried to say anything to her.

The sound was constant: an aerial whistling, a moment of silent dread, a booming thud. Any one of those could take them all out. They exchanged looks whenever they heard it: someone else's tragedy this time, not ours. In the silence following the shells that fell close, the ones that rocked the building and echoed in their heads for hours afterwards, once or twice Rose thought she heard a man sobbing.

Every day brought death. Ilya reported the worst of it: an entire house flattened, killing everyone inside; people shot in the street in twos and threes; a mother felled by a single piece of shrapnel to the heart; a four-year-old caught in a blast staring out of a window. Sometimes a sharp crackle of machine gun fire and a scream carried on the air told an unknown story. The medical centre was the closest they had to a field hospital, that and whatever was at the barracks. Rose hadn't yet discovered where they were taking the bodies.

No one had mobile signal. For news, there were radios, and rumours from the barracks. Tbilisi hadn't fallen, although the bulk of the Russian army was encamped on its outskirts. Big words from foreign leaders. Ilya set great store by the threats of the NATO powers, the Americans, the Germans, the British. The EU, Georgia's neighbour across the Black Sea, to whom they looked. Rose, privately, had her doubts.

For messages out, a few of the land lines worked, Ilya said, if you knew who to ask. The barracks had a satellite phone. Rose asked Ilya to request a message to the Embassy in Tbilisi. They should at least know she was still alive. She remembered Peter saying that he'd do what he could, but didn't expect much. At a time like this, a sole stranded officer wasn't going to be top priority. She was expected to look out for herself.

During her nightly prowls she used a number of viewpoints to observe the Russians herself, wondering if she could slip past them. Getting out of the town was possible. She was convinced from what Marta brought back from the market that food was getting in. Who during peacetime would have a crate load of powdered milk lying about? And they weren't army rations. So getting a person out could be done. But what about the miles of occupied territory beyond the town? For something like this, officers like her would normally have military support. Should she go it alone and risk being caught, or was it better to stay here, behind at least some layer of defence? This was constantly on her mind. Meanwhile she could make herself useful getting supplies for the family. She could do that much at least.

One night she returned lugging huge catering cans of tomato paste and olives. A man in uniform was there. Marta's husband, Rose assumed, until he turned and she saw that it wasn't. Marta's face was blotchy. Katya lay head down on her lap, silently shaking. Ilya was pale, thin-lipped, staring at nothing.

Rose put down her gear. "Your husband?" she asked softly. Marta's look of pain confirmed the worst.

Ilya jumped up. "Ilya!" said his mother. "Please, stay!"

But he left, slamming the door. The soldier stayed and lit a cigarette. Marta stroked Katya's hair while tears rolled down her face. Rose expressed her sympathies as best she could and went to sit in the bedroom. She'd never felt more alone.

46

Yuri was the best of the bunch. Yuri was the only one who told Fairchild his name. It was Yuri who stepped out and stopped the captain from firing that day. What if he's right, Yuri had muttered to his superior. How does a guy just show up like this? On his own? He's not just some ordinary bloke, is he? A couple of others grunted agreement. The captain gave up in bad faith, swore at his men, stowed his gun and stomped off. Since then, Fairchild had been locked in a windowless inner room that smelled of shit. Not animal shit: human shit. Stuck in a shithouse for the best part of a week. Wasted, wasted time! And all because of his own utter stupidity.

But they brought him rations and water, and Yuri stayed to chat. He would roll his eyes and his droopy jowls would work while he wondered at why the big guys from the front were taking so long: they're tied up down there, lots going on! This whole thing's more difficult than they thought. And we're stuck here with only one vehicle and the stores getting thin. Maintain territory gains, they say! That's why we're in these forsaken villages. There's no one here! All the villagers ran away before we got here. Guarding a bale of hay and some chickens. What's it all for, anyway? Why are we even here? We've got chickens back in Russia, don't we? I mean we're all just people, all the same really, wanting to make a living, look after our own. I'd be more use back in Omsk with my wife and son, only two years old but so smart already. Still, we're soldiers. We do as we're told.

And he'd talk about the captain and his instability. He's getting impatient now, Ivan. You be careful with him, Ivan. As if Fairchild had some means of avoiding him. Then the captain came to see him. There was only space for one other person in this tiny shithole of a room. So the others waited outside and the captain squatted in a false show of camaraderie on the dirt floor. Fairchild sat, back against the wall, saying nothing.

"You see my problem," the rat-faced officer was saying. "They won't send anybody. Too busy. They don't believe us, maybe. They can't spare anyone. So they're saying to me, get him to talk to you. He can tell you what he knows, can't he? Maybe if I could give them something. A little snippet, something to show you are who you say you are?"

Fairchild looked at him blandly.

The captain raised his hands in helplessness. "I mean, look at it from their point of view. We only have your word for it, that you're this *super-spy* with all of this *top-secret* intelligence. They could be thinking, maybe he only said all of that to avoid getting shot. Maybe it's all a big story. He's just stringing us along, and here we are having to keep guard and share our rations, and in fact he's just a worthless traitor playing us all along."

Fairchild maintained his gaze.

"Or maybe," said the captain, "they're thinking it's even worse, that this renegade is spying on us! Getting all friendly with the more gullible of our soldiers and pumping them for information, so you can feed it back to the Americans, or whoever it is he works for. Why are you putting up with that? That's maybe what they're thinking, the big chiefs. Those idiot troops pandering to a guy who has no evidence, none, that's he's anything special, and just sits there staring all day!"

The raised voice had no effect. The captain clicked his teeth and got out his gun. He played with it thoughtfully, checking the cartridge, rubbing his finger along the barrel.

"You know, last time," he said, "I was going to shoot you in the head. But there are worse places. Yes!" He held the gun up, examining the trigger. "There are worse places."

His eyes widened as the gun skittered across the floor. Fairchild's boot knocked the captain's chin back, and the back of his head hit the wall. Fairchild shoved him down onto his front, bent both his arms up behind his back and pushed the man's head into the foul-smelling dirt. He didn't give the guy a chance to cry out. Maybe he was trying to say something but his mouth was full of grit and muck. Fairchild felt an overwhelming impulse to make him convulse with pain, snap off his fingers one by one. He was white-hot, thinking of lying on the tarmac, his eyes closing as the captain's finger squeezed on the trigger, thinking no, no, not now, not this time, not now there's somewhere I need to be, something I have to put right.

The captain wheezed, trying to draw breath as Fairchild's knee jammed down on his back. But there was no time for all this. Fairchild reached forward, grabbed the gun and shot the captain in the back of the head.

He got up and opened the door of the inner room. Everyone outside would have heard the shot. He passed into the doorway of the next room, hovering out of sight of the windows. The door of the building flew open and a soldier made straight for the inner room. Fairchild shot him in the side of the head as he went past. Right behind him was Yuri. Yuri, it had to be Yuri. Their eyes met for a moment. Yuri lifted his gun, but he was slow, the big lout. Fairchild shot him in the shoulder. He fell, groaning and squirming. No one else followed. The other three would have had second thoughts and retreated, finding cover and waiting for him to come out.

Fairchild raided the pockets of the dead men, taking money, ID, cigarettes, another weapon. He crossed the front room past the window, getting a fleeting glimpse as he went by, a reminder of the layout. There were only a certain number of places someone could go. He braced himself, and ran.

The shots didn't start until it was too late. Three or four seconds and he was in the barn opposite. By then he had a good idea of where two of them were, and an impression of their marksmanship skills. The third, as it turned out, was in the barn. He heard the guy move, heavily, and was ready to fire by the time he stepped out. He shot him three times in the chest. The other two, on the other side of the street, had boxed themselves in a shed with only one door. He ran straight for it, firing without stopping. One of them was already down by the time he got there. The other cowered in a corner, breathing fast. Fairchild finished them both.

The store room. He needed food, water, weaponry. A uniform would help. He found all of this in the most sturdily-built house in the village where the truck was parked. Fairchild considered the truck but dismissed it. He could get further undetected on foot, if he took more care this time. Some charts of the area confirmed what he knew already of his current position. He had a way to go. Back in the trees he could make some progress before nightfall. He stepped out of the store.

"Ivan." Yuri's voice trembled but the gun in his hand was steady. One arm hung, the shoulder bloody. "I can't let you go, Ivan."

He fired, but Fairchild had already moved, darting in front of the truck. He got out his gun and called out.

"You're going to shoot me, Yuri? After you fed me all week?"

"You should have taken my gun, Ivan." He was in pain, weakening.

"I should have killed you. But I didn't. Because this is all nonsense. This whole thing, right? What are we even doing here? I'm not a spy, Yuri. I don't care about this war. But I need to go now. I need to look after my own."

He waited, tensed, then rose up on the other side of the van, closer to Yuri, gun in hand but pointed upwards.

"Just let me go, Yuri," he said softly.

Yuri swung and fired. Fairchild moved. The bullet whizzed past his ear.

"I can't do that, Ivan!" Yuri was almost crying. "I'm a soldier! We do as we're told! I tell you, I —"

Fairchild stood and shot him in the head. He walked up to the fallen body, emptied the bullets out of the dead man's gun and pocketed them.

He glanced at Yuri's open eyes, and walked off towards the trees.

47

Rose ran from doorway to doorway. It was starting to get dark but plenty of light remained for the distant snipers. Her darting movements generated no *ack-ack* of gunfire, but it could happen any time. She followed the road as it wound down to riverbank level. She needed to be quick. This was the first of three or four places Ilya could be, these lookout points as he called them. A long concrete block rose up as the road bottomed out, amorphous apartments facing the river. The roof was ripped off, walls missing, floors and staircases exposed. Around bent metal window frames the front of the building sat at an angle. A giant lump of concrete dangled from metal pins. This was the front line, immediately facing the Russian barrage. That Ilya was hanging out in a place like this was horrifying. He'd barely been at the flat since the solider came with his news.

Rose walked along its length. The basement windows below the level of the road were barred, all except one. She crouched next to it.

"Ilya?" Her voice echoed. She heard shuffling, shapes moving. She sat, swung her legs round and let herself in feet first. The gap was only just big enough for her. She lowered herself to the floor of the room.

Eyes were looking at her from all directions. It was a long, low room with little natural light. As well as Ilya, four or five other children were sitting or lying around. Next to the walls were old cushions, mats, sleeping bags and blankets. On the floor were magazines, bottles of water and sweet wrappers.

"Who are these kids, Ilya? This isn't a safe place for you to be. This building's dangerous."

Ilya was standing in the middle of the room. "Everywhere is dangerous."

"You're right on the front line! They'll be watching from over there day and night. They'll shoot anything that moves."

"They can't shoot us in here." Ilya pointed to the river-facing wall. No windows, just high narrow slits for ventilation. This basement must have been a storage area only, not living space. "They can't shoot through those. They're not that – crack-shot." Ilya's English was heavily influenced by comics and TV action drama. He had a comic book in his hand. He was right, though; the children wouldn't even be visible. Hell of a view from those slits. Rose could see how observations from here might be valuable up at the fort.

Some of the children turned back to each other, talking, reading, whatever they were doing before.

"They're sleeping here?" she asked Ilya.

Ilya pointed. "Those two, their dad was killed by a bomb and their mother was shot in the street. The three there were in a cellar, with strangers, but they ran away. It was…" – his face went dark – "not very nice. It's better here. Safer."

Rose was about to ask what everyone was eating when she caught sight of a bag of sweets that she herself had lifted the night before. She'd been wondering where it had gone. Ilya was looking out for these people.

"Why are you here?" he asked.

"Looking for you. Seeing where you're spending so much time."

"What does it matter to you?" He was hostile, hurting. And he was right. Rose had no calls on this young man. At least, not until this morning. Now, maybe, she did.

"It's time to come back, Ilya." He scowled, sat on the cushions and picked up a comic.

Rose sat on the floor next to him. The children kept glancing at her. They ranged in age from as young as Katya to older than Ilya. Ilya's eyes were on the page in front of him, but he wasn't reading.

This was a lot to throw at a twelve-year-old, but what choice did she have? "Your mother went for water this morning. She hasn't come back."

Now Ilya looked at her. Rose had tried to persuade Marta not to go out. She was distracted, unfocused. But she'd insisted. She just seemed to want to walk, some space to herself maybe.

Ilya's eyes were wide. He was working it through in his head. "Where's Katya?"

"I left her on her own in the flat to come and find you. She needs you, Ilya."

Ilya blinked and swallowed. He was too young, too young to grow up like this. He put the comic book on the floor and got to his feet.

"So let's go," he said.

She let him lead them back; he knew the best route by now. She didn't tell Ilya that she'd left Katya alone once already that day. She'd gone out earlier to retrace Marta's steps, and found no sign of her except their water bucket, punctured and twisted, lying by the side of the road. Where were they taking the bodies?

Nearing the flat, to avoid a sniper spot they cut through a narrow alley made up of steps, high walls on either side. It was almost dark now. Footsteps and an animal roar made them jump. A man lunged at them, in his hand a shard of glass, half a jagged bottle. He'd come up behind them, cutting them off. His clothes were grimy, like everyone's; it was the wildness in his eyes and quickness of his movements that sent Rose's heart to her throat.

He swept the shard in front of them. They were backed up against a wall. He smelled of alcohol and the stale air of the cellars. He uttered something.

"What's he saying?" Rose asked.

Ilya's voice was steady. "He says, give me what you've got."

"We don't have anything."

Ilya answered the man. He growled back.

"Does he want money?" Rose asked.

"Food, clothes, fuel. Anything."

The man stared at them both. He grunted and brought the sharp edge right under Rose's chin. He seized her wrist, a strong grip, a grip of desperation. She knocked the shard aside and twisted his hand to grab his arm and twist. He cried out. She kneed him in the stomach. He yelped, clutching himself, and staggered. The bottle dropped with a crack. She pushed him to the ground and kicked. He rolled down the steps, coming to a halt face down, unmoving.

Rose bent over him. Something wasn't right. She pulled his shoulder back and turned him over. His coat fell open. His shirt was a mess of dried brown blood and yellow pus. It smelled rotten.

"Shit." She could see fresh blood soaking into the shirt. Ilya stepped up beside her, his twelve-year-old eyes watching this.

"What should we do?" he asked.

"He needs treatment. If it isn't too late. But how do we get him there?"

The man was stirring. He started mumbling. His eyelids flickered. He gave a low moan. His eyes opened wide and he looked straight at Rose.

"Waaargh!" An aggressive growl. They backed off. He was struggling to his feet now. He bent and picked up the broken bottle, grabbing the sharp edges in his palm. Blood oozed from his hand.

"Waaargh!" His eyes were huge, unfocused. He charged towards them holding the bloodied shard out like a rapier. They turned and ran.

They pelted up the steps and along the street at the top, and stopped at the next doorway. They looked back. No sign. He hadn't even made it to the top of the steps.

"Not a well man." Rose's statement was obvious; less obvious was whether his problem was mental or physical. Either way, they couldn't help. They carried on in the usual stop-start way. Ilya looked at her from time to time, with something like curiosity or even respect.

"Where did you learn that?" he asked.

"Self-defence classes."

"Really?" He didn't sound convinced.

"It's nothing to be proud of. The guy's as desperate as everyone else."

"Can you show me that?"

She hesitated. The way things were going, it wasn't a bad idea. On her nightly scavenges she'd had to fight once or twice to keep her findings. Too many people, not enough food. Too many close encounters with death, too much of this callous everyday suffering that could turn anyone's mind inside out.

"Do any other adults know about that place?" she asked.

"Only the soldiers."

They seemed vulnerable in that wreck of a room, blocking it all out with comics and sweets and each other's company. She thought about it, silently following Ilya darting through the streets.

Katya was asleep by the stove when they got back. Ilya squeezed quietly next to her, snuggling down, appeasing her somehow as she half-woke, persuading her back to sleep again. The morning would bring terrible scenes. Rose sat sleepless on her cushions and waited for Marta to return, while knowing already that she wouldn't.

48

Nothing much was happening. Night-time fireworks, as usual. Stubborn, these Georgians. Same old story for weeks now. So it was no surprise that the two Russian conscripts on night watch lying on the sloping riverbank were taken by surprise by the man's appearance. He just seemed to materialise, him and his gun and his neat efficient move which managed to disarm the two of them. The confusing thing was, how did he get this far? Over the road and through the blockade and through the whole encampment?

GRU, the man said. Special Ops. That would explain it, then! Those guys could do anything. It looked like a standard issue uniform, though. What do you expect, he said. We have to blend in, don't we? And how did he know about the boat? What boat, one of them asked, getting a slap for it. Well, on an army salary can you really blame people for doing a bit of business? Everyone was at it, anyway. Take me to it, he said, and I won't report it to my superiors. It seemed fair enough. It would help the war, he said, this secret mission he was on. So this achingly boring siege would be over sooner. Just don't tell anyone. It's top secret. He even gave them cigarettes.

Shortly afterwards, in a lull in the barrage, Fairchild drifted downriver on the tiny craft, lying down, an occasional sweep of his hand nudging himself shorewards. He'd seen which stretches of the bank were undefended by Georgians. They'd largely fallen back to the fort, but were ready to come out again to repel an offensive. Still stalemate, for a while anyway. So he slipped between them, these warring forces, unseen by anyone who was going to say anything.

In shallows he stepped out, his feet sinking into mud. He pulled the boat up into swamp and reeds and sank it out of sight. A flash above and an echoing report accompanied his arrival. Fairchild slipped along the beach and up into the streets of the citadel.

In no way could he have prepared himself for what would happen there.

49

Boris was in the bathroom, levering tiles off the wall with a penknife. Hundreds of tiny tiles, maybe a thousand. One by one he dug underneath and pulled them away. He tried to stop thinking about food, or vodka, or Tatiana. It kept him moving, helped with the cold. Oh, it was so cold now! Even wrapped up with blankets in the tiny room, his fingers and toes were like ice.

He didn't want them seeing him. What are you doing here? they'd ask. You shouldn't be here. You should be dead. You should be on the other side. You should be in Russia. And he knew that, he knew. But somehow he was still there. He thought he was dead when it happened, the roaring that came bursting through, light and wind and smoke and dust! He was asleep in the bed, then he was on the floor. When he rolled over he saw, but couldn't believe. The street outside, the building opposite, they were right there! The whole room, opened up for people to see him. He didn't want that. So he moved into the bathroom. He was invisible there.

He only came out to eat. To sit and eat every evening with Tatiana. We must be careful, he said, as he served up some tiny portion. We're running so low, so low. I'm sorry, my love. Could you not bring something back for us? Maybe one or two places have something to sell? Just a few juicy red tomatoes, a couple of pale cucumbers? I would make us such a refreshing salad, so cold and crisp. Or how about cheese, one of those rounds of strong salty pale cheese that we used to have? What a feast it would be!

But then he remembered that her chair was empty. He sighed and cleared up the plates which served nothing but the minutest tin of meat, one less from the dwindling supply.

Then he went back to the bathroom and shivered and yearned for her warm body.

You should go out, Tatiana seemed to be saying. Call yourself a soldier? Call yourself a man? Just go, down the stairs, into the street. No one will turn their heads even. But the thought of it made him sweat, and churned up his stomach and took his breath from out of his lungs. They were okay inside. They could live. They had what they needed, for now.

No vodka either. His hands started to shake by the middle of the morning. He could feel the cold rim of the bottle at his mouth, smell the fumes, taste the liquor. He clutched at himself and doubled over, eyes clenched shut, and stayed like that, sometimes for hours maybe.

Tatiana made him cry. Everything made him cry. He had never loved anyone except Tatiana. When he first caught sight of her in the schoolyard with her hair tied into a long plait and her broad smile, he wanted to stare at her all day. He watched her as they grew up, and as she turned into a beautiful woman he knew that he wanted to marry her and be with her forever. He felt a sob of happiness rise up inside him and his neck and face started to glow. He always let his emotions show. His stupid pale face that flushed at the smallest thing, how they teased him in the battalion! But now it didn't matter. He could sit here and cry all day if he wanted, until they arrived. But Tatiana wouldn't like that.

He had an idea. He went to the living room, to the bureau where he knew there was paper and pens. He opened the desk, feeling a kind of pride, wishing that someday he could have a desk like this. He was going to write Tatiana a letter. He was going to tell her exactly how he felt about her. He would tell her how much he thought of her during the worst ordeals of the training, and how it was that he was still alive, how she made his life complete. Maybe she would never read this letter. But perhaps she would, and it would make him happy while he was writing it. He could lose himself in the world he would create. There was so little hope now, that a few hours of happiness may be all that any of them could expect.

He took the pen and paper back to the bathroom. He wrapped the blankets around himself. Something was happening outside. He had to block it out. In the street a rumbling sound started quietly and grew, then changed into giant crashing and people screaming. He pulled the blankets tighter. His hands were shaking.

Think of home, Boris. Think of warm summer nights, and kompot, and her. Remember every detail, and where there's nothing to remember, imagine.

He started to write.

50

It wasn't an explosion that woke Rose. It came from the street. A series of booming crashes, people shouting out, a woman's scream. It was morning; she'd been out most of the night and didn't even try and sleep until the early hours. The noise penetrated her dream. When she jerked awake, it still echoed. Dust was rising through the windows, despite all the coverings. Ilya and Katya weren't by the stove; she checked the flat and they weren't there. Shouts were still coming from the street. She went down and realised why.

Half the building opposite was gone. In its place lay a heap of smoking ruins. Its entire front was torn away, leaving exposed rooms and staircases. A few were trying to climb over the unstable rubble. Most stood and watched.

On those scenes on TV, there'd be a rescue team, thought Rose. Flashing lights, fire trucks, ambulances, rescuers with gear swarming all over this mess, a round-the-clock exercise that would go on for days. Here there was no one to call, no sirens approaching, no equipment, no paramedics, no TV cameras. Tired, half-starving people, staring at a pile of bricks and concrete, wondering how soon they'd be next. Buildings were in a state of semi-collapse all over the island. Would there be anything left of the place by the end of all this? A stuttering of weapon fire somewhere close by hurried the footsteps of those who were already turning away in despair.

The flat next door to theirs had a gaping hole where the bedroom used to be. Was anyone in there? The door to the flat was still barricaded shut from the inside; Rose had discreetly tried it one night. They should all go into a cellar, but Ilya was adamant they were still too crowded. If that were true, or whether he was saying that to avoid putting Katya through the trauma, or because of what happened to those other children, she didn't know. She had no authority with them, and when Ilya announced yesterday he was taking Katya with him to the lookout point, she only requested they come back before nightfall, and tried not to appear as anxious as she felt. Same with her state of relief when they did indeed return by nightfall. Today Ilya hadn't even woken her up to tell her they were going. In Marta's absence, Katya's clinginess had transferred to her older brother. They spoke to each other in low voices. She had no idea what they were saying.

Back in the flat Rose went through the supplies she'd brought back that morning. Quite a lot of it was missing. Knowing where it was going, she didn't begrudge it. She sat and ate some food herself. Marta had been good at making things out of Rose's unappetising offerings, soft flat breads and sweet pastries from the flour and powdered egg and milk. Rose tried to fill up on crispbreads and tea made on the stove.

She was putting more time into her nightly scavenging, bringing back as much as she possibly could. She'd made several forays during the night, returning from each to dump her stash at the flat. The easy-to-access supplies were now gone except for mould-encrusted bread and foul-smelling freezers. Now she was basically a burglar, a night-time food thief, cruising the town for balconies that could be scaled and windows that could be prised open. All the while every sense was on alert for the tell-tale whistling above, not that there was time to get away. You just had to take your chances.

And these places weren't always empty, either. Rose was quiet and discreet; sometimes she entered and exited without even seeing anybody else. At times she dropped herself into a room to find it full of sleeping bodies. Whatever happened then, she usually managed to persuade people it was better for them to let her take what she wanted and leave. Occasionally she'd find herself up against enough brawn or determination to beat a hasty retreat. It was often a battle of wills more than an out-and-out fight. She was no different now from the guy who'd tried to mug them in the alleyway – just better at it, and more focused.

The siege had lasted a couple of weeks now, she didn't know exactly how long. Her mobile phone had run out of battery long ago, and a lot of the radio receivers had too. News came in the form of rumours from the barracks. Rose did ask Ilya to check for any messages for her. No word so far. But who knew if the messages were getting through?

Whoever had been sweeping bodies off the streets was now too overwhelmed to keep up. If they weren't moved, the dogs would help themselves, ripping into a stomach or an abdomen. More and more dogs were roaming free, some thin and hungry, others bold, well-fed, glimpses of sticky gore on their jowls. Those were the ones she avoided. If Rose happened upon a corpse lying in the street, if she could she would drag it and leave it out of sight, behind a wall or inside a culvert. Each time, she looked at the face, wondering if it might be Marta. But Marta was probably already similarly stowed, rotting away somewhere unknown. At the barracks they were trying to keep a list of names, but Marta's name hadn't appeared. Ilya checked every day.

The situation seemed hopeless; she had no idea how many soldiers were in the barracks – fewer, probably, than everyone was assuming – but they were using up ammunition against the Russian positions which wasn't being replenished. The Russians, on the other hand, had supply lines in place. The rumours from Tbilisi were of a stalemate, but here they seemed to be going in a particular direction. It was impossible for anyone to get out, she'd convinced herself, ignoring the small voice inside her which kept asking her whether she'd even tried. But how could she go now, and leave Ilya and Katya to starve?

She lay down and failed to sleep, tried to work out how long the children had been gone, thought about the mugger from yesterday, his shard of glass pointing under her chin, her back against the wall, Ilya by her side. Ilya was brave, but not equipped for that. How was she expected to sit here and wait to see if they came back? She couldn't. She got up and left.

It was warm and sunny, she noticed, navigating cratered streets below forlorn frameless windows. In other years Lali might be basking, celebrating the arrival of spring, but this year it merely tempered the night-time chill and rotted the bodies more quickly. Just as she neared the sloping road down to the lookout point she spotted Ilya and Katya some way beyond, walking hand in hand in the opposite direction. Where on earth were they going? She hurried after them and called out. They stopped and turned. She carried on and they started coming towards her.

When she recalled it afterwards, she could picture all the details: the long street between them striped light and dark where the sun shone through the gaps; Ilya tugging Katya along, his white T-shirt a dirty grey; Katya trotting trustingly next to her brother, her free hand looping an untied belt on her dress around her fingers. It lifted her spirits that they turned to come to her, that she mattered to them after all in some small way. But that moment was brief.

A low-pitched growling off to the side made her turn. A dog was coming towards them down a side street directly between them. Its generous haunches rippled. Its eyes held Rose in a stare, its lips were pulled back to show thick pointed yellow teeth, and drool gathered in folds of skin along its jaw, dripping as it padded closer. The dog raised its nose in her direction, as if the creature were hungry for her in particular, eyeing up her body parts. Patches of its face were matted and brown. Transfixed by this horror, Rose took too long to realise that the children were also standing and staring, their two little hand-holding shadows cast before them in the road. They were in the sun; Rose was in the shade. They were standing stock still where the sun shone through a gap, a gap which also made them visible from the river. In slow-motion her brain called on her lungs and mouth to form a sound and commanded her to leap towards them, arms flaying. She'd started turning already, her mouth opening to form a word. Right in that second came a thunderclap, and the ground erupted into fountains of dust.

She found movement, she found words. "Run! Run!" Was she waving them away or towards her? It didn't matter – they just had to move! Four eyes looked up at her. Now she was in the light as well. What would a Russian soldier see? A woman and two children? Would he care that they were children? Would he pull the trigger anyway, or would something inside make him pause?

Before she reached them the thunderclap came again. Ilya turned and twisted to the ground. Katya knelt, pulled down by his hand. Rose was there, between them and the sniper. Ilya was missing half his face, red lumps and spatter over his neck and T-shirt. Katya stared, expressionless. Rose circled Ilya and grabbed Katya under the armpits but she wouldn't let go of her brother. Rose was shouting at her, she didn't know what. She took the girl by the waist in one arm and with the other hand prised her fingers from around her dead brother's hand. She ducked and ran for the shadow, as another salvo erupted around them.

She put Katya down and fell to her knees. She gasped desperately for air. Katya trotted forward and stood staring at the body. Specks of blood dotted her face. Rose reached out to stop her stepping out again into shot. She recoiled, shaking Rose off as if she were a swarm of flies. She carried on staring at Ilya, as if expecting him to stir and wake up. Rose sat back. She realised that the reason she couldn't breathe was that she was sobbing. She couldn't stop. Katya's wide blue eyes were on her now and she still couldn't stop, had nothing she could say, no word or expression, that would make sense of what just happened.

She didn't know how long they were both there like that. Eventually she stood and held out her hand to Katya. What else could they do but go home? But Katya just looked at her, turned, and ran straight past her.

51

It was a challenge Rose hadn't not faced before, tracking a six-year-old. First of all Katya just ran, randomly it seemed, criss-crossing the damaged remains of the town, never looking around. Rose kept her distance. Had she ever done a more important surveillance op than this? She mustn't lose sight of her for a moment, and Katya couldn't see her, or all was undone.

Her heart rose in her throat whenever Katya approached an exposed area. But with her height and erratic speed she would have been a hard target, and there was no explosion of shots. Only once did she stop, distracted by some early blossom, delicate white flowers on a thin tree in the grounds of a church. Then she worked her way back to the street where Rose had seen them. Ilya's body was still lying there. Katya came to a rigid halt some distance away, staring at it. She stood for a very long time. Then she turned back. Rose knew where she was going now. She kept her in sight all the way, watching her crawl fully inside the window of the lookout point. She could understand, she thought. This was a place Ilya liked, that he took her to. There would be something of him in there. Rose curled up in a doorway and waited.

It was a few hours before Katya emerged again, getting late but not yet nightfall. Now she was walking, not running. Rose gave her some space, but came a little closer when she realised where Katya was headed. She knew the way, this girl, knew where she was going. At the entrance door to their block she was almost directly behind. Katya went up the stairs to the flat door and looked around with an expectant expression, as if she'd known all the time that Rose was there and was summoning her forward now to let her in. Inside, Katya went and lay down by the stove. She showed no signs of wanting to eat, but Rose made food anyway: fish ladled out of a tin and some crispbreads. She put it on the table and lay on her sofa cushions.

She only realised she'd fallen asleep when she felt Katya's weight against her. The girl was snuggling in next to her. The last, the very last person in her life, a stranger who didn't speak her language, who tried to protect them and failed, Rose was all she had left now.

Later, when Katya was sleeping soundly, Rose slipped out from under her and crept out of the flat, locking it behind her and uttering a silent prayer for calm for the next couple of hours. Another child needed her now.

Ilya's body was still lying where he fell. She picked him up and carried him to a corner she'd passed which was more rubble than standing buildings. Climbing awkwardly over the ruins she found a quiet spot, laid Ilya out and piled stones and bricks until he was completely covered, a little barrow, an unmarked grave.

No dog was going to feed on this body.

52

Boris heard something. A scuffling noise. He held his breath. A door opened. Footsteps in the corridor outside. Was this real now? His dreams were so muddled with his waking. He couldn't make sense of it. The front door was still blocked with furniture. But someone was in the flat.

They must have seen him! When the wall was blown away they saw him, and now they were coming to get him. His heart thumped so hard it hurt. He was a disgrace, sitting there amongst tiles and plaster wrapped up in blankets, his head against the wall. Please go away, please go away! He should defend himself, like a real man. Where was his weapon? He didn't even know. What kind of a soldier was he?

The footsteps came into the hallway. Two steps then nothing. He clutched his stomach. The footsteps moved away into the lounge. A pause, then back again. Now the other way. He clenched himself even tighter and his heel shifted, grating against broken tile. The footsteps stopped. He closed his eyes. It must be a dream.

The door opened and a voice spoke.

"Do you live here?"

It wasn't a dream. He opened his eyes. Standing in the doorway was a tall man, brown skin and brown hair, thin cheeks.

"I said, do you live here?" He was speaking Russian.

Boris said nothing. Don't say anything to anybody. It's too dangerous.

"Is this your apartment?" The man glanced at the damaged tiling.

Yes, yes, it's my apartment. Boris bit his lip and a whimper came out. The man was staring, appraising.

"Is that your army uniform back there? Are you Russian?"

He was waiting for a response. Boris stared directly in front. This man had ruined everything.

"Answer me! Are you Russian? What are you doing here?"

The voice boomed in the tiny room. Boris let out a sob.

"What are you doing inside Lali? Where's your battalion?"

The stranger knelt in front of him. Rough hands grabbed his jaw and forced his face to the front. Boris looked into fierce grey eyes, inches from his own. The man smelled of the outside, of sweat and unwashed skin and hunger.

"You tell me. You tell me who you are. Are you a sniper? Or a spy? Are you GRU?"

The grip tightened. The man was breathing heavily. There was something frantic about him.

"I don't like you," he said. "I don't like that you're here. I know you're up to something. What are you doing in this flat? It's just a coincidence, is it?"

Boris didn't understand what he meant.

"Are you working for him? Are you working for Khovansky?"

Boris shook his head. The stranger pushed his face and knocked his skull into the wall.

"What, then?"

His desperation gave him an idea.

"I will show you," said Boris. "I will show you who I work for."

The man went quiet. He let Boris get up. Boris went out and pointed him into the living room. "Please, after you."

The stranger went in. Boris followed and picked up a chair. He lunged at the man and swung it fast, smashing it into the side of his head. The man staggered. Boris ran out, slammed the door and rammed the chair under the doorknob. He started to pull furniture away from the front door.

The man hammered on the door. "Let me out!"

He could break out, it wouldn't take long, but Boris only needed a few moments. Piece by piece he flung all the furniture aside and opened the door, and he was on the landing outside making for the stairs, but already the man was out, and grabbed him by the clothes, and Boris fell to his knees. His head cracked on the bannister. Oh, they've all come back again, all the nightmares! Then he was looking at a gun, pointed at him.

"Who are you? What's your name? What are you doing here?"

His bladder gave way and he felt warmth all round his crotch. He shouted out, no longer caring. He was dead anyway, he knew.

"I'm Boris! Boris Egorov! Russian army! Fourth Battalion, Second Motor Rifle Division! That's who I am! I am a Russian! Russian!"

The gun didn't move. Boris knew he was going to die.

Someone opened the door of the other flat. The man turned his head, and his face changed.

53

"Fairchild! What are you doing?"

Rose was right in front of him. Looking at him with disbelief on her face. Fairchild lowered his gun. The Russian soldier on the floor was sobbing like a child.

Fairchild already knew she was there; he'd been in the town several days, working from street to street asking about a British woman, or when that didn't ring any bells, any foreign woman at all. One rumour had pointed him here and he'd lurked, catching sight of her in the street. She looked gaunt, pre-occupied, but she was alive, thank God. If she'd been dead already, if he'd got here too late, it would have crushed him. Now she was standing here eyeing the gun in his hand. The Russian had wet himself; he could smell it. The soldier was curled up, shivering.

"Did you know he was Russian?" he asked Rose. "What's he doing here? What's he doing right here, under your nose?" He could hear something like hysteria in his voice.

"You think he's a threat? Look at the guy. He's terrified. I've not seen him before. He's been barricaded in that flat the whole time. It's him I've heard crying in the night."

She was right, of course. She bent and put her hand on the man's shoulder.

"Your name is Boris?" He jumped and looked at her. "Boris, it's okay. This man isn't going to hurt you. Please, go back inside."

She helped him to his feet. Fairchild stood aside feeling like a spare part. He stowed his gun while Rose guided the Russian to the door of his flat. Behind the closed door came the sound of furniture being piled up against the door, and the occasional sob. They looked at each other.

"He's broken," said Rose. "Like everyone else here."

"You seem okay."

"Do I?" There was something in the way she said that. "Well. Maybe I just haven't reached breaking point yet. It's only a matter of time."

She didn't ask about him.

"So it's time to get out?" he said.

"That's what you're here for, is it?" She frowned. "How did you get in?"

Fairchild was going to answer but stopped. A girl had appeared at the doorway, six or seven years old, messy blond hair, wide blue eyes. She looked up at him shyly.

"It's a long story," said Rose.

Fairchild crouched. "Hello," he said in English. The girl stared.

"She only speaks Georgian."

"Do you speak Georgian?" Fairchild asked Rose.

"No."

"Then how do you…?"

Rose rolled her eyes.

"What's your name?" Fairchild asked the girl in Georgian. She didn't answer but looked straight at him, curious.

"Her name's Katya," said Rose. "I don't have your flair for languages but I've picked up a little. Come inside."

The flat had avoided the worst of the shell damage. At least it was secure. Boris Egorov's barricading of the front door was irrelevant given how easy it was to climb up the remains of the frontage straight into his bedroom.

"I think I can manage tea," said Rose, busying herself with water bottles and a stove. He could see supplies of food.

"Are you hungry?" she asked.

"No."

It was a lie; he hadn't eaten in twenty-four hours. She looked at him and passed him a packet of plain biscuits.

"We've got enough. Don't expect a feast. But I'm sure you weren't, coming into a town that's been cut off for almost three weeks. Did it take you that long to find a way in? Or did it take Peter that long to have the idea of sending you?"

Fairchild put a biscuit in his mouth. It was the easiest way of not answering. Convenient that Rose was assuming Peter had sent him; it saved him having to invent another reason. Or tell her the truth.

Katya sat on the sofa and watched him eat.

"Is this your home?" he asked. She shook her head sadly. When Rose appeared with tea, she sat on the sofa and Katya curled up against her.

"You've made a friend there," said Fairchild.

"Not really. I'm all that's left." Rose stroked Katya's hair as she told Fairchild the story of the girl's family and everything else that had happened. Her voice was low and strained.

"This Grom character lured me here. It was a trap. And I fell for it, like an idiot."

"It was Grom," said Fairchild, "who had my parents killed."

She stared at him. "You found the monk? The Russian?"

"Dimitri told me everything. But now he's dead."

"Dead? How?"

"He was murdered. Brutally. With the aid of the FSB. They had a go at me on the train on the way back to Moscow, too."

Rose fell silent, pouring tea. "Grom and Khovansky. Are they the same person?"

"I believe they are. How did you get that name, by the way? Khovansky?"

"It was written on a piece of paper. Which I found at the Morozov house." Her face was a picture of innocence.

"A piece of paper in the pocket of my jacket, maybe?"

She shrugged. "You were in no state to argue."

"I was paralytically drunk. That piece of paper is the reason you're here."

"I'm the reason I'm here. I stole the name from you and passed it to Peter. He got all excited about the idea of such a big name wanting to turn. That's why he authorised it so quickly. The man played both of us. Whoever he is, I hope I live to thank him for the experience. Sounds like you have some issues with him too."

"You could say that." Fairchild could have said a lot more given what Walter had told him in Moscow. But here in the middle of a siege, a story of old scores from long ago seemed unimportant.

"This place seems doomed to me," Rose said. "Every day more shelling, more shooting. Less ammunition, less food, more injured, more dead."

That was Fairchild's reading also. "The Georgians have done well to last this long. Their artillery has held off a ground attack and their anti-aircraft capability has deterred Russia from coming in by air. But they're cut off here."

"Do people outside know what's going on here? The shelling is completely indiscriminate. They're not even trying to avoid civilians."

"I've been a little out of touch. I ran into some difficulties getting here."

"How did you get into the citadel, anyway? There can't be many options. Two heavily guarded bridges and Russian troops sitting on every inch of riverside all the way round."

"There's always a way in. Boris got in, didn't he?"

"I suppose so. You still think he's some kind of Russian GRU type, sent here for me?"

She made it sound like a stupid idea. Over the last few days he'd perhaps become a little over-vigilant.

"I guess not. But he must have got in, somehow."

"By accident, I expect. Maybe he was part of the first offensive that was pushed back. Or else he was trying to desert."

"You think he crossed enemy lines to get away from his own side?" asked Fairchild.

"You must have heard the dire stories from conscripts in the Russian army, the hazing that goes on. Hard to know if he's sitting here hoping the Russians will gain entry, or dreading it."

"Well," said Fairchild, "getting out will be more difficult than getting in. How's your swimming?"

"My swimming's fine," said Rose, "but if we're going to get out, it needs to be all of us."

Fairchild looked at the sleeping girl whose head rested on Rose's lap. Ideas spun through his mind.

"That might be do-able," he said.

"No," said Rose. "I mean, all of us."

54

The lookout point was busier. Eight of them were there now. Word was spreading. Judging from the sleeping bags and blankets, it was becoming more of a place to sleep and shelter than just a hangout. On the way, Katya started talking to Fairchild, quietly. Rose listened to her little voice, which gradually became more confident. Every now and then Fairchild would tell Rose what the girl was saying. It was nothing profound – observations about the streets they were passing through – but something tightened inside Rose when she saw how Katya was drawing towards Fairchild. Already, the girl had found another person to cling to.

Fairchild struggled to bend himself enough to get into the basement room, and seemed too tall inside it. The kids were fascinated that he spoke their language although most of them knew a fair amount of English. Fairchild's main interest, though, was out of the window; he peered out across the river for quite some time. Outside, he went down to the riverside and disappeared. When he got back he was covered in dirt.

Rose had some special skills training but was happy to leave the planning of an escape like this to Fairchild; she'd read his file. He kept his thoughts to himself until they were back at the flat.

"The boat I used to cross is still there. It's not big enough for all of us, though. And we can't go over in the open, like I did to get in. It won't work in reverse. Certainly not with these numbers."

"Well, we need another plan, then."

"The best I can think of is a raft. Launch it on the bank underneath the bridge. Tow it after the boat. Stay right under the bridge all the way out. There's enough wood and plastic lying around to knock something together."

"What would happen on the other side? Even at night it's busy over there. Possibly even more than during the day."

"Some places further along the bank are less well guarded. We'd have to walk along the beach on the other side and come up in the right place."

"And then? The whole area's being held by the Russians."

"Steal a truck. Load everyone in and hope we don't get stopped. From the viewpoint you can see where their vehicles are over that stretch, so we'd know what we were aiming for."

Rose shook her head. "That sounds like an incredibly risky plan, Fairchild. A huge amount could go wrong."

"I agree. It would also take a few days to organise. I can't think of anything else right now, though. Is it better than sitting it out? That's the question."

As if on cue, a whistling noise stopped abruptly overhead, followed by a heavy thud not far off.

"The bombardment's getting worse," said Rose. "They're preparing to come in, aren't they?"

"Maybe."

They fell into silence. Katya appeared around the side of Fairchild with a book in her hand. She was asking him to read to her. Marta used to do this. The books lying around in the flat were too grown-up for Katya to read, but okay if someone read them to her. Fairchild looked up at Rose.

"Go ahead," she said. "I need to go out and find food now it's dark. I don't like leaving her on her own."

She stepped out of the flat, glad to be gone. Why did she feel like such a spare part? Ridiculous, to be so put out by the wavering attentions of a traumatised six-year-old. Of course Katya connected more with someone who spoke her language. Was that the whole of it, though? Or was Katya instinctively picking up on something about Rose? Was she cold? Unmaternal? She'd never worried about this before; her career had always been enough. So what was bothering her now?

She was pocketing her keys when a click behind her made her jump. Boris appeared at his front door. No scraping of furniture: he must have been waiting there. His face was calm, but red and blotchy.

"Hello Boris. Are you okay?" If Rose couldn't be motherly, she could be neighbourly.

"I am okay. I am okay."

"I'm sorry about my friend. He thought you were some kind of spy."

"That's all right. No problem. I want to ask you something."

"Of course."

"I have a letter. To my girl. Back home in Russia. Well, she's not really my girl, but I always hoped, you know. That I could do something to make her notice me. I have written to her, about everything that's happened. Will you take it? Will you make sure she gets it?"

He held out a thin white sealed envelope with a handwritten address on it.

"Of course I can take it," said Rose. "But why are you giving it to me?"

Boris gave a tremulous smile. "Well, your friend, he will get you out of here, won't he? That's why he's here?"

"What makes you say that?"

"He came into the town, through the enemy lines. He must have a reason. He knows how to get in and out of places. Like my flat. I think you are leaving. I hope you are leaving, and you take my letter with it, so Tatiana will receive it. Will you take it?"

Rose took the letter. "Yes, I'll take it. I'll do my very best. What are you going to do?"

"I will wait here. I believe my countrymen are coming. You think so too? The nights, they're terrible." His voice cracked. "They will come in, and I will explain what happened. It was an accident, me being here. I thought I was going to die in the river. I often wish I did. But – I am alive. There must be some purpose to it. So I will wait here, and see what happens."

Rose nodded and wished him luck. He flushed suddenly, and went back inside. She listened for the sound of furniture being rammed behind it, but heard none.

The shelling was incessant, raw flashes and shattering explosions everywhere, a great overhead battle. Every place she went she found burning, fresh destruction, people running, people crying. Something really had changed. She came back empty-handed, thinking that they needed to give Fairchild's idea a try however risky it sounded. But that all went out of her head as she rounded the corner into the street.

There was a hole in the middle of the apartment building. In place of the stairwell was a pile of smoking rubble. No entrance door, no stairs, just jagged edges of flooring and hanging floorboards. Some fist squeezed her heart as she looked at the huge heap of tangled metal and stone. It was pitch black. People were standing in the street muttering, moving away in groups to seek safety elsewhere, or just staring. A man and a girl. A man and a girl, she needed to see, somewhere amongst these dusky figures. But she couldn't. Where were they? Please, don't be in that pile of rubble, that huge pile that kept drawing her. She stumbled trying to climb on it. Panicking, breathing too fast, it was foolish what she was doing, but she couldn't stop herself. Her foot gave way and she fell, grazing her face on the rough stones. Someone put a hand on her shoulder. She turned.

It was Fairchild, and he was carrying Katya, her arms draped around his neck. Something inside Rose came undone, became untethered. She couldn't control it.

"We're okay," he was saying. "It missed us. We climbed down. We're okay, Rose."

She barely heard him. She was crying, maybe. She wanted to hug Katya, but the girl's arms were firmly clasped around Fairchild as she stared silently about her. Fairchild patted Rose's arm awkwardly. She took a breath.

Pin it back down, Rose. Hide it away. They're okay, after all. They're okay.

They sheltered for the rest of the night on a narrow set of steps leading down to a locked cellar door. It was much like the first night, with Marta and Ilya as well, but without the snow. This had to, this absolutely had to be their last night here. Rose couldn't take any more of this.

55

As soon as it started to get light, the three of them headed for the lookout. Its occupants had multiplied, either due to rumours of an escape plan or forced there by the heavy bombardment. Fairchild sent them, bleary-eyed, searching for planks of wood, metal barrels, rope, plastic containers, anything that might float if tied together the right way. Others were sent for supplies: easily portable food, water, torches, tools if they could find them. Rose took some of the older ones with her; she could get them into places they couldn't otherwise access. Rose also found a good place to assemble their craft: a secluded yard away from prying eyes, but close enough for their constructions to be carried down to the waterside after nightfall. And there would need to be more than one, looking at the number in their gang now. They were all hungry and tired and stressed; some had minor injuries. But the day's purpose gave everyone a quiet energy; they were nervous but excited. Fairchild had given them hope. That made him nervous. Rose too, he could tell, although they didn't stop to talk about it. It was only the increasingly hopeless situation here that could justify such a risky enterprise.

They didn't talk about last night either. All was business-like and focused, but Rose's display of emotion when she turned and saw them there marked him somewhere deep. He was under no illusion, though; it was Katya who had drawn the tears, Katya she'd been so moved by the sight of, not him.

From the slitted basement vents, he watched activities on the other bank. He was starting to rethink the idea of stealing a truck. It couldn't be done quietly or quickly now, not with the numbers they had. A better plan would be to identify a thin part of the line, a place that would be dark, away from the action. He'd have to come back later to check on that. Rose and he could take out some of the guards and provide cover. He had guns and ammunition for them both, though only one silencer. Only one Russian army uniform as well. A diversion was what they really needed. He'd been up to the barracks when he first arrived, tried to make conversation with a couple of grave-faced smokers outside the gate, but was met with suspicion and a kind of defensiveness. He suspected the situation up there was worse than people thought.

Mid-morning he left the lookout, deserted now, and went up to the yard. The kids had done well; spread out across the ground was a collection of mismatched pieces, the widest possible interpretation of his instructions. Grouping them together in ways that would result in floatable objects was a team effort, with Rose and some of the older children pitching in with good ideas. They worked with purpose, everyone doing something, taking turns at keeping guard to distract curious passers-by. Katya overcame some of her shyness and trotted round offering water to people as they struggled with fixings and rusty metal. It was warm enough in the sun to break into a sweat. The barrage seemed to be on hold for some reason. The expression on Rose's face when she looked at Katya did something to Fairchild. He knew she was imagining this girl, paddling and drifting silently in the dark, right into the midst of a hostile armed unit. It was unnatural, counter-intuitive. He felt it too. But the rational part of him said otherwise. They had to get out. She'd said so herself.

Despite the circumstances, working alongside Rose like this changed him, loosened a part of him that had always been clenched and taut. Around her, he could be different; what he thought was important before, so critical, so all-consuming, he could feel how maybe it wasn't. Maybe he could do without all that, if he were with her.

They configured the junk into two sufficiently sturdy craft, big enough for three or four small people on each. The others would fit in the boat. They stacked the rafts up against a wall and covered them.

"Shame we can't test them," said Rose, checking that the fixing on one of the barrels was tight.

"It'll take all the hours of darkness we have to get across and away. And we want to go tonight. If there's a problem we'll have to work around it."

Meaning, if there were a problem with one of the rafts they'd have to load up the other craft, or persuade some of them to swim. Or leave some of them behind. They stood in silence, a similar thought process going on in both minds. Getting these children out, he realised, would make this whole episode meaningful for Rose, make up for the deception that landed her here in the first place, make up for the whole miserable, punishing experience.

"Here's something else I found," she said, holding out a grimy black plastic canister. He leaned in and sniffed.

"Petrol?"

"Petrol. You said something about a diversion."

"Good thinking."

They sent everyone back to the lookout to wait for nightfall and try to sleep. Even if they were too nervous for that, they would be rested at least. Rose stayed by the rafts in case anyone took a fancy to them. Fairchild went back with the gang. In the basement he talked with them for a while. They asked a lot about the plan for that evening and he told them what he could, but they were also curious about him. That apathy, the withdrawal he'd seen before, a defence against this impossibly hostile world they found themselves in, dissipated for a while. He persuaded them all to sleep, or at least to lie down. He'd come back for them as soon as it was dark enough. Doubtless tonight the bombardment would resume.

He followed the route he'd taken before to the shoreline and shuffled down to the water's edge on his belly. The jagged edge of the lookout building was side on to him. Taking his time, he surveyed the far shore. He could see one or two potential good spots to break through the line. But he needed more height; the angles weren't clear enough, particularly as it was now dusk. He crawled up the shore to get back onto the lane, coming up slightly as he changed direction.

An explosion of machine gun fire sent him down flat again. The sound broke off but rang in his ears. Stupid! You can't be off guard for a moment. He lay motionless. Now they'd spotted him, he'd be seen if he moved at all.

A rumble caused him to re-angle his head on the shingle. Something was different. In the fading light it took him a moment to figure it out. The profile of the riverside building was a different shape. A thin remnant of wall jutting up before was gone. As he stared, he realised that the structure was in motion. The back wall was leaning forward. A long groaning sound reached him. He scrambled to his feet, no longer caring about the sniper, and ran flat out, heading straight for the window. A thundering crash made him duck. The upper wall was coming apart. Blocks tumbled down onto the top of the basement ceiling. Rocks landed in the street. A cloud of dust expanded. He didn't slow down; he had to get to the window.

He was ten metres away when an immense crack split the air, the sound of beams giving way, concrete hitting concrete. The wall bulged towards him, spewing out a weight of dust particles, splinters of mortar and plaster, lumps of brick. He covered his face with his arms as he was forced back. When the assault lessened, he ran into the dust cloud, eyes streaming. In front of him was a massive pile of brick and concrete. The window frame was just visible, its edge poking out, twisted. Lumps were still cascading down, covering every inch of what used to be the basement, where a dozen children were bedded down.

He stood, looking at the window, as if there could still be some way in through that half-buried twist of metal, that the metres-high rubble could somehow be lifted. Then the hammering started up again, a clatter of machine gun fire, flashes now visible from over the river. It forced him to the ground again. He lay, his eyes stinging. Something made him look at his shoulder; he'd been hit, just caught enough to bleed badly. He wanted to climb all over that heap of bricks, pick up every one and toss it aside, dig, dig, dig, in case there were one small body, just one, which could be pulled out. But still the gunfire kept coming, and he lay there shaking with rage.

It was fully dark by the time he had mustered something in him to move. But he couldn't face her straight away. His feet led him back to the cock-eyed ruin of the apartment building. He stood and stared up at its remnants, an old curtain flapping gently on half a window frame. Opposite yawned the gaping hole of Boris' bedroom. It was time.

When she heard him coming, she emerged from her corner, expecting him. But when she saw his face, the dust all over him, the blood on his shoulder, her expression changed.

"What happened?"

He had to lean on a wall while he told her. He heard her exhale, saw her hands go up to her face, her skin blanch as she bent. The fortitude, the resolve that had kept her going through the past weeks, through God knows what else in her life, he watched it ripped away from her like skin torn from flesh, by this cruellest, this utterly unbearable mischance. She made a sound, a guttural cry of disbelief, fury, anger, a sound he would never forget. He couldn't stand it. Finally this siege had broken her, left her shrivelled, gasping, dry of hope. And by breaking her, it had broken him, too. He crouched, wrapped her in himself, rested his chin on her head and cried as he held onto her, feeling her shuddering sobs as the bombardment started overhead.

56

It got so bad they had to move. Rose would have just stayed there. She no longer cared. But Fairchild had come here for a reason and he would fulfil it, or die trying. So he pulled her to her feet and led her through the streets, as the bombs dropped and the shrapnel ripped through what fabric of the citadel was left.

He found a cellar with some space, and they bedded down wordlessly in a corner. She gripped his arm and turned onto her side away from him. Her head found his shoulder. He lay, cocooning her, feeling her hair brush his face, thinking of nothing but the sensation of her hand on his skin.

Later, when the bombardment relented, he shook her awake.

"Time to leave," he said.

They no longer needed the rafts, but they had to go back there for something else Fairchild had stashed with them. He felt around under the covers and brought it out.

"Russian army uniforms. For you and me."

She stared, dazed. "Where did you get these?"

"I wore one on the way in. The other belonged to Boris."

"You stole his uniform?"

"I went back there earlier. I left him his gun."

He was unrepentant. Boris would get a new uniform, if he lasted that long.

They dressed, then Rose disappeared briefly. She came back with the canister of petrol.

"Come on," she said, and led the way.

He couldn't fathom her purpose. He was just glad she had one. But he could have guessed they'd end up back at the lookout. He let her go alone, clambering the rubble, shaking the petrol over every inch of it, tears streaming. She had matches. He thought for one frenzied moment that she was going to just strike and drop, right at her own feet as she stood up there. If she'd done it, there'd be nothing he could do. But she paused, matchbox in hand, and looked up. Not at him, of course not: past him, at something distant behind, or perhaps at nothing at all. A flash of artillery fire lit up her face: thin, cold, hollow. Then she descended and lit a fuel-soaked rag, throwing that out onto the ruins. The heat rushed at them, black smoke belching out from the wall of flame. They stared up at it for a moment, a worthy pyre, but then they had to move. On the shore hauling out the boat, tipping out the weeds and mud, dragging and launching, they were dark shadows cast into shade by this giant furnace, barely visible through the billowing smoke as they drifted low and silent across the river.

They were ready, weapons in hand, coming up to the bank on the other side, but no one was there. The distant bridge seethed with walking figures. The tanks were grinding, the barrage had ended, the gunfire silenced. It was over. The Russians were going in. The enemy was filing into the citadel.

In the end, they just walked away.

57

He couldn't hide any more. In the night, the bombing deafened and drowned. He shook and cried under the blankets, locked in the bathroom, hiding away, little boy Boris. But then it stopped. Nothing, for hours. He slept. Slept! Then he woke. From the crack under the door he could see that it was light.

He crept out and peered down. The street was empty. But in the distance he saw a tank, crawling through the streets, coming this way. And soldiers! They were going into every building. When they arrived here he needed to be ready. In the bedroom he searched frantically for his uniform. Where was it? No! Not here! It was stolen! But who…? No matter. He still had his gun. He would address them in Russian. He would shout out his name and battalion. He would show them his gun. They would recognise him then.

He hurried to put on a coat and shoes, clothes of the man whose home this was. For a while this place was Boris' sanctuary, his home, but today he saw what a pitiful mess it was. No more hiding and festering in the dark. His countryfolk had arrived. They were downstairs, already in the street. For days and days he'd feared this moment, but no more. He would explain everything. What will be, will be. He heard the stranger's voice in his ear: *who are you?* I am Russian, Russian. I am a Russian soldier.

He left the apartment for the first time since entering it. He clambered down what remained of the stairs, letting himself down onto the heap of rubble at street level. He hesitated, but only for a moment, before stepping out onto the street, at last no longer hiding. The tank rolled towards him, making a terrible roar as it tore up the road surface.

Walking alongside were soldiers, infantrymen like him, their eyes on the doorways and windows, guns ready in their hands.

"Hey! Hey!" He ran towards one of them, shouting, waving his gun. "I'm Russian! I'm one of you! I'm in the Fourth Battalion! Second Motor Rifle Division! I'm a soldier like you! I'm a soldier!"

He tried to shout over the noise of the tank which kept grinding, grinding towards him. He shouted till his voice hurt. The soldier stopped. He was looking at Boris. He was readying his weapon.

"No! No!"

Boris sped up. He had to get closer, so the soldier could hear what he was saying, could hear that he was Russian. Boris started running flat out. The tank kept coming. The soldier raised his weapon, aimed, and fired.

Two huge blows in the chest. The force threw him backwards. He fell. He couldn't move. He couldn't breathe. Above him, the soldier appeared, looking down at him. He stepped over Boris, stowed his gun and walked on.

Boris shivered. Everything turned white. The tank ground on and faded away.

Russia

58

Roman turned to Vadim.

"Are you sure this is the place?"

Vadim nodded. It was a warehouse in a commercial zone, outer Moscow, a place for trade. Not for hookers. Roman expected to find her in a nightclub, pouting and preening, looking for her next victim.

They pulled in by an open truck and some wrapped crates on pallets. Whatever was in those crates belonged to him. He got out of the car and looked through the window. After almost a month of searching, there was Kamila Morozova, standing in an office with a scarf on her head, speaking on the phone. She turned when she heard the car doors closing. Her expression changed as they approached. Fear, yes: but a calm resolve that suppressed it. She ended her call and waited for them to come in.

"One of you must be Roman Morozov," she said.

"And you are the woman who married my son," said Roman. "Finally, we meet."

He sat down. Vadim hovered by the door.

"You're not afraid?" Roman asked Kamila. "You have no bodyguards, no locked doors. Did you not expect me to find you?"

She looked at him, a thin, clever face. Beautiful, yes, but not showy. No bright red lipstick, no big long lashes.

"This place isn't part of your business. You wouldn't find it trawling through the Morozov paperwork, or asking any of your people there. Whoever told you I was here, they have more knowledge and influence than that."

She was right. Roman had been wondering who gave them the information. Whoever it was chose to do it anonymously, a simple phone message.

He looked around. "If this is your place, and you bought it with money stolen from Alexei, then this is really mine." He picked up a file lying on the desk and flicked through it. She sat still and watched. The paperwork was neat, well-organised, thorough. He could smell a well-run business.

"What are you trading?" he asked.

"I'll show you." She stood up.

Vadim put a hand on his weapon. Roman shook his head.

"It's okay, Vadim, it's okay." The man was like a fussy old woman sometimes.

Kamila walked out and across to the open warehouse door. Roman followed, then Vadim, a bad-tempered shadow. Kamila seemed at home in this place. She was not what Roman expected.

A guy was standing outside the warehouse smoking, another inside leaned on a fork lift truck reading a clipboard. Kamila went over to a wrapped crate, got out a knife and cut the packaging. Roman caught a bitter, rancid smell. She pulled out a wooden box with western writing on it and levered open the lid. The smell got stronger. Inside were large cylinders coated with something like chalk. She lifted one out.

"Cheese. French cheese. You know what Muscovites will pay for this? But they can't get the real thing because of the trade embargo with the EU. Luxury food, delicatessen food. German sausage. Parma ham. Greek olives. Artichoke hearts. There's plenty more. People will pay ten times more for the genuine item than a similar product made in Russia."

Roman heard excitement in her voice.

"You set this up already?" he asked.

"This is the first shipment. I've found plenty of buyers in Moscow. This is already sold, everything you see here. And they want more." She was pleased, bragging.

"It's not possible. Not possible to find product like this in just a few weeks."

Kamila paused. She called out to the warehouse man and asked him to go. Then she repacked the cheese and turned to Roman.

"These people came to Alexei. He wasn't interested. Women's stuff, he said. Handbags and dog treats. Morozov's not like that any more. We're in a higher league now. That's what he said."

She stepped closer. So did Vadim, his hand ready. She did have a knife, after all.

"Your son had no sense of business. He was an angry man, sometimes cruel, sometimes just like a child. He married me because I made him feel important, special. That's what he yearned for. But he was destroying the business. I saw that, and I took advantage."

"You stole," Roman said.

"Yes. I stole. I stole money, and I stole information, contacts that I knew I could use. I could see their value. Alexei took it all for granted. He thinks a business like Morozov runs itself. And he was blinded by what the government people were offering. They would have taken control of everything. He was giving it away to them, and he didn't even realise. So yes, I stole. But I didn't kill him, if that's what you think. The people who told you where I am, is that what they said?"

"Then who did?" said a quiet voice.

"Vadim!" Roman turned on him. He'd never seen the man look so furious. "You keep out of this."

Roman turned back to Kamila. "Who is helping you with this? You didn't do all this yourself."

"Why not? Because I was a prostitute?" She spat the ugly word. "Once you're a whore, that's everything you'll ever be, everything you ever were. But I had a life before, in Chechnya, before your countrymen destroyed everything I'd known. I did what I had to do to survive. And I still am."

She held her arms out high. "You're right. This is all yours. Have it back. But let me run it. I'm good at this. I'll show you every transaction, share every margin with you. I'll keep nothing back. I can help Morozov grow, see new opportunities."

"You think we'll do business with a thieving slut like you?" Vadim again, spitting contempt. Roman turned once more.

"I told you to keep quiet. This is not your concern."

Kamila carried on. "Those fat corrupt blood suckers in the Kremlin. I know how much you hate them too. They killed everyone I loved, and they almost destroyed me. But I fought back. I will keep fighting back. I can help you keep them out. They're not as invincible as they think. They have their weaknesses, even this Grom, this man who likes to manipulate people. He is a complicated man, a strong man, he likes to think. But maybe not so complicated."

"You've met him? The one who so blinded my son? You know him?"

"Yes, I've met him. He realised I was taking money out of Morozov. He spared me in exchange for something. I had to do what he wanted and he promised I would stay hidden. But – I think he has now betrayed me."

"What did you have to do for him?"

"I had to send the British agent to Georgia."

Roman frowned. "John Fairchild?" Several times he'd tried to get in touch with his friend Fairchild, but hadn't heard anything in weeks.

"No, not him. The woman."

"The woman?"

"Rose Clarke. But it was because of the man. It is a shame. I liked her. But Grom likes to play games with people. That's what he does. He sends them running off after what they want, but it's because he has tricked them. Alexei was easy, for a man like that. Alexei was vain, he thought he was clever, especially if you told him so. He had so many needs, so many wants. You only had to —"

The bullet blast echoed in the empty space, took Roman's breath away. Then another: one, two. Kamila fell to the ground, hit in the head and the chest. Vadim's hand shook as he lowered the gun. He turned to Roman, eyes wide.

"That scheming little whore! How can you listen to that?"

"Vadim!"

His voice trembled with anger. "Trying to save herself by turning a father against his own son. She's a Chechen! A thief! A murderer! She stole from Alexei and then she killed him. And you listen to her while she puts her claws in you!"

Roman punched him in the mouth. He fell to his hands and knees, the gun skittering along the floor. Roman kicked him in the chest. He slid to the ground.

"*I* am Morozov! *I* am Morozov! Not you!" Roman walked away and kicked the wall. Vadim breathed hard, starting to pick himself up.

"You're a lonely old man. You don't need her."

Roman turned and punched him again. Vadim slammed into the ground. There was blood in his mouth, but still he wouldn't shut up.

"This is all yours now. You came here to kill her. That's what you came here for. But she knew how to turn you. Can you tell me you didn't notice, how much she looks like her? Looks like your wife, on the day you got married? You can tell me you didn't see it?"

Roman kicked him in the stomach. He heaved. He didn't try to get up. Roman faced the wall and listened to Vadim's breathing come back to normal. The whining voice started up again.

"I won't fight you, Roman. How many years have we known each other? I won't fight you. You can kill me if you want."

Roman strode over and picked up the gun.

"Get up."

Vadim got to his knees, then his feet. He wiped the blood from his face and stood, facing Roman.

"You came here to kill her, and now she's dead. That's what you wanted."

He waited, his sad eyes watching. Roman could end him. He should. In years gone by, he wouldn't hesitate. But from those years gone by, Vadim was the only one left.

He looked at the gun in his hand. He held it out. Vadim stepped forward and took it.

Roman cast a final look round, at the cases of cheese and the body on the floor.

"Let's go home," he said.

59

Several days of strenuous cross-country trekking got them to the Russian border. They walked at night, hiding during the day, short of food and water with inadequate kit, but Rose felt nothing. Fairchild knew the route; she followed blind, not finding it in herself to contribute or question. At the border, Fairchild's contact, a dark-eyed young Georgian, escorted them across, and then to Nalchik and a long train journey back to Moscow.

They shared a carriage and a lot of silence. Rose slept or stared out of the window, staring at the passing scenery: wide rivers with scrubby banks; clusters of concrete tower blocks; soggy marshland with puddles reflecting the low grey sky; massive concrete silos joined by conveyors, smoke billowing out of vents. Every now and then something would remind her of Katya's messy straw-coloured hair, or Ilya's earnest young voice, or Marta and her quiet presence, and she would battle against tears. Fairchild pretended not to notice. Good: she didn't want sympathy, or company.

She had vivid dreams. Once she was in a flotilla of boats crossing a river at night, flashes and bangs overhead, but when she looked up she realised they weren't missiles but fireworks, vibrant colours and patterns painting the sky, watched by hundreds of upturned faces. And when she got to shore and stepped out of the boat they were all there, Marta and Ilya and Katya, and they hugged her and everyone smiled. When she woke in her narrow bunk in the airless, rocking carriage, she sobbed silently, face to the wall.

They got news of what was happening en route. Tbilisi was still a stalemate, but the taking of Lali and the river crossing strengthened the Russians' supply lines.

International condemnation was widespread, with a handful of pro-Russian (ie anti-American) nations prevaricating, calling on "both sides" to find a peaceful solution. The only news coming out of Lali itself was via Russian media channels. God knows what was really happening there.

By the time they were pulling into Moscow, things started to seem heart-achingly normal. She'd managed a phone conversation with Peter and a meeting had been arranged for the following day. From the train, Moscow looked grey and gloomy. All the snow had gone. She didn't want to be back here, to recognise these familiar sights, take up her life as if nothing had happened. Fire was what she wanted, a great roaring, sweltering, hissing, crackling, raging force to take over and eat it all up, turn this whole miserable thing into stinking, smoking ash.

Walking up the platform, Fairchild muttered something about sharing a car. One of his executive fleet, no doubt. Rose shrugged. The idea of going back to her goldfish-bowl flat had no appeal. He left her standing at the pick-up point saying he needed to buy a new SIM card to call for the car. It sounded like an excuse, and clearly it was because he wasn't back after twenty minutes.

She didn't blame him for regretting the offer. She could hardly look him in the face and he knew it. At times back there she'd relied on him, needed him. He knew of her weakness now. He'd seen her passion, her desperation, and there was no unseeing it. He'd glimpsed inside her, discovered things about her that no one knew, that she hadn't even known herself. You don't expose yourself in this trade, not to anybody. Especially not to someone like Fairchild. In some ways she hated him for showing up in Lali. She'd prefer to be dead right now, crushed in the same pile of rubble as Katya and all the others. But she wasn't. She was here, waiting for a car that wasn't going to arrive and it was cold, and getting dark.

She gave up on Fairchild and headed for the Metro.

60

It must have been obvious it was an excuse. Fairchild walked away from her, exhaling slowly, barely looking where he was going. He needed a moment to himself, a moment to think, try and clear his head.

The train journey had been agony. He knew she didn't want him there. She was so fragile, so silently despairing, so keen to hide it, that he worried about what she might do. Having seen her in her fury and shock and rage, to watch her draw it all in, internalise, suffer it alone while he was right there, was almost unbearable. He remembered every detail of that night lying in the cellar, her body warm and solid and real, her breathing, her hair, her touch. Every cell in his body wanted to hold her now, comfort her, tell her she wasn't alone, that he'd been there too and that he thought he understood. But she'd pulled back and withdrawn from him quite deliberately.

He understood why, respected it, admired her strength in some ways, but it was a dangerous kind of strength, the kind that might lead her out into a desert and leave her there, stranded and parched. He'd been there himself so often, concluding a long time ago that he could trust no one with his soul. But he had an outlet for his loss, he had a mystery to solve, a puzzle to complete, the puzzle of *what happened that night.* He'd turned his inner grief into an intellectual exercise, conducting ever more research, digging ever deeper, building a bigger and bigger network, convincing himself that all he needed was to know what happened and everything would be better. And now he knew, but it wasn't better. He was even more alone than before, mocked by the life he'd built. What was the point of John Fairchild? He had no purpose.

She could be his purpose. He'd use it all for her. If he had it in his ability, if it fell within his gift, if he could do something that would mend her, give her peace again, it would make everything meaningful once more. But that wasn't what she wanted. Mile after mile the elastic binding him internally grew ever more taut. As they drew into Moscow it tightened and squeezed so that he couldn't even keep still. He couldn't stand this. He couldn't stand the idea, after what they had been through, of things between them simply returning to how they were before. He had to say something.

He wanted to say this: I understand how you feel because I was there and I know what happened. I feel like that too, and it's okay. It's okay because I'm not going to use it against you, or foist myself on you, but don't ever think that you're alone. Because I'm here for you, forever, whenever you want me. And if you don't want me, that's fine as well. Just know that I'm yours.

But they pulled in and got off the train and walked up the platform, and still he didn't say anything. So he offered her a lift, to give himself more time. But he needed to get away for a minute and think, think what to say, plan something while she wasn't there in front of him, something perfect, something that exactly expressed how he felt.

He walked past the arcade of shops out to the back, an access road for deliveries and a hidden spot for smokers. Nobody was there. He leaned back against a wall and closed his eyes.

Footsteps. He opened his eyes. Hands gripped both his arms. Two men were standing either side of him. Two big chunky guys.

"You come with us, please," one of them said.

"I don't think so."

"No, you come."

He tried to pull out of their grip but it was solid. Before he could try anything else a car squealed to a halt in front of them. Another thickset guy got out. He opened the back door and pointed Fairchild in. All three of them stood, waiting.

Fairchild twisted both arms and ducked, sliding backwards between them. He turned, but the third was in front of him already, and shoved his head backwards. A blow in the stomach winded him. They lifted him up and threw him bodily into the back of the car. He slid on the leather seat into the lap of a fourth heavy.

The door slammed shut and the car accelerated away.

61

A man standing on the platform was wearing a trenchcoat and reading a folded newspaper. Rose noticed him just as her train built speed. She stared at him as the train went past. They plunged into a tunnel and he was gone. It was such a familiar image, a stereotypical spy from Cold War days, a Moscow shadow.

He was nothing. Modern day street watchers didn't dress like extras off a film set, even the FSB. But that image somehow penetrated the fog she'd been walking around in since arriving back in Moscow. She was a fool to go back to her flat. If sending her to Lali was a trap set by Grom, it had a purpose to it. They might be waiting for her. Part of her didn't care, but another part, now awakening, protested. You're going to give them what they want? After what they did? She wouldn't make it that easy for them. She focused on the Metro map in front of her and made another plan.

The hotel looked decent enough, but explaining at the front desk that she'd lost all her ID but did have quite a lot of cash, the room options became more limited. Her room key number took her through the lobby, along a corridor with plush carpets right to the end, round a corner into a corridor with no carpet at all, where the lights were bare bulbs and the room doors were badly fitting, to the end of this one too. Her room had a single bed with a threadbare blanket, a washbasin with a tiny bar of soap and two pieces of paper towel, and a tiny rickety wooden desk and chair. After an extensive search she located a toilet at the end of the corridor, in the corner of a room used for cleaning materials.

She sat on the bed. No relaxing steam bath for her then. It didn't matter. A charger would be useful, though, for her phone. She eventually found a socket under the bed. Then she lay on the bed having nothing else to do, no place to be, no plans or ambitions of any kind.

She closed her eyes, dozed, maybe for a minute. She woke with a start and sat up, thinking she was on the sofa cushions in the flat in Lali. For a moment she was right back in that room, looking round for the children, checking they were okay. She lay back down again, empty. But in that moment something else popped into her head.

Boris. What happened to Boris? Sensitive, damaged Boris, another innocent in all of this. She dreaded to think, but she still had his letter somewhere.

She emptied her bag on the floor. It was odd to think that these trivial personal items, hurriedly packed three weeks ago, had endured intact. The letter was among them, wrapped up with her paperwork inside an improvised dry bag. She looked at the writing on the envelope, reliving the conversation they'd had on the landing. She prised the flap open carefully and drew the letter out. It ran to four pages, neatly printed Cyrillic on old-fashioned gossamer-thin writing paper.

She read it. She put the letter down, lay back on the bed and stared out of the window at the night sky, her thoughts in another place. Then she sat up suddenly. In the same bundle of paperwork she still had the business card of Jannes, the journalist she'd met on that first night in Lali. She found his card and thought for a while, looking at the words on the card. Then she retrieved her phone from under the bed and called the number.

62

Fairchild was escorted out of the car and led by a man on each arm into the tired lobby of one of Moscow's towering Stalinist skyscrapers. One lift took them up to the twentieth floor, the next, round the corner with its own security code, up another two floors. There, two more men were already waiting as the lift doors opened. The door opposite led into a large room, overheated and stuffy. A row of dirty windows offered a magnificent view of Moscow. The thick brown carpet and wooden furniture probably dated from the 1950s. There was not enough furniture for the room, which stretched alongside the windows like an empty gallery. Towards the far end was a single armchair and a coffee table.

The door closed. The men stationed inside the door made it clear that Fairchild was expected to stay. He sat in the armchair, put his feet on the table and drifted in and out of sleep sitting there overlooking the city lights. When awake, his eyes would trace the streets below wondering where she was. How long did she wait for him? He thought of phoning her and got his phone out, only for one of the goons to snatch it out of his hand. He fell into a deeper sleep and dreamed he was in a cellar, with Rose, and the sound of falling shells was so loud that he couldn't hear what she was saying. She was agitated, trying to say something important, something that mattered to her, but he couldn't make it out. A thud, as a shell landed near them. He woke with a jump, the sound echoing in his ears. Standing by the door was a familiar figure, a large well-built man with an air of authority.

"Sleep is a good thing," Roman Morozov said. "It will help you heal. I imagine you will need to recover from the last few weeks." He placed a hand on Fairchild's shoulder. "But it will take time."

A guard brought an upright chair, and a bottle of vodka and two glasses were placed on the table.

"I apologise for how you were brought here," said Roman. "We have an urgent need to talk."

The Bear sat squarely opposite him, and poured the shots. Despite the vodka and the greeting, there was no doubting the situation; Fairchild was in the man's custody.

He took his feet off the table. "How did you know we were back in Moscow?" he asked.

"I have people watching every train going through to Baku. Anything unusual, I hear about it."

"It sounds like you're back in charge already." He shifted in his seat.

"You are injured?" asked Roman.

"Just a flesh wound." Fairchild indicated his shoulder, which was still sore.

"My friend! You should have said. You need a doctor?"

"No, it's okay. It's healing."

"That's good. You are not defeated by pain. You can endure it, knowing it will come to an end. I was hoping the army would give such a mentality to Alexei, but it was not to be. He was always in the moment."

"Perhaps I should be grateful to you for bringing me here and looking after me so generously."

Roman ignored his irony. "We have important things to discuss." He raised his glass.

"I thought you weren't a big drinker."

"Ha! Well, maybe I am these days. People change. To good health!"

They both drank. It had been weeks since Fairchild had drunk anything. He felt lightheaded straight away. Roman poured again. The bottle seemed very large. He hoped this wouldn't be a repeat of their last encounter.

"Do you know why you were lured into a war zone?" asked the Bear.

"Was I?"

"Yes." Morozov settled into his chair. "I now know, I now understand, who it is you and I are against. We have a common enemy, and he is a dangerous person."

Fairchild waited. He'd begun to suspect something like this. Roman leaned forward.

"The state is taking over everything, you know this. We used to have balance, different sides. Yes, there was violence, fighting, but because we had something to fight for. Now, everyone gives their soul to the government. Some for money, others because they see no other option. Why try? they ask. They will take it anyway. I may as well get what I can. So they do whatever they are told, become puppets, outwardly the same but behind the scenes following orders. We're going back to how things were before, all power in the hands of a few, our great country at the mercy of individuals who decide on a whim who will live and who will die. You don't believe me?"

Roman had picked up on the tiniest change in Fairchild's expression. His eyes glittered; his face was set. This was the man who terrorised Siberia, built the Morozov empire on the bodies of his rivals. This was the man Fairchild was afraid of. But the Bear was waiting for an answer.

"You've killed people too," he said.

"Never on a whim. For a purpose! We had a code, Fairchild. Those people, they have none." He stared out of the window as if glaring down on the Kremlin itself. Then he continued. "It's not inevitable. People shape events, strong people who step in and influence things. The man they call Grom is a strong person. He is not known, he keeps himself hidden, but he's at the heart of this. He feeds on the power in the Kremlin. He uses it for his own purposes. He's a puppeteer, Fairchild. A master puppeteer. He was testing you. He wanted to see what you were made of, what kind of a man you were."

"And what kind of a man am I?"

"You were not afraid to go into the heart of the battle, and you survived. You are a hunter, strong and fearless. You disagree? This man Grom will be impressed. But he also knows you have weaknesses. He knows what these weaknesses are. He knows," – Roman swilled his glass – "he knows *who* these weaknesses are."

Fairchild drank, feeling the fiery liquid in his mouth. This was exactly what he didn't want to hear.

"He tricked Rose into going to Lali because he knew I'd go after her. But Roman, I've never even seen this man."

"But maybe he has seen you. You take a lot of pride in being able to hide your feelings. But when you're not prepared, you give yourself away. I saw it. I saw how you looked at her, when you weren't expecting her to be there. Only for a moment, but it was enough. Somehow, he's witnessed this and has realised how you feel about her."

Fairchild felt his mouth go dry. His gaze went back to the view of Moscow outside. Where was Rose? Had she gone back to her flat? The FSB would surely know where she lived. He glanced around. The heavies were still by the door. Whether he liked it or not, he would be here for as long as Roman wanted him here.

Roman was watching Fairchild, following his thoughts. "Her dealings with you have put her in danger, my friend. This Grom, this Khovansky, I know now it's the same person, his issue is with you, not her. But he used her to get to you. You might wonder, if you are a problem to him, why he hasn't just had you killed."

"He tried," said Fairchild.

"Ah! But he did not succeed. So now he wants to find out who you are, give you a test. By doing that, he has told us a lot about himself." Roman paused to pour again. "John, tell me this. Are you a threat to the Russian government?"

Fairchild smiled. "I could be, if somebody paid me enough."

"Exactly! You do the bidding of others. You're not a danger in your own right. So why does this Khovansky play these games with you? I tell you why. He has access to a lot of power, in his very-high secret service role. But he is using this power to serve his own ends. He has a grudge against you, because of your parents, because of something they did. Something they did, not you! You were only a child. But he doesn't care. He still wants to end you, or punish you."

Fairchild was only half-listening. *Why does this Khovansky play these games with you?* Why did his parents play games with him? Why were their tricks and riddles so important, their perpetual insistence that he fill his head with knowledge, their constant testing and challenging? He'd often thought, looking back over the years, that they'd been preparing him for something. Now he thought he understood what it was. It was this man: Grom, Khovansky, Sutherland. They anticipated that he would someday come back for them – and for him. They were trying to make sure Fairchild was ready. He wished he could ask his parents about it, find out for sure, but he'd never be able to now.

"How do you know all this?" he asked.

"Ah! Well, while you were away, I had an interesting conversation with someone. A person I didn't know before, Fairchild. This person, though, had a very good

277

understanding of how things work, how people work. She met him, this Khovansky. And she understood him. Yes, she opened my eyes. Now I understand more fully the situation I'm in."

She? Fairchild was thinking hard, but there was only one person it could be.

"Kamila?"

Roman's voice sounded strained. "It was Kamila who persuaded your Rose to walk into the lion's mouth, you know. But she was only doing it because she was under pressure. This Grom likes to make everyone dance his dance. Meeting Kamila was a great benefit to me. Sadly, she did not survive our encounter." A shadow crossed his face.

Fairchild thought of the delicate woman he'd met at the reception. It seemed that everyone had under-estimated her. Roman's response was puzzling, though.

"But Kamila stole from the business, didn't she?"

"Yes, she did. She was clever. More so than I thought."

"You don't think it was Kamila who killed your son?"

"Oh, no. Kamila did not kill Alexei. She hated him, but she did not do that."

"Then who did?"

"Russia killed my son," said Roman. "The Russia we've become. It tempted him in and poisoned him. It turned him bad like it turns everyone bad, and then it wanted more. Grom is one of them. He is one of the worst."

"But who pulled the trigger?" asked Fairchild quietly.

Roman was looking into the far distance. His words dropped like stones.

"I tried to reason with him. Think of the business, I said. The people we protect, what they need. But he laughed. He didn't understand where it all came from, before things grew so large, before we became so respectable. I tried to show him, to make him understand, when he was growing up, but I failed. It was my fault."

He turned to look at Fairchild. "We all have to sacrifice things. But we need to hold in mind what's important, our role in the lives of others, many others. So I did the most difficult thing a father can do. I sacrificed my own son."

His eyes filled with tears. It was Fairchild this time who filled the glasses. Silence invaded the room. They both drank. Fairchild stared at the carpet. What Roman had done was gross, horrific, against nature and all human instinct, and yet for him, for the Bear, it made sense.

Eventually the old man spoke. "Was I wrong, my friend? Would you do that? Kill your own kin for something bigger?"

"I really don't know," said Fairchild. "I don't have any kin."

"So you have no words of comfort for an old man. Well, no matter. I made my own choices. You must be strong too, Fairchild. You must separate yourself from this woman. As long as she's important to you, she will be in danger."

Fairchild couldn't imagine a time when Rose would not be important to him. Roman leaned towards him.

"He will try to destroy you now. He will get to everyone you are close to. He will try even harder, now he knows what you are. And you must end it. You must kill him."

They both drank, looking at each other.

"Why me?" said Fairchild. "Why don't you kill him?"

"I'm old. I'm not as strong as I once was. And my men – they're good and loyal, but they're street fighters and ruffians. He's not threatened by such people. He knows them too well. You, on the other hand, are up to the challenge. You are a match for him."

His voice had become low and gravelly. There was no other sound, no movement in the room. "I will help you. My people, everything I have, we are at your disposal. Take your time. Form a plan. Do your research. Don't be predictable. Don't go where he would expect you to go. Stay clean, stay alert, stay alone. And when you finally get to him, when you finally get the chance, when he's there in front of you, don't hesitate. Whatever he says. Finish him, otherwise he will finish you. Do you doubt it? Look what he did to your parents, what he tried to do to you. He will try to flatter you and trick you. Don't give him a chance."

He poured, set the bottle down and drained the glass. "You need to get out of Moscow. Out of Russia, for now. While you form a plan. He's too powerful here. I can arrange it. Transport, paperwork. It takes a couple of days. It's becoming more difficult. You could get these things from government departments if you knew the right people, but it's more dangerous now. They call it anti-corruption. It means, only government corruption is allowed."

"Two problems with that," said Fairchild. "First, I don't have a couple of days. If what you say about this man is true, I need to get out of Moscow now. Second, so does Rose. She's in as much danger as me."

Roman waved his hand. "She's a diplomat. Her people can get her out."

"Not necessarily. The Kremlin doesn't always respect these niceties, especially at times of great international tension. And her people might not realise the situation. I take your point about keeping distance. To be honest, I think that's something she'll decide, not me. But I won't abandon her in the middle of Moscow. It's my fault she's in this mess. I at least need to get her out. What she does after that is up to her."

Roman was weighing it up. "You will promise," he said. "You will promise to kill him. I made a sacrifice. I did not hesitate. You will do the same."

He held Fairchild's gaze with a look of steel.

"I promise," said Fairchild.

63

Rose walked in through the main entrance of the British Embassy, in doing so putting herself back on the Russian watchers' radar again. The cash-only back room of a central hotel was a good place to hide, but the FSB would be keeping tabs on who came in and out of here, that was certain. In the secret briefing room were Peter, Zack, and a familiar face she wasn't expecting at all.

"Walter! I didn't know you were in Moscow." They air-kissed as they had last time they met, in a hotel room in Kathmandu. She got a strong whiff of his familiar after-shave. He seemed out of place here, with his small spectacles and threadbare brown jacket. He looked more like a retired academic on an historical city break.

"Didn't John tell you I was here?" he asked. He watched her response carefully. Walter was getting on these days, but she knew from experience that he didn't miss much.

"No, he didn't."

He registered this as though he'd consider later whether he believed it or not.

Rose's debrief was shorter than she thought it would be. They didn't need the everyday detail of how they all tried to survive the siege. She met some people, they died. Done. Of more interest was the Georgian defence, the Russian forces. But what she knew here was more limited, and out of date by now anyway.

Then it was her turn to ask. "So what's the likely outcome? How long can this stalemate carry on? Surely there'll be some intervention."

Zack got in first. "Well, you know how this works. Everyone condemns it, then sits on their butts and waits for the USA to lead. Right? Even though this is basically Europe."

"It's not Europe, Zack." This was Peter. "Georgia links Russia with the Black Sea and Turkey. What's the other side of Turkey? Iraq. Iran. Beyond that, Saudi Arabia. These are places the USA has no interest in?"

"Okay, okay, it matters to us. But it matters to you guys as well. You just don't want to do what it takes. What's the point having armed forces if you don't use them?"

Peter shrugged. "That's up to the politicians, but direct military engagement risks the situation escalating. There's more interest in squeezing Russia even tighter on sanctions."

"Sanctions, right. That sure scared them after they invaded Crimea. Which they still occupy, by the way. So scared a couple of them turned up in some small town in England to carry out a hit under your noses."

"The UK has plenty of issues with Russia and we're not pulling any diplomatic punches. That episode damaged them, as you know, Zack, because we spoke out about it. But the view in Westminster and elsewhere seems to be that direct military intervention isn't in the public interest at this time. In the meantime there are active negotiations going on for a ceasefire."

Rose came in. "So that's the official position. What about unofficially?"

"Yeah, well, discussions are being had," said Zack.

She felt the need to press the point. "I mean, this isn't a separatist issue like Chechnya. Georgia is actually an independent country."

"So's Ukraine," said Zack.

"And it's a neighbour of the EU, across the Black sea from Bulgaria and Romania."

"So's Ukraine," repeated Zack.

"Conversations are ongoing," said Peter firmly. "And all of these things are being talked about."

Zack shifted impatiently in his inadequately-sized chair while Peter continued.

"What's more relevant to Rose is the circumstance that took you to Georgia in the first place and what that means."

"Well, clearly that was a trap," said Rose. "Engineered by the FSB officer who's the Morozov liaison. Known as Grom, probably also known as Mikhail Khovansky. Kamila was under pressure to persuade me to meet him in Tbilisi. She was looking out for herself, and I'm not sure she had much of a choice. Did Roman catch up with her?"

"Unfortunately for her, yes," said Peter. "Our police contacts tell us she was found dead a couple of days ago at an industrial unit in the outskirts of Moscow. Shot in the chest and head. A clean kill. An execution."

Rose thought of their last conversation, probably in the same place where she died. Kamila was so focused, so keen to make it work, pull herself up from a past of such heavy tragedy, find some meaning and happiness. But even then it had seemed fragile. Ultimately she was, like so many women, crushed underfoot by the will and aggression of the men around her, her life unimportant compared with their struggles.

"Are we sure it was Roman?" she asked. "It could have been Grom."

"The police seem to think it was Roman, although they're struggling to track down any witnesses. They don't seem to be in any hurry to make an arrest. Roman has taken over the Morozov business. Asserted control, we're told."

"That won't please Grom very much," said Rose. "He had Morozov in his hand. You'd think he'd want to get rid of Roman. A murder conviction would do the job nicely."

"What we need to understand," said Peter, "is how the Russians pulled off such a feat of misdirection. They masked this invasion from us completely."

"I think I can help there," said Walter. "Clearly they've been planning it for some time and set up the training manoeuvres as a smoke screen. But as well as that, the Kremlin has the benefit of a sharp and duplicitous mind. Someone who knows exactly how to appear to give people what they want."

"You're not trying to claim that he doesn't exist, then?" said Rose. "You're talking as if you know him, Walter."

"What did John say to you about him?" asked Walter.

"He thinks this guy killed his parents. And that he recently tried to kill Fairchild himself. That's all."

"Nothing else?"

"No."

Walter fell silent. Peter looked towards Zack, and then back to Walter. Zack sat up in his chair.

"Is this British-speak for you'd like me to leave? Look, whatever Fairchild knows he'll tell me, so I'll find out anyway. He knows the guy's real. He tried to have Fairchild killed. That's real enough, isn't it? So don't mind me."

"It might be useful to have him here, Peter," said Walter. "If he can treat certain things confidentially? Avoid posting them on the CIA intranet, ideally?"

Zack waved a hand. "Yeah, yeah." It was the best they were going to get.

"So we're calling Fairchild by his name now, are we?" asked Rose.

Peter stepped in. "We conversed earlier about our work with the Morozovs and there was mention of a contractor, but no mention by name. That contractor is no longer working for any of us, is he, Zack?"

"Nope. Went off the job a few weeks ago."

Rose looked at Peter. "So who sent him to Lali?"

"Well, he must have gone for his own reasons," said Peter. "We're discussing him now because he's very pertinent to this new threat which has emerged."

"For his own reasons? You mean, you didn't send him? You said you'd speak to some people, see if you could get me out."

"And I did," Peter said. "But it didn't go anywhere, I'm afraid. I couldn't get a confidential message through to let you know. It was considered too high-risk, the chances of the British being seen to be involved. And if it went wrong, questions would be asked about what you were doing there, of course."

"So why was he there?" Rose asked.

"Didn't he tell you, my dear?" asked Walter.

"I just assumed he'd been sent. That he was on a job."

"You really don't know?" asked Zack. He looked at the others. "This is one of your best people? And she doesn't know that?"

Walter came in. "I think what Zack is saying is that you have yourself a guardian angel, my dear. I did suggest something like this earlier, I believe. When we last met?"

She felt her neck and ears going red. This again? "For Christ's sake. I could have got myself out of there if I'd had to."

"So why didn't you?" asked Peter.

Rose had no answer.

"The point is," continued Walter, "Grom, Khovansky – I think we can assume it's the same person – his modus operandi suggests that he is indeed the Soviet agent who managed to infiltrate MI6 and work for us decades back, during the Cold War."

Rose thought she'd misheard. "Excuse me? Khovansky worked for MI6?"

"Get out of town!" said Zack. "A British spy turned out to be a Soviet double-agent? There must be a special club for them all over here. If I put that on the CIA intranet, people will yawn."

"Yes, all right, thanks Zack," said Peter.

"But this is different, though," said Rose. You're saying this guy wasn't even British? That he was Russian?"

"Why don't we let Walter carry on?" suggested Peter.

Walter did. "This officer was known to John's parents during their days in the Service. His name then was Gregory Sutherland. The Fairchilds investigated him. But the investigation ceased because Sutherland died in a car crash. The Fairchilds formulated the theory that his British identity and his death were both faked, and that he returned to the Soviet Union and became active within the KGB. I have to say I had some sympathy with that view, though others considered it far-fetched."

Rose was thinking all of this through. "Khovansky killed Fairchild's parents because years earlier they'd exposed him as a deep cover Soviet agent?"

"They were going to expose him, but they didn't get a chance because he staged his own death to return home. But that seems to be enough for Khovansky to seek them out from behind the Iron Curtain and have them killed. It also seems to be enough for him to target their son as well, now he knows of his existence, even though Fairchild was only a child at the time. The man bears grudges, clearly. Given his influence within the FSB and access to their power and resources, Fairchild is in a lot of danger. It also means you are, I'm afraid."

Now Peter came in. "You'll have to leave the country, Rose. There's no way you can operate here with this hanging over you."

"You're joking!" Rose couldn't believe what she was hearing. "Pack it in and go home? No way! Not after what I've done to get this post. Walter!"

"I fear Peter's right, my dear. This is a very serious situation."

"But it's got nothing to do with me! This Grom, this is all Fairchild, not me!"

"You're right," said Walter, "but clearly John has feelings for you, and Khovansky has latched onto that."

"How? How could someone who's never met either of us know that?"

"He must have seen you together somewhere. Or, more precisely, seen Fairchild's response to you. He can be read, Rose, if you're good at these things. As I said to you before, I've known him a long time."

"There were FSB agents all over the place at the reception in St Petersburg," said Peter. "Half the waiters were probably FSB. That's the first time I've seen Fairchild in Russia for some years."

"Well, I didn't notice anything." Rose knew she sounded sulky.

Walter spoke mildly. "I appreciate you don't welcome the attention, but in actual fact, that's by-the-by."

"Don't welcome the attention? I've lost my job! Again!"

"Not your job, Rose," said Walter. "Just this posting."

"And why was I posted here, Walter? Because of him? Because you knew he'd come to Russia searching for Dimitri and you wanted me here too? Are you telling me this? Because I said to you, didn't I, that I didn't want to spend my career chasing him around the place!"

Walter met her agitation with blandness. "Your posting here served a number of purposes."

"Oh, great. Listen, Peter, surely this can't be the right time to send me home. We're in the midst of a political crisis. I'm running other agents here, I can do useful work."

Peter sighed. "It's too great a risk to you now, Rose. With the attention of this man it's unlikely you'd be able to operate in secret anyway. We'd be risking the agents as well. Besides, there's been talk already of diplomatic expulsions. A few rounds of tit-for-tat expulsions and we may all be getting on a plane home."

Rose couldn't accept this. "They're already watching me. They've been watching me since I arrived, you know that."

"Not like this," said Peter. "This isn't just normal FSB intimidation. This is a much bigger threat."

"And seriously, this is more important than what's going on in Georgia right now? The whole Anglo-Russian relationship? The whole *NATO*-Russian relationship? This one man?"

"Potentially, yes," said Walter. But instead of explaining how, he turned to Zack.

"Where is Fairchild right now?"

"No idea," said Zack. "He told me he'd be back in Moscow last night but I couldn't reach him."

"We both got back last night," said Rose, "but he did a disappearing act at the train station. I haven't heard from him since."

They all looked at each other. Peter spoke first.

"I'm thinking that Rose should get over to the airport right now."

"Is that safe?" asked Zack. "I mean, they're watching the Embassy, aren't they? They'll know she's here."

A knock at the door and a head peered round. "Car here for Rose Clarke."

"What car?" asked Rose. "I didn't order a car."

"He says sorry for the delay."

The head disappeared. The penny dropped.

"It's Fairchild," said Rose. "He offered me a lift last night before he vanished into thin air."

Walter and Peter looked at each other.

"Go with him," said Walter to Rose. "Stick with him if you can."

"Walter, are you sure?" asked Peter.

"She's probably better off with him than with anything we can offer."

This sparked something in Peter's normally sedate self.

"You can't say that, Walter. Are you doing this for Rose's safety or because you want eyes on Fairchild?"

"Yeah, and let's not forget Fairchild's wellbeing here," Zack intervened. "I can tell that's high up on all your priority lists."

"I think we're all done here," said Walter. "Rose, you can escort Zack out and wait in reception. Peter and I will finish off."

It was a voice that extinguished all debate: quiet, hard, utterly authoritative. Rose got a glimpse of Peter's rigid face as she closed the door on the way out. Walter, of course, outranked Peter. No doubt that point was about to be made to him.

At the security desk she said to Zack: "I really don't welcome any of this, you know."

"Yeah, you made that clear enough." He took off his security badge and threw it unceremoniously onto the desk.

His resentment niggled her. "I'm marked, now, because of him. I've got to move, start again somewhere else. I didn't ask to come here. I didn't ask for him to show up in Lali. I didn't ask for any of it."

"Well, neither did he. And I seem to remember you coming after him in the first place."

"To get my job back, Zack! That's why I did that. It wasn't personal."

"Well that's okay then! You're all heart, aren't you?"

"That's what I'm supposed to be, am I? Why's that? Because I'm a woman?"

Zack performed the classic eye-roll all men in the industry did when anyone mentioned gender. Out of the doors through the security gates she could see a sleek black limo with tinted windows parked on the other side of the road. She turned to Zack.

"Look, you're his friend. Go out there and tell him to go without me. I can look after myself. Tell him that's what I want."

Zack hesitated.

"Well, that's what you think as well, isn't it?" she said. "That I'm bad news? That he should forget about me and look out for himself? Go out there and tell him! Quick, before Peter and Walter get down here!"

Zack's large brown eyes contemplated her. "You think I haven't said that already?"

"Well, try again."

She knew she sounded irritated. But Fairchild's attentions were an embarrassment as well as a liability. Zack shrugged and went out to the car. The back window slid down. She couldn't see Fairchild but Zack was talking, pointing, gesturing. A slight pause, then the same with more energy. It wasn't going well. How could he be so stubborn? She really didn't want to get in a car with him. Hurry up, Zack, she said to herself. Just make him go before the others get here.

But it was too late. Peter was already walking towards her.

64

"Well," said Peter, "I have my orders. But you don't have to do this, you know. Walter's obsessed with Fairchild, was blamed for him ever since he went off-piste in his teens and caused so much trouble. It defined Walter's career somewhat."

"Well, I just hope it isn't going to define mine," said Rose. Outside, Zack gave an extravagant shoulder shrug and walked off. The car remained. "But Walter's word is final, isn't it?"

Peter paused for a long time before answering. "I'm not the rebellious type, Rose. But I think he's hanging you out to dry here. How can he say you'd be safer driving off with Khovansky's main target than with any kind of plan we can put together? I'll back you up on this. If you don't want to go with Fairchild, don't. Send him away. We'll think of something else."

Rose's pause was shorter than Peter's. Craven's leadership and the resources of Moscow Station, the people who had her back, against one man with no loyalties who was already a walking target? There was no contest. Of course she'd stick with her own.

"I'll tell him," she said.

She stepped out through the security gate. Peter followed. But before she could cross to the car, a sharp squealing filled the air, tyres skidding on tarmac. A tatty old hatchback careered towards her, accelerating fast.

"Get down!" shouted Peter, but Rose had already seen the open window and the end of a gun barrel sticking out. She threw herself onto the ground and covered her head. Machine gun fire hammered. Bullets clattered on the iron gates. The car tore up the street, braked and reversed. Peter was lying on the ground next to her. The car's engine revved. It pulled out. It was coming back for another run. Behind her an alarm was going. Footsteps were running, but they weren't fast enough. The hatchback was accelerating towards them.

The limo door opened.

"Get in!"

It was Fairchild, shouting. Beside her, Peter didn't move. The hatchback was gaining ground.

"Now!" shouted Fairchild.

Rose got up and pelted across the road in the path of the oncoming car. She threw herself into the limo and slammed the door shut behind her as the hatchback ripped past, another salvo strafing the gates. The limo took off. Rose looked behind. Security guards were running out into the road now. They formed a huddle around the body on the ground.

"Peter!" The limo turned a corner. The Embassy was out of sight.

"There'll be more of them," said Fairchild. "We need to get out of Moscow."

Rose turned back. The choice had been made for her.

"I really hope you've got a bloody good plan."

"Yes. And some help. I'd advise you to fasten your seatbelt."

They swung round another corner. The driver's arms were solid and muscular. Her face was intent on the road with frequent glances up at the mirror. She was large, not young, in a jacket and shirt with permed dark hair. She braked suddenly to take a narrow side street. Rose noticed flecks in the glass window next to her.

"Is this bulletproof glass?"

"Standard on all our vehicles," was the response.

They came out on an expressway, blocked with traffic. They crawled to the next junction and turned off.

"Where are we going?" asked Rose.

"Nowhere. Not for a while, anyway."

"Behind us." That was the driver addressing Fairchild in Russian. They both turned. A black saloon was several vehicles behind.

"They've found us again," said Fairchild.

"Great," said Rose.

"Don't worry. She's one of our best drivers."

As if to prove it, they jumped a red light and turned twice in quick succession while the saloon was held at the signal.

"So what happened to you last night?" she asked.

"Sorry about that. Roman Morozov wanted to see me. I didn't have much choice in the matter. He's the one who's helping us."

"Helping us do what?"

"Get out of Moscow. Then out of Russia. Safe passage, paperwork."

"In exchange for what?"

Fairchild's hesitation was slight. "He wants me to kill Grom."

"And will you?"

He looked at her, his eyes grey and bland. "Yes."

"Again," said the driver. Another saloon was behind them now, closer than the last.

"Are they tracking us?" asked Rose.

"I don't think so."

"They're talking to each other, that's for sure."

"How far are we?" Fairchild asked the driver.

"Not far."

They gained a few seconds, then turned into a long narrow street. The driver braked sharply and reversed the car into a narrow gap between buildings. After a few seconds the FSB car shot past them. The driver waited a few more seconds, pulled out and turned the other way. Several turns later she pulled up in the middle of the road.

"The van," she said.

They got out. A rusty white van was parked in a driveway, its back door open. As soon as they got out of the limo, it moved off. They climbed into the van and shut the doors. The van set off in the opposite direction.

"I hope your driver's prepared, when they catch up with her again," said Rose.

"She'll lure them to a very public place."

"What, more public than the British Embassy, you mean? They just gunned down the Deputy Head of the UK's Mission to Russia!"

"Somewhere where they can't stage a drive-by in an unmarked car and then blame it on some dissident group. Once they realise we're not there, they'll lose interest. By which time, hopefully…"

"We're now in Roman's hands, I take it?" They were moving at a normal pace on a smooth road. No windows at the back so she couldn't see out, or see the driver beyond a headrest in the front.

"Very much so. He wants this guy dead as much as I do."

"Make that three of us," said Rose.

After a few minutes the van accelerated smoothly. They were on an expressway, one that wasn't clogged this time. Their speed was steady but not fast enough to draw others' attention.

"If Peter's dead…" started Rose.

"You'll read about it on the news."

"I can tell you're touched by it."

"What do you expect? I suppose Walter was in there with you?"

"Yes, he was. I didn't even know he was in Moscow."

"And what did he have to say for himself?"

"He talked about Grom."

Fairchild looked round at her. "What did he say about Grom?"

"He wanted to know what you said."

"Right. What else?"

"He said Grom was dangerous. But then, we already know that."

"So he didn't really say anything, then."

She wasn't in the mood to tackle Fairchild's animosity towards Walter. They lapsed into silence. After a long time they slowed again, coming off the expressway and turning left then right. The road surface was bumpy, not a city road.

They slowed to a halt and the driver got out and swung the doors open. The quiet after the noise of the engine was striking. They were in a goods yard next to a railway line. Stacks of timber were piled up in the distance. Rose smelled freshly cut wood and sawdust.

"You're to give me your mobile phones," said the driver, a portly man in working clothes.

"Why?" This Rose didn't like.

"Instructions from the Bear." He held out his hand and waited.

"Probably not a bad idea," said Fairchild. "We can't be sure the hackers haven't got hold of our numbers."

"Did you know about this?"

Fairchild shook his head and handed his phone over. They both waited. With a sigh, Rose did the same.

"Wait here," said the driver.

"What for?" asked Rose. He'd already turned back to the van. He looked round at Rose as if she were an idiot.

"The train."

He got in the van and drove off. They moved towards the rails. A short standalone wooden platform was positioned for loading. Elsewhere the ground was level with the tracks. No buildings or features, no one else around. They stood in the silence waiting.

She'd lost track of time when eventually she heard a distant clatter. A blot appeared in the far distance, seeming for ages to be coming no closer, but then the sound intensified and the shape grew larger. As the train came nearer it loomed above them. The engine roared as it passed them, although it wasn't moving quickly. Behind the engine were open cars piled with gravel and sand, cylindrical containers, box cars.

"This is a freight train." Rose turned to Fairchild. He was staring up at the cars.

"I suppose Morozov is all about freight," he said.

"What exactly did he tell you to do?"

"Come here and get on the next train. That's all I have."

"We're supposed to ride on this?"

"Well, it's the next train."

They were having to shout as the huge ironwork rolled past them. The cars seemed to carry on forever. The train was rolling slowly but Rose could hear no squeezing of brakes. Fairchild was frowning. Now she could see the end of the train in the distance, the last car.

"Although," said Fairchild, "he didn't actually say that the train was going to stop."

She stared at him. "You're joking." The fifth carriage from the end was passing them now.

Fairchild held his hands up. "What do we do? We can't call him and check."

The fourth car from the end passed by. He was waiting for her.

"Oh, for fuck's sake."

She started jogging, running alongside the carriages. She looked up at it, the one third from the end. It was a cylinder, with a metal ladder half way along it stopping at the top. In front of her at ground level the loading platform loomed, a wooden structure extending right across her path. She sped up. She could hear Fairchild behind her. The car second from the end started to come past her. She put on a spurt. Running flat out, she reached up and grabbed the grip bar at the back of the car and lifted her feet off the ground. She swung into the medal side. Her feet kicked out until they found the bottom rung of the ladder. The platform was five seconds away. Fairchild was running alongside the last car of the train. He reached for the last grip bar at the back of the carriage, and grabbed on. His legs came up just as the wooden floor of the platform rushed under them.

The sound of the metal wheels on the rails just below her feet was deafening. She manoeuvred herself and stuck her head out between the carriages. Fairchild was gone. She climbed up the ladder and turned backwards. Fairchild was on the roof of the car, lying flat. They caught each other's eye.

Away from the loading bay the train sped up, the rhythm of the moving parts below her feet getting faster, the wind getting colder. She found a way of perching on the ladder and wrapped her coat more tightly, looking out at distant roofs and chimneys across fields, criss-crossing power lines overhead. They went onto a bridge. The sound doubled in volume, echoing upward. The iron spans of the bridge flew past close enough to touch. She leaned out to see the river below.

Whether this was part of the plan or not, they were at least out of Moscow.

65

Roman rubbed his eyes after closing the last of the ledgers. It had been a long day, but despite everything he enjoyed being back. Retirement felt purposeless. He piled up the ledgers and pushed them over to Vadim to store in the safe. The office was back to how it should be. Kamila was right. A business like this didn't run itself.

On the desk in front of him was an envelope for Fairchild and the woman Rose. Vadim would organise getting it to the man who was looking after them. Vadim knew every subtle shade of the business. He had a hand in everything. In all types of endeavour, it was necessary to trust people, unavoidable.

Getting the paperwork was not easy. But if it were the last time Roman could do it, good that it was to free Fairchild. The net was closing. All Roman could do was hope that Fairchild would somehow find a way through it, and that his own hurt and obsession would push him onward. That he would not be tricked and flattered as others were. And that his feelings for this woman would not distract him.

Vadim moved about, putting everything in order for the night. Roman poured himself a shot from the bottle he kept on the shelf. A single shot at the end of an evening's work helped to calm him for sleep. He offered it to Vadim who declined. Roman had never seen Vadim drink. The vodka tasted clean, earthy, like home.

Roman moved to the window, stretching his legs. How many other *vory* bosses stayed up to the early hours like this, reviewing every detail? These days they were too willing to leave things to well-spoken subordinates who told them what they wanted to hear. No wonder it was so easy for the long fingers of the government to reach so far.

"You were right about her, that woman," he said to Vadim, who was slowly locking up. It was a sop, a peace offering. Until now he hadn't mentioned it. Vadim looked up sharply, but then nodded. He always was a man of few words. Roman knocked back the rest of the vodka, feeling it burn in his throat. He handed the glass to Vadim. One shot at night was enough, when drinking on his own. Outside the window the car was parked, sleek along the pavement. He looked at his own reflection in the window, an old man.

His stomach twinged. It must be tiredness. Behind him, Vadim seemed to be moving more slowly, checking every lock on every cupboard. Roman wished he would hurry up. But Vadim always wanted to do everything thoroughly, correctly. Roman was lucky to have him. Such a silent, obedient servant. Always so loyal, always.

"Ready," said Vadim briefly. Just as well, as Roman was feeling weak, sweaty. He turned and put a hand on the table to steady himself. Vadim was fastening his jacket. Roman took two paces and his gut exploded. He fell to his knees and bent over, grinding his teeth.

"Vadim." He needed help. He was never sick. "Help me, Vadim." But Vadim stayed where he was, watching, waiting.

That was when Roman knew for sure. He suspected it, ever since what happened to Kamila, but at that moment he fully understood. Everything fell into place. Oh, Vadim.

His insides burned and he tasted blood. His ears roared. He fell onto his side. He didn't think it would be like this, not like this. He tried to speak again but couldn't. Vadim wasn't moving. Roman couldn't draw breath. His heart was racing. His mouth was wet with spit and vomit.

If Vadim had to betray him, why like this? Why not a gun, a knife? All their time together, then to kill him like a woman would? This was not how the Bear should die. He wanted to weep. He looked up. Vadim stood staring down, his eyes no sadder than usual.

That was the last thing Roman saw.

66

Vadim stood and watched his employer die. Not just his employer: his lifelong friend, the centre of his existence for more years than he wanted to count. Roman was a fool. Roman should never have come back to Moscow. He should have left Alexei to his own devices. But he had to meddle and disrupt everything. And it cost him his life.

The world was changing. Alexei, for all his conceits, understood that. Roman, stubborn old fighter that he was, tried to stop it. But it would not be stopped. The brute force that was the will of the Russian government swept in like a tidal wave, destroying whatever it found in its path. If the Kremlin wanted your money or your supply lines or your silence, you gave it or you lost everything. The biggest mafia gang of all, it showed its strength and you got into line. Roman of all people should have understood that. But he would never have accepted it.

Oh, he wouldn't approve of the method. A stabbing or a shooting, please, Vadim! But Vadim had to be sure, couldn't risk it going wrong. Vadim had his orders now. Grom had sought him out, explained what was needed. Vadim could see what was coming. Roman was finished, had been since the moment he decided to come back to Moscow. The only question was how. An arrest, a show trial, a trumped-up charge, a phony sentence in a filthy prison? That, for the Bear? No. In younger life he could have managed it but he was old now, would waste away in such a place. Better this, painful but quick. It was his own fault. Same with Kamila: that's why she had to go too. They thought they could resist, but no one can.

In the Russian story, everybody dies. Roman used to say that. But this way Morozov would live on. Vadim could keep the business intact. Paying dues to the government, doing what was needed to survive. But still here, still serving the people, helping ordinary Russians make ends meet and live their lives. It wasn't what Vadim wanted, for himself or the Bear. But of all the paths open to him, this was the best, the cleanest.

Well, it was over now. Roman's bulk lay still on the office floor. Vadim picked up the envelope that was on Roman's desk, switched off the light, closed the door behind him and left.

67

Some hours later the train came to a halt in another goods yard. Fairchild couldn't feel his face. His fingers ached from gripping cold metal. From his position on top of the box car he couldn't see Rose, but he knew she was there, down between the carriages, hopefully more sheltered than he was. They were travelling east. Roman had shared nothing of his plans from this point forward.

The attack at the Embassy was a much closer call than Fairchild would have liked, for either of them. Grom was afraid of no one. Power like that was chilling. Roman was right about leaving Moscow to regroup and form a plan. When his heavies had picked Fairchild up at the station in Moscow, the old gangster had probably saved his life.

Some unhitching and shunting was going on with a formation on the next rails. It looked as though they would be here a while. He climbed down. Rose already had, and was stamping her feet on the ground. She had a 'what next?' expression on her face. Clearly, he had a 'I've no idea' expression on his, because she didn't even ask the question and walked off saying she needed to find somewhere to pee. Fairchild hung around watching the unhurried rearrangement of goods cars, and keeping an eye on the slow approach of a man in a dark jacket, who was walking steadily up the length of the train smoking a cigarette. By the time he got close, Rose had returned. The man wore a train driver's uniform, of sorts.

"You are our guests from Moscow?" he asked. Fairchild said nothing. "Don't worry," said the driver. "Roman asked me to look out for you. You can trust me. Come."

He led them to a box car and invited them to climb in through the side door. When Fairchild's eyes adjusted, he saw mattresses in the corners; this carriage had been used for similar purposes in the past. The driver disappeared but came back with warm meat-filled sweet pastries in a paper bag, and bottles of Coke. Rose asked him how far they'd be going.

"You'll know when we arrive."

He left. Shortly afterwards, the train jerked into motion again.

They ate the pastries. When Fairchild screwed up the paper bag he found something inside, a key with a fob on which was written a street name and house number. He showed it to Rose then put it in his pocket. No doubt all would be revealed when the time was right.

It became the pattern of their existence, hour after hour of rumbling along in the dark followed by a few minutes' light and air in another freight yard. Fairchild tried to keep track of time. After several days, possibly somewhere between Yekaterinburg and Omsk if they were still going east, Rose, from her dark corner of the box car, started a conversation.

"Did you know," she said, "that Kamila was forty-two years old?"

"I would have said she was younger," said Fairchild carefully. "Why?"

"There's a lot we never knew about her. She lied to me about everything, not just the false information. Her whole persona was an act. And yet, I can't be angry with her. There's something about her that made you see the human in her."

He hesitated. Damn it, he thought, I'll risk it. "I wasn't her lover, you know."

He expected something – defensiveness, denial that she'd ever thought that – but there was none.

"I know. She told me about him. It was someone she met in Moscow, in one of the bars. They were going to set up together. That's why she stole the money and did all the things she did."

Something was surfacing in Fairchild's mind, something that had been submerged in there for some time.

"Roman told me that Kamila had a good understanding of Khovansky, that she'd opened his eyes about what a danger he was. As if he realised, when he finally met her, that there was more to her than he'd assumed."

"Didn't stop him killing her, though."

"He didn't actually say he killed her. He said she didn't survive their encounter. He sounded like he was sorry she was dead."

A slight pause. "Our source at the police said it was a clean kill. One shot in the head, another in the chest."

Fairchild tried to isolate exactly what was troubling him about his conversation with Roman. "It doesn't make sense that he would execute her like that. It doesn't fit with what he said."

"But Roman thought she killed Alexei, didn't he? Surely he killed her for that. For his reputation if nothing else."

"Kamila didn't kill Alexei," said Fairchild.

Another pause. "Then who did?"

"Roman did."

Her surprise was tangible, even in the dark. "He killed his own son? After giving him the business? Why?"

"It was *because* he gave him the business. And Alexei messed it up. Roman wanted to give Alexei the freedom to grow into a man, by making his own decisions. But he couldn't bring himself to stand by and watch Alexei make the wrong decisions. Freedom to become a man, but a man like Roman, not a man who was intent on doing the very things Roman didn't want. That's why Roman came to Moscow, to try and influence Alexei. But clearly it didn't work. He realised he had to do something drastic to seize back control and rectify his mistake, even if it meant sacrificing his son."

A long silence as they rocked along steadily. "The history of Russia," said Rose. She was lying on her back sounding philosophical. "A brief period of freedom followed by a change of heart and an even more totalitarian regime than before. That's Peter's analysis. So if Roman feels that strongly about keeping the Kremlin out of his business, and he thought Kamila could help, it doesn't make sense that he killed her."

"Maybe he didn't," said Fairchild. "Or maybe he did – but it wasn't really his decision."

The atmosphere changed. Rose was computing what he'd just said, the same implications forming in his mind as well. What if Roman Morozov, despite his best intentions, were no longer in charge? What if the FSB, controlled by Grom, had already swallowed him up? What did that mean for the two of them in this train carriage? What was going to happen when they finally got off this train, if they had an opportunity to get off it at all?

Someone had to say it out loud. He was glad it was her.

"John, if Morozov is that compromised, if Roman's effectively no longer in charge, we're heading straight into another trap."

It was some time before he could think of something to say, the only line of hope he had to cling to.

"Roman wants this to work. He wants Grom dead. He's a clever man, a survivor. If he knows how tight the net's drawn, he'll think of a way through." He tried to sound more positive than he felt.

More silence. Another stop, another goods yard, more shunting and hanging around. It was dark outside this time. Fairchild recognised something about the horizon, how the train line ran alongside the river.

"I think," he said to Rose, "that this is Irkutsk."

He first met Roman in Irkutsk, years ago. This was the Bear's home turf. He'd brought them to the centre of his empire, three thousand miles from Moscow. Fairchild chose to take comfort from it.

They cleared Irkutsk at five thirty in the evening Moscow time, nine thirty local time. But before they'd got back up to speed the train started braking again. They couldn't have another scheduled stop this soon. They both got to their feet. Was this good or bad? Fairchild reached into his bag for the spare gun; Roman had equipped him well.

"Take this." He handed the gun to Rose as the train eased to a halt. They stood either side of the door, waiting.

Silence. Then a loud metallic *tap-tap-tap* on the outside of the car. They did nothing. More silence. *Tap-tap-tap*. Fairchild, his gun hidden from view, slid the door open a crack. Below stood a maintenance engineer holding a steel rod, the kind used for checking the train undercarriage. The guy gestured him out. Fairchild scanned the area, a long siding almost directly on Lake Baikal itself. He couldn't see much in the dark. Rose moved closer to him, gun ready.

"I'll cover you," she said quietly. Fairchild dropped to the ground, kept low and hurried away from the door, no longer trying to hide the gun. The engineer muttered and backed off when he saw it. There was no other sound. Rose jumped down and moved in the other direction. They both paused, listening. The engineer tutted, strode up to the car and slid the door shut with a clang. He wandered off shaking his head and the train lurched back into motion.

"Hey!" Rose called after him, her voice battling the crescendo of the train. "Which way?"

Without stopping or turning, the engineer pointed towards the lake. They went that way. A single road ran between the railway line and the lake, lined on both sides with cabins. Rose used a head torch to find the numbers of the houses. Fairchild shadowed her, gun in hand, straining every sense as they moved around in the near-darkness. The train faded to silence. Their footsteps made the only sound.

"Here!"

Rose was standing outside a small single-storey cabin on the lake side of the track. She'd found the number that matched the key fob the driver had given them. He gave her the key and she tried it in the lock. It fitted. She pushed the door open slowly, silently. They waited. Nothing. Guns ready, they crept in, circling to check each of its rooms. Nothing and no one.

Rose flicked on a light. The place was plainly furnished and had a sitting area with table and chairs, an ancient-looking kerosene heater, a kitchen, a tiny rudimentary bathroom and a bedroom. The kitchen was empty of food except for two bottles of beer in the fridge.

They looked at each other. "So what do we do?" asked Rose.

"Wait and see what happens, I suppose. Getting this far is a good sign, surely."

There was only one bed, a double. Rose slept first. Fairchild spent three hours combing the cabin for any signs of bugs, booby traps, surveillance. Nothing. Then Rose emerged and he went to bed fully clothed. He wasn't expecting to sleep, but he must have done because the sound of shouting woke him up. He could hear Rose and a man. A door slammed. He jumped up, grabbed the gun and ran out. Rose was standing astride a man face down on the ground, her gun digging into the back of his head.

"He was coming up to the door," she said.

"Is he armed?"

"Cover him. I'll check." She drew back and frisked him while Fairchild pointed his gun at the guy's head.

"What's your business here?" he said to the guy in Russian.

"I told her! I'm here to give you the package! The documents! From Roman!"

"He's clean," said Rose. Then, to him: "Sorry. We have to be careful."

The man sat up, revealing a padded envelope he'd been carrying in his hand. He could have been the brother of the engineer who tapped on the box car. Maybe he was.

"Yes, I know, I know. Roman called me. He said things were bad. Don't trust anybody, he said. He changed the plans. First you were staying in Irkutsk. But he said take them somewhere else. And careful who you tell! Make sure you're not followed. You'll get the package as arranged, but when you get it, hide it. Take it to them alone. Check no one is watching. So here I am. Here is the package. Please, I'd like to go now."

Rose took the package off him, turning it over to examine it. The man got up and brushed himself down.

"You're sure you weren't followed?" asked Fairchild.

He held his hands up. "This is a tiny place. Just some cabins, one road. There's nobody here. See for yourself."

Rose had opened the envelope. Inside were two passports, visas, tickets and printed itineraries. She turned to the Russian.

"You should go, quickly. And take care. Spasiba."

He left. A few seconds later an engine turned and caught, and the sound faded as he drove off. Fairchild sat on the table opposite Rose. He rubbed his arms. It was light outside, but early.

"So Roman was locked down," said Fairchild. "But he managed to get a message out in time."

"That saved our lives, probably," said Rose. "I'm not sure how long we would have lasted in Irkutsk." She was looking at the paperwork. "Mongolia."

"It's the nearest border from here. I think I might have that beer now."

"At this time in the morning?"

He didn't care. Now they'd established they were still hidden, he felt almost lightheaded. He opened the fridge. "You?" he called.

"Go on, then." He got both beers out and began a search for a bottle opener. The kitchen wasn't equipped for actual cooking of any form. Rose, at the table, was examining the padded envelope. With a penknife she tore along one of the long seams. Fairchild hit paydirt: a sticky opener in the back of a drawer amid an odd collection of non-culinary tools. He opened both bottles, set them down on the table and sat. Rose was now working her way around all the seams. She pulled the back away, revealing the dark fabric of the padding material inside. Fairchild lifted the beer to take a swig. But before the liquid hit his mouth, he froze.

From within the padding, Rose's fingers had isolated an object. She held it up: a flat round disc of circuitry. A tracking device.

They looked at each other. "How long do you think we've got?" she asked.

313

"If they were already following that guy, they'll be here already."

A smash of glass was followed by a clatter and a low-pitched *whump!* They both dropped to the floor. The ceiling flickered. A wave of heat washed over them.

The kitchen was on fire.

68

Rose could feel the heat on her back as she crouched. She could smell petrol or some other accelerant. Flames licked the panelled roof above their heads and smoke leached out of the kitchen. Her throat itched.

"There's no way out at the back. They're trying to flush us out of the front," she said.

"There's nowhere to go down there. It's just the lake."

"There's a boat. I checked it out earlier while you were asleep."

He looked at her. "Can you get it started?"

"Yes." She'd already hot-wired it. It was only a simple motor launch. But it seemed prudent to have the option if they needed it. "We just have to get to it," she said.

He looked around. "Okay." He suggested a plan. It wasn't much of a plan, but good enough if they got the timing right.

"Let's do it."

She emptied the beer out of the bottles, tore the tablecloth in half and stuffed half into each bottle. Fairchild pulled over the kerosene heater, took out the fuel reservoir and poured it into the bottles. The room was full of thick smoke. Fairchild crawled towards the door with the bottles. Rose bent low and ran to the bedroom. She knew as soon as Fairchild opened the door; an explosion of gunfire started up. He was ready for them, out of shot behind the door. But these people weren't going to hang around outside.

The bedroom window wasn't designed to be fully opened. After a few seconds playing with the casement she closed it and smashed the glass with the handle of her gun She ducked and froze, waiting for a reaction from outside. But by now Fairchild was engaged in a firefight, emerging from behind the door long enough to get several shots off each time. The answering volleys got closer and closer. That and the roaring fire covered the sound of breaking glass. She wrapped a bedsheet around her hand and worked quickly to clear all the glass out of the pane. Fairchild was drawing the shooters further and further in. He'd crawled into the bedroom away from the cabin door and was firing off burst after burst, the responses moving ever nearer. The thin dividing bedroom wall was scorched and smoking. Flames danced above the headboard of the bed. Rose grabbed the mattress and positioned it like a ramp below the window. She spread the remaining bedsheet along the bottom of the pane and folded it over on itself. For this to work, speed was critical.

Fairchild was fully in the bedroom now. A shadow passed beyond him through the doorway. One of them was in the house. Fairchild picked up a bottle and threw it. It smashed on the opposite wall and ignited in the flames. Someone screamed. This was the moment.

"Go!" Fairchild shouted. But she was already up on the sill, then out. She landed and ran. She heard another smash as Fairchild threw the other bottle. She stopped by the boundary fence and turned to cover him. Smoke was leaching out of the window. A shout started up from within: they'd realised what was happening, but Fairchild was at the window and down on the ground before the shooting started. Rose aimed several shots over Fairchild's head into the window, turned, and ran.

She had to trust he was right behind her: no time to check. She pounded down to the beach, then along to the jetty. Something on the land side caught her eye for a split second, but she didn't have time to process it. Her steps hammered along the jetty to the boat. She slipped the knot that she'd retied herself earlier, and turned the starter. The rudder was in the water ready to go. Fairchild was sprinting up the jetty now but he had company, a man twenty paces behind and another further back. Rose turned the boat and had her hand on the throttle when Fairchild landed in the boat. She flung the gear forward and they powered away. Fairchild turned in the bottom of the boat and fired relentlessly at the figure now lying prone on the jetty. She kept going full throttle until they were well out of range, then slowed down and looked back. A giant plume of smoke towered over what remained of the cabin, and was drifting over the shore. She couldn't see any moving figures. Fairchild was sitting up, reloading his gun.

"You picked up the paperwork?" he asked.

"Yes." Rose patted the zipped pockets of her trousers. Then she remembered what she'd seen. She realised what had caught her eye, and a lot more.

She pulled back the throttle so that they were idling. Fairchild looked up.

"There was a man sitting on a bench. Just above the jetty."

"What was he doing?"

"Nothing. Just sitting there. As if he were – supervising. I've seen him before, Fairchild. Near my flat in Moscow. He was watching me. Not trying to hide it. Just sitting. It's him, isn't it?"

She could hear the fear in her own voice. Even immobile, from a distance, the man had something about him, a presence. Fairchild stared back at the shore. They were too far now to make out a person. He turned to her.

"Take me back," he said quietly.

"That's what he wants you to do."

It was peaceful now, out so far on this vast lake, the only sounds the lapping of water and the engine ticking over. The smoke was drifting further out over the lake and gathering over the water. Fairchild scanned the lakeside.

"Drop me downwind of the smoke. Don't try and wait. Go east, to the other side. Or back to Irkutsk, up the river. They won't expect that."

It was as if he didn't hear her last remark. She turned the boat and slowly powered up.

"You want this passport?" she asked. He shook his head.

She went as close as she dared but he still had a hell of a swim. The shoreline looked hazy from there. He'd packed his gun and a few other things into a drybag that he tucked into his waist. She put the gear into neutral and he slipped into the water.

"Goodbye, John." He looked up at her, then turned and started swimming.

She didn't try and dissuade him. It was his life, his decision. He thought he could get a shot off, surprise him somehow, but he could have no realistic hope of getting away himself.

She understood, she thought, why killing Grom was worth that much to him. But she did feel, as she powered up and steered towards Irkutsk, a certain emptiness at the thought that she would probably never see him again.

69

The coldness of the water made him gasp. He shouldn't have been shocked, should have remembered that Lake Baikal was still frozen solid three weeks ago. Exactly the kind of geographical fact that his parents crammed into him like they were stuffing a turkey. His limbs seemed to fade away as he swam. His face went numb and his head throbbed. Keep moving, keep moving, even if you can't feel a thing. He forced himself to do it, moving smoothly without splashing, keeping low in the water.

He aimed east of the cabin to work back on land towards the jetty. All he had was the element of surprise. But if Rose was right, he didn't even have that. Grom would be expecting him. This was a man who seemed to sense what people were thinking and keep ahead of them. Combine this with the might of the FSB within a barely accountable global power, and Grom was something very dangerous indeed.

If Fairchild valued his own survival he wouldn't be doing this. He was doing this for his parents, for thirty years of his life wasted, for Dimitri, for Roman, maybe even for Kamila. For Rose and what she went through in Lali, for Katya and all the others. Besides, what would there be for him after this? The edifice of his life had crumbled to ruins. He was in love with a woman who could barely look at him. For it to end today, on this shore, as long as he could place one judicious bullet, would be meaning enough. Just one bullet would do.

The shore was a steep climb. Baikal, shaped like a test tube, plummeted for a mile below its surface: more useless facts. He started shivering as the air cooled his wet clothes. He stripped down to the waist and jettisoned everything except the gun. Barefoot, he weaved further inland and double-backed above the smouldering cabin to the jetty. People were still moving around by the cabin as he skirted above. There, on a bench overlooking the jetty, sat a man facing out to the lake.

Fairchild slowed. He approached and paused. This was all too easy. But no one was watching, no one was near. He was shaking from the cold; he needed to get closer to be certain of the shot. He had to get this right. There'd be no second chance.

He took three more paces, four. He raised the gun and aimed.

The figure on the bench stood, turned, and looked straight at him.

70

"So you came back," said a low-pitched, hearty voice. "You made a promise to the Bear, didn't you, John? That's why he helped you. Drinking buddies, are you? They're the closest buddies of all. Except maybe killing buddies. People you drink with, people you kill with. That's a special bond. But you don't have to honour a promise to a dead man."

Fairchild lowered the gun. The man's English was absolutely natural, no hint of an accent except a possible slight Scottish drawl. He was wearing a smart dark woollen coat, suit and tie. Sixties, seventies, maybe, but in good shape. White hair, healthy skin, something very solid and direct about him. Likeable. A decent bloke, that's what you'd think. He stood with his hands in his pockets, totally relaxed.

"I'm not armed, don't worry." He gave Fairchild a glimpse of his gloved hands before pocketing them again.

"Did you kill Roman?" asked Fairchild. He kept the gun primed. He could shoot the guy any time. May as well satisfy his curiosity first.

"Me personally? No. I may have given other people reason to. How do you persuade a young chick to leave the nest? Coax it gently, supervising every tentative step, heaping encouragement on its downy little head? Much quicker just to set fire to the nest. But you know this," said Grom. "You're a manipulator too. I've been doing my research. You've done a lot to be proud of."

"I'm not like you," said Fairchild.

"Aren't you? You don't use people, get them to do what you want?"

Fairchild didn't want to talk about himself. "What about Kamila? Someone else did your dirty work there as well?"

"Ah! So you know it wasn't Roman. You're clever, more so than I imagined." If Grom was expecting some kind of response, he didn't get one. "Kamila was a slight miscalculation. I was sure Roman would destroy her for what she'd done. But I didn't reckon that when she and Roman finally met, they would click. He saw her true strengths, beyond the labels she'd been given. They would have worked well together. And we couldn't have that. Lovely girl, though."

"You're all heart, aren't you?" Fairchild couldn't help the sneer. The man took such pride in pushing people around like pieces on a chess board. His tone sparked a flash of anger, resentment, in the older man's eyes.

"No, John, that's you, remember? It was the first thing I noticed about you, when I saw you at that gathering in St Petersburg. The way you looked at her. You were so eager to hide it, and yet, you didn't quite manage it. It got me interested. And that was before I knew who you were."

Fairchild went back to that evening in the Winter Palace, his sense of being observed. Sutherland was there? He must have kept a low profile.

"And that question she asked you, about the Russian with the missing fingers," the man continued. "That rang a bell when one of my people reported it back to me. Yes, we had a few people listening. Those networking evenings can be very worthwhile. Once I'd done some digging into your background, I realised what that little comment of hers meant. Until that point I didn't know where Dimitri had disappeared to, but you led me right to him. You and she."

His expression was indulgent, patronising. "You shouldn't wear your heart on your sleeve, John. It'll get you into all kinds of trouble. And her. I knew she'd take the bait, trotting off to Georgia, starry-eyed with the notion that she'd bag some mega-agent and bask in the glory. Her boss lapped it all up as well. It's just too easy sometimes. And you! What an old romantic, inserting yourself into a hopeless siege to rescue the love of your life! I was curious to see what you'd do. Impressive you both got out. Pity she was less than grateful. She doesn't even seem to like you very much. Climbing the greasy pole, that's her game, isn't it? Never mind. That's the way it goes. I bet you're wondering about my accent, though. Or lack thereof. You're right there. We're both speaking our mother tongue."

Fairchild tried not to react, but there must have been something, a blink, a twitch.

Grom smiled. "How much did Walter tell you? He's the only one who really got close to the bottom of it all. Pity no one much listens to him these days. Did he tell you my real name?"

He should shoot the guy right now. But maybe he had a chance first to get to the truth, discover all the things he knew Walter had never told him.

"Your name is Gregory Sutherland," he said.

"Good to meet you. It seems we've only recently become aware of each other's existence. Come, sit for a while. Let's catch up. You can shoot me afterwards. Plenty of time for that."

He turned away from Fairchild and sat on the bench. Fairchild edged round to the side of him, keeping his distance. No way was he going to sit down next to this guy. He was still shivering. The vast lake rippled in front of them. Was Rose still out on it somewhere?

"It's pretty impressive, really," Sutherland was saying. "They were careful, Mum and Dad, keeping you at boarding school, at arm's length. Then I suppose they got sloppy. Maybe they thought after ten years I was well and truly off the radar, buried somewhere the wrong side of the Iron Curtain. Maybe they even convinced themselves that the car accident was real after all. But you got lucky that night. Of course you realise that. Just a quirk of timing, that you went walkabout just as my rent-a-mob showed up. Dimitri helped, of course. Deciding not to say anything. He gave you a second lease of life. If I'd known about you I'd have been after you from that moment on. What was that, thirty years ago? I'd never forget about the Fairchilds. I liked my life back then, and they took it away from me. No, Dimitri's silence saved you. He wasn't silent at the end, I have to say. There are times when one has to carry out these matters oneself. It just seems appropriate."

Fairchild stood as if hypnotised. Why didn't he just raise the gun and fire, stop this callous voice? Somehow he couldn't.

"You strike me as the hands-on type, John. This set-up you have, all these companies across the world, it's very discreetly run. As I said, I've been doing my research. With the resources of the Russian government, ferreting out information about who owns what isn't difficult. These people will do anything if you persuade them it's to tackle an enemy of Mother Russia. But it's your personal skills as well, John, all those languages, all that knowledge you've amassed, the contacts that put you right at home anywhere in the world. Anywhere but your actual home, of course."

Fairchild lowered the gun. Sutherland had been busy. He'd got a pretty good understanding of Fairchild's whole operation and had even figured out Fairchild's aversion to the UK.

"They haven't treated you at all well, have they?" continued Sutherland. "They never told you the truth. They've let you tie yourself in knots, more interested in covering their own backsides than doing right by you. The more fools they. They could have brought you inside, made good use of you. What an asset you would have been! But instead they turned you into an enemy."

"Is that what you think about yourself?" said Fairchild. "That they didn't appreciate you? That's why you had it in for my parents. Maybe it was more that they didn't appreciate being betrayed by one of their own. Or someone posing as one of their own. Whatever you are."

Sutherland ignored Fairchild's contempt. "There's a lot you don't know, Fairchild. You think Walter's telling you everything, even now? Come on. Wait for them to be honest with you, you'll be waiting forever. I can put you straight. I'll give you a fresh perspective. You might find some of it hard to believe. Maybe you'd prefer not to know. Just go around for the rest of your life wondering why you're banging your head against the same brick wall. You must have a pretty sore head already by now. You kill me now, you'll never get to the truth."

Sutherland was looking at him. The man's eyes flicked from left to right. Fairchild reacted straight away, but the click of a catch told him he was already too late.

There were two of them. One was the man who'd chased him onto the jetty. Both were aiming straight at him. If he thought he could lift his gun and get a shot away before they could fire, he'd have done it. But it was too late. He'd let this mind-manipulator soothe him into inaction, until the opportunity passed. Once again, he'd been played. He'd failed.

"Drop the gun."

Fairchild did so on the jetty man's curt order. The man stepped forward and kicked it away. A pause. Fairchild clenched every muscle. He hoped it would be quick. But something happened that didn't make sense. Jetty man turned and pointed the gun at Sutherland.

It was no trick; Sutherland's eyes widened. His jaw clenched and he swallowed. This was not something he was expecting.

"You. Run." The other man was talking to him. Fairchild didn't understand.

"Run!" shouted the man, and fired high, over Fairchild's shoulder.

Fairchild turned and ran.

71

He pelted flat out along the track, expecting any second to be thrown to the ground by bolts in his back. Surely that was what they wanted. They wanted it to look as though they shot him trying to escape. Or else it was just sport. But as he sprinted, no bullets came. He ran round the curve of the lake until his legs were burning. He stumbled and fell to the ground, heaving for breath, lungs aching.

Still nothing. He lifted his head and looked back. Three figures were standing by the bench. Two of them had guns aimed at the third. None of them was looking in his direction.

He crawled into the undergrowth and watched. Sutherland was talking, gesturing. Remonstrating. The others stood solid. Sutherland seemed to weaken suddenly. He reached out for the arm of the bench. One of the men lowered his gun, about to step forward.

What happened then was so quick Fairchild didn't catch it. A man was on the ground. Two men grappled with each other. There was a shot. Someone else fell to the ground. It was Sutherland who was still standing, with a gun in his hand. He aimed and shot again, once then twice.

That was it. One old man stood over two bodies. Then his eyes lifted. He was looking for Fairchild.

Now Sutherland had a gun and Fairchild didn't. Fairchild looked around him. All he could do was run, try to draw him somewhere to gain advantage. He tensed, about to get to his feet. Sutherland was already moving in his direction. But then the old man slowed, looking up.

He was staring into the sky beyond Fairchild. A distant droning got louder. Fairchild turned and saw it. A helicopter was approaching, coming from Irkutsk. The surface of the lake roughened. It was flying low. Sutherland paused, staring up. He was some distance away but his posture seemed to change. It was as if in that moment it was sinking in. Something had happened beyond here, back in Moscow, that changed everything. Whatever it was, Sutherland was no longer the hunter. He had become the prey.

The helicopter kept coming, the sound growing all the time. Sutherland turned and strode away. A flash of something on the other side of the railway. Sirens. They were sending in police, everybody for this guy. Whether the helicopter could see Fairchild or not he didn't know, but it was Sutherland it was tracking. Another long goods train was snaking its way along the railway line, separating Sutherland from the road. His black coat was just about visible as he made his way alongside the train. He disappeared from Fairchild's view behind the row of cabins. The helicopter hovered above.

Squeals of sirens now, and vehicles were congregating around the station platform. The train kept moving slowly, steadily, right through the middle. Fairchild heard shouts, gunfire. Still the helicopter hung there, its hammering deafening. The train kept going. More shouts, men in uniform running.

The train cleared the platform. Uniforms swarmed across the tracks, invading the road where the cabins were, covering every piece of ground, kicking down doors. The helicopter moved up the shore, did a slow turn and came back.

The search slowed. The copter lifted and turned back to Irkutsk. The uniforms were standing now, pointing, looking around.

Their prey had escaped.

Fairchild waited until the last of them had gone. He got up, rubbing his freezing body. The warmth from his burst of running was long gone. He walked back to the bench. The bodies and weapons had been taken away. He walked along the road between the cabins, moving silently, listening and watching. Every cabin had a door hanging open. Fairchild crept up to each one, combed every room inside, checked every piece of fencing, every shed, every wall. The burned cabin was a blackened mess. Along the railway he worked his way up the platform, checking every storage unit and gully. The searchers hadn't missed anything. Sutherland was gone.

Fairchild sat on the jetty staring out at the lake. He should have shot the guy. Why didn't he? Because Sutherland knew that Fairchild didn't trust MI6. Sutherland played on Fairchild's alienation from Walter and the Service. He used it to talk his way out. There was nothing in what he said. There were no further secrets to discover. The guy was just a traitor, so enraged at being uncovered that he'd taken it upon himself to exact revenge. And when it finally caught up with him, he hinted at conspiracies and cover-ups just to protect himself. Fairchild's anger at himself warmed him. After everything Sutherland had done, Fairchild had let the man go.

The only upside was that the Russian authorities now seemed to be after him as well. Hopefully they'd find him. But if they didn't, Fairchild would be ready next time. He wouldn't make the same mistake again.

72

Ulan Bator, the concrete capital in the middle of Mongolia's sparse plains, probably had its points of interest, but Rose was there purely because that was where the train went and it was the first place of any size outside Russia with an airport. It was well able to provide what Rose most needed – sleep, news, decent food – and she didn't have to wait long before Walter arrived and they were catching up inside one of the city's many decent Chinese restaurants.

"So you got out of Russia quite easily, in the end?" asked Walter, delicately folding a duck pancake.

"Yes, and I'd like to know why." Rose was working her way indelicately through a mountain of prawn crackers. Her metabolism was still playing catch-up after Lali. "Even if they weren't expecting me at Irkutsk there should have been patrols at the station, extra checks on the train. The passport could have been flagged. I had none of that, Walter. I don't understand it."

"Things changed, that's why. They were called off. It all happened rather quickly."

"All what?"

"Well, as you know, there's always been a question mark over Sutherland's real identity. The Fairchilds developed a theory that Khovansky was a sleeper agent inserted into the UK, who managed to convince everyone that he was British and rise up through the ranks of MI6 to a fairly influential position. I went into all this in huge detail and eventually had to draw a different conclusion. The reason why his legend was so perfect, so beyond suspicion to the intelligence service researchers, is that he really was British. He was born there, grew up in Scotland, family, education all exactly as per his record. His achievement therefore is even greater that we thought. Rather than a Russian who persuaded the British he was British—"

"He's a Brit who persuaded the Russians he's Russian?"

"Precisely, my dear. No mean feat. We might never know exactly how he did it. When he was working for us and passing secrets to the Soviets, did he persuade his handlers that he was Russian? Or did he concoct a legend later, after he'd already crossed over? He must have had some help either way. And a great deal of foresight and nerve. But that's Sutherland. He gave the KGB a good period of his life and in exchange built up a considerable power base. He deceived them for decades and gained their complete trust to use for his own ends. He also weathered the regime change. The KGB became the FSB, but Khovansky, really Sutherland, remained in place. Well, until now."

"Until now? Is this what's changed?"

"We had ourselves a perfect storm, you see. Sutherland with the Russians dancing to his tune, making use of the inner machinery of one of the world's most corrupt and oppressive governments. Peter and I had a little discussion and agreed to address the issue. We do of course have our own ways of influencing the FSB. We introduced the idea that Khovansky's Russian identity was a fake, and that he is in fact British. We also managed to implicate the man in a couple of recent leaks. Quite handy for us, as it deflected attention away from our own people. As you know, the best kinds of lies are those that are close to the truth. Their own checks clearly verified our story. Which resulted in an instant death sentence for Sutherland."

Rose's progress with the crackers slowed. "He was there, by the lake, you know that, don't you? Fairchild could have got away with me, but he went back to confront him. Kill him, in fact."

"Our best guess is that news of Khovansky's real identity surfaced during the course of the operation to track the two of you down, which led to the FSB agents who were there under his direction being ordered to turn on him and arrest him."

"But that's not what happened."

"No." Walter spooned hoisin sauce and rolled his last pancake tightly like a cigar. "It seems he got away, even though they sent a sizeable team to apprehend him. Slid out and vanished when there seemed to be no way out. Something he's good at."

"How old is this guy?"

"Older than me, my dear. But his strength comes from the mind games he plays, not physical force."

"Well, Fairchild may have had an opportunity to get away as well. Not that he was trying to. I have to say, Walter, I assumed he wasn't going to make it. He could be in the lake, for all we know."

"Indeed. They could both be. But somehow…" Walter's voice trailed off as a waitress approached with a tray of food, most of which Rose had ordered.

"If Fairchild is alive, he could be anywhere," she said after the waitress left. "What would Sutherland do? Where would he go now?"

"Anywhere in the world except Russia. He's effectively in exile. His power base is destroyed. Given Russia's global reach, he may have to go into hiding, change his identity. Hopefully he'll remain impotent but he's lost none of his manipulative abilities."

"Will he try and go after Fairchild, do you think?"

"Well, my dear, there's a reason why for all these years I never shared any of this with John. He would have tried to find him, the man who killed his parents. As a consequence, Sutherland would have discovered him. While both Fairchild and Sutherland were unaware of each other's existence, Fairchild was safe from him. Fairchild will never believe I kept things from him for his own protection. But that's by-the-by now. Sutherland will pursue him. He's not a man who forgets. He may even try to use you again."

"You think that Fairchild's in danger from Sutherland? Surely it's the other way round. Fairchild went back to kill the guy. He promised Roman he would kill him. That's why Roman was helping us."

"He'll try, I expect," said Walter. "He may even succeed. Or Sutherland will. But there's something worse than one or other ending up dead."

"Such as?"

"Why do you think Sutherland engineered the whole Lali episode? He knew exactly where you were back in Moscow. He was testing. Playing a game. Experimenting, just to see what Fairchild would do. He was curious about him. Instead of trying to kill Fairchild, Sutherland might try to recruit him."

"Recruit him?"

"Talk him over. Get him on side. Play on his bitterness, how let down he's been by the British. Fill his head with lies about what happened all those years ago, Cold War shadows no one can ever really refute. They're both highly competent people. Imagine what they could do if they started working together. And who do you think all their bile and fury would be directed at?"

"Us," said Rose. "Britain. MI6."

Every now and again Walter's inner machinery made itself visible through his dainty exterior: a mind that anticipated, weighed up consequences and possibilities, considered options far in the future.

"So you see, I doubt this is over," said Walter. "In fact, this may still end up being one of the biggest challenges our Service has ever faced. I know you never welcomed being a part of this story, Rose. But if the issue does come back, you will be uniquely placed. Uniquely placed."

"So you're telling me I'm now of strategic importance to the Service?"

"In my eyes, yes. It would be helpful, let's say, for you to be on hand should this flare up. Of course it would be better if it didn't, and we never hear of Sutherland again." He patted his mouth with a folded napkin.

Rose wasn't sure how she felt about that. It wasn't at all clear what Walter had in mind. In due course he would probably reveal some long term plan and her role in it. But she knew what she wanted.

"How's Peter?" she asked.

"Making a full recovery. He took a couple of bullets but it could have been a lot worse."

"And has this persuaded him that it's time to retire?"

"He said he's given it some thought but doesn't feel ready quite yet. So no, he's still our Station Head, though not for many more years. This will have taken its toll on his health."

Rose hoped he had a few more years. There were bosses far worse than Peter.

"I imagine all the heat is off in Moscow given the Russians' decision to pull back from Tbilisi."

"To some extent. Of course the international press is saying that the Boris letter and the outcry back home shamed the Russians into retreating, but others are suggesting that they were losing the game anyway. They were particularly troubled by some covert operations which destroyed a number of their strategic positions."

"Really? Who was behind that?"

"Publicly, no one knows. Privately – well, you can't expect to gun down the number two British diplomat in Russia and pay no consequences. Of course the Kremlin is saying the shooting was a dissident group, but no dissidents we know are claiming it. And I've heard Zack is in the region as well."

"Ah! He'll be pleased about that. The Russians have only gone back as far as South Ossetia, though. They could try again."

"Indeed. They could try again. Relations, as they say, remain tense."

"Well, if the Boris letter prompts them to reform their military obligation programme, at least one good thing will have come of it."

"Yes, my dear. It does seem to have caused something of an outrage, and has prompted numerous questions about the human cost of the siege as well. It significantly weakened the Russians' position at the international negotiating table. I wonder how that letter got out of Lali and into the hands of the media. It's assumed Boris himself was killed in the siege."

"I expect we'll never know." Rose ate a mouthful of pork. Passing information to the media was not something her superiors would approve of. Walter may have his suspicions, but they'd never find out for sure.

Jannes had done well, finding Boris' home village and getting his mother to read out the letter on camera, with the rest of the family and a subdued but beautiful Tatiana in the shot as well. The letter was tragic, sincere, horrifically frank and incredibly moving. Hearts across the nation were touched. The clip went viral, with millions of online views in a matter of days. Activist groups of soldiers' mothers seized on it and campaigned vigorously. Russian politicians found themselves facing a barrage of awkward questions, not only on the plight of Russian conscripts but the purpose of the Georgian conflict itself. It was gratifying that even a government with this much power found itself knocked back occasionally by the will of its own citizens. Far too occasional, that was the problem.

She changed the subject. "What's happening with Morozov?"

"Well, Roman was found dead as you know. He was poisoned. We've heard it was someone close to him, his driver and bodyguard, who's now running the network in close cooperation with the authorities."

"Vadim? So Vadim turned traitor. Poor old Roman." She thought about them all: Roman, Alexei, Kamila, Boris, Marta, Ilya, Katya, all the others. Such a Russian story. The babushkas had it right: *dead, dead, all dead.*

"It's thanks to Roman that Fairchild and I made it," she said. "He managed to get a call out to us. He must have realised Vadim was working against him. Fairchild will…"

Walter carried on eating as she tailed off. Fairchild will what? Never give up. Transfer all his efforts from finding his parents into ending the person who ended them. But that was him. What about her? Fairchild will turn it into a feud, something personal. This was bigger. As Peter said, there will never be a time when Russia doesn't matter.

"Walter, I have to go back. I can help with this. Now Sutherland's out of the picture it's all different, isn't it? The personal element is all gone. I get back to business, doing what I'm good at, running agents."

Walter lowered his fork. "Rose, I'm terribly sorry, but going back to Moscow is out of the question. The FSB know you're in intelligence. Our contacts have told us as much. It would be impossible for you to do anything covert, even without Sutherland on the scene. You've done well there in very difficult circumstances, Peter only has praise for you, and this will be reflected in your record, don't worry about that. We know that much of this is not of your own making. But staying in Moscow just won't work."

Rose sat back. Why was all this happening to her? For her first ten years she'd been a model intelligence officer. Still was, in fact. But this thing she'd got caught up in didn't want to let her go. She just wanted to get stuck in, bury herself in a role, get back to where she was. What she wanted, in fact, was to go back in time to before she'd ever heard the name John Fairchild, or Grom, or Khovansky, or Sutherland.

She wanted to be the person she was before Lali, the one who'd never seen a child shot in the face – not a child, a young man, a boy as brave as any soldier – never felt the warmth of a girl's head on her lap, felt the ache of knowing that child was suffering, was relying on her, never had it all snatched away in an instant, feelings crushed as soon as they'd formed, leaving her with nothing, with only what she had before except that she knew, now, what she'd lost, what she missed, why she felt so empty. To un-know this, to fill the emptiness with purpose, that was what she wanted, what she needed.

Walter put his fork down and dabbed his mouth again, sensitive enough not to say anything for a space, not to look at her until she'd composed herself. He was waiting for her.

"So," she said eventually, her voice sounding impressively close to normal, "If not Russia, then where?"

He put the napkin down, folded his hands on the table and looked at her with his thoughtful, knowing eyes.

"I do have something in mind," he said.

The Clarke and Fairchild series

Thank you for reading *Moscow Honey*! If you want to stay in touch and hear about new releases in the series before anyone else, please join my mailing list. Members of the Clarke and Fairchild Readers' Club receive exclusive offers and updates. Claim a free copy of *Trade Winds*, a short story featuring John Fairchild and set in Manila. It takes place before *Reborn*, and before Fairchild and Clarke meet. Another short story, *Crusaders*, is set in Croatia and features Rose Clarke's fall from grace from the British intelligence service. These stories are not available on Amazon but are free for members to download in e-reader formats or as a pdf file. You can unsubscribe from the list at any time. Visit www.tmparris.com to sign up!

Reviews are very important to independent authors, and I'd really appreciate it if you could leave a review of this book on Amazon. It doesn't have to be very long – just a sentence or two would be fine – but if you could, it would provide valuable feedback to me to and to potential readers.

Other books in the series are *Reborn* (Book 1, set in China and Tibet), *The Colours* (Book 3, set in Monaco and the French Riviera), and *The Secret Meaning of Blossom* (Book 4, set in Japan). Subsequent novels will be based wherever there are interesting political stories to tell. Both characters grow and develop over the series: Fairchild will eventually discover everything about his past and Grom's motivations. My inspiration for Rose is the Judi Dench interpretation of M in the later Bond films, and an imagining of what this M would have been like earlier in life when she was in the field. Some of the other characters will make appearances in later books:

Zack and Walter, and probably others. I hope you stay with us for the journey.

Author note

In the summer of 2011 I travelled by train from London to Beijing via Moscow, Irkutsk and numerous other places. Having seen it in the summer, I then decided to repeat part of the journey in the dead of winter, a highlight of which was a walk on the solid ice of Baikal, the world's deepest freshwater lake. I also went to Georgia in 2016, both Tbilisi and the Caucasus mountains, but the town of Lali doesn't exist. It's partly based on Gori, Joseph Stalin's home town which was invaded by the Russians in 2008, but the location and geography have been completely re-invented to fit the story.

My research for Moscow Honey included the following books, which influenced the story heavily:

Russia by Martin Sixsmith (2011). This book covers the sweep of Russian history, repeating themes of brutal events, mass suffering and the cycle of suffocating central control, then a promise of release followed by even tighter control again. Plenty of events in Russia's history such as the storming of the Dubrovka theatre siege in 2002 which left over 100 Russian citizens dead, not to mention the USSR's cover-up following the massive radioactive leak at Chernobyl in 1986, demonstrate that human life is indeed held cheap in this part of the world.

Nothing Is True and Everything Is Possible by Peter Pomerantsev (2015). A journalist and broadcaster's experiences working in Russian media. From this book I learned about the allure of the oligarchs and the women who seek them, as well as the status and respectability of provincial mafia leaders.

Mafia State by Luke Harding (2011). A journalist's short-lived stint in Moscow before being thrown out by the Russian government. From here I learned about the FSB's home incursions as suffered by Harding himself, the secret room in the British Embassy (which has passed into folklore), and the village made up entirely of women, two of whom were indeed called Olga.

One Soldier's War in Chechnya by Arkady Babchenko (2006). A conscript's experience serving in Chechnya, the brutality of hazing and the whole experience of war. In one episode the writer enters an abandoned flat and imagines it's his own, which gave me the idea of Boris holed up in the flat in Lali.

The Angel of Grozny by Asne Seierstad (2007). This fearless journalist showed up in Grozny alone just after the start of the first Chechen war. I have nothing but admiration for her. She writes about a blond girl in an orphanage, who is in some ways the inspiration for Katya. Some of her descriptions of post-war Grozny I've used for Lali, although the circumstances are quite different.

Besieged by Barbara Demick (1996/2012). This focuses on one particular street in Sarajevo over the course of its three-year siege during the Balkan War. Again the situation in Sarajevo, a large city supported by UN airlifts, was different from the fictional stranglehold of Lali, but I've used many of the details of life under constant fire and the arbitrary nature of who lives and who dies.

I did plenty of other reading in addition to this, but at the end of the day the story comes first. I intend for these books to be accurate but impressionistic, with the focus on the story and the characters. Many things may have been changed to fit, but the inspiration for the stories comes from the research, from real places and real events.

About the author

After graduating from Oxford with a history degree, T.M. Parris taught English as a foreign language, first in Budapest then in Tokyo. Her first career was in market research, during which she travelled extensively to numerous countries and had a longer stay in Hong Kong which involved visiting many of the surrounding countries. She has also taken sabbaticals for a long road trip in the USA and to travel by train from the UK through Russia and Mongolia to Beijing and around China to Tibet and Nepal.

More recently she has played a role in politics, serving as a city councillor in Brighton and Hove on the south coast of the UK.

She currently lives in Belper, a lively market town near the Peak District National Park in the centre of England.

She started writing seriously in 2011. She published her first novel, *Reborn*, in 2020, the first in a series of international spy thrillers. She is drawn to international settings and the world's most critical political issues, as well as the intrigue, deception, betrayal and secrecy of clandestine intelligence services.

Crime and action thrillers are her favourite book, film and TV choices. She occasionally plays the trumpet or the Irish flute. She enjoys walking, running, cycling and generally being outdoors in beautiful countryside, as well as cooking and baking and, of course, travelling.

Email: hello@tmparris.com
Facebook: @tmparrisauthor
Twitter: @parris_tm

Printed in Great Britain
by Amazon